HIT

MALLORY HART

For Tommy Shelby, the first man to make me realize I have a thing for men on the other side of the law.

And to Cillian Murphy, for looking so damn fine while you played him.

OCTOBER
1988

PROLOGUE

———

PINA

Nothing but open desert and hot sun yawned before us. The last town we drove past was fifty miles behind us, the last car we passed, twenty. Cacti and dried, cracked earth stretched in every direction, as far as the eye could see. As far as I was concerned, we drove through the end of the world.

Neither of us said a single word. You'd think ten hours of silence would be enough to process some of what had happened, but apparently not. Because I still had no goddamn clue what just went down.

So far, I had only three solid facts to go off of:

One, Darragh somehow knew I tried to turn him in. My suspicions were with the bartender, but knowing him, who knew. I underestimated him badly. I couldn't do that again.

Two, someone wanted the both of us dead. Who and why was still a mystery.

Three, and this was the fact that puzzled me the most, Darragh kept me alive.

I hugged my arms closer to myself and laid my head between my knees. Paulina once told me that's what you were supposed to do if your plane was about to go down. This was a

1

rusted Honda and I was already on the ground, but I couldn't help the feeling that everything was about to crash and burn.

Nothing, and I mean *nothing*, made sense right now.

The silence pressed on until we rolled up on a town that seemed abandoned for decades. Weathered wooden stores groaned in the hot, desert wind beside dusty, old cars. Not another human was in sight. Darragh pulled the car to the curb. Besides the haunted storefronts, there was nothing but an old payphone erected from the sidewalk, bleached white from the sun.

I turned to him, the question bubbling in my throat, but the glare he sent me snapped my mouth shut. Sticky blood caked the entire front of his shirt and splattered up his neck. None of it was his.

"I'll be right back." He stepped out with the car still running. Then, thinking better of it, took the keys out of the ignition and strode for the payphone.

I watched in empty silence as he dialed.

I took a deep breath and slowly uncurled my arms from my waist. The car was empty when we found it. Now, Darragh's duffle and my destroyed, red dress lay in the backseat. I don't remember how it got ruined, but a rip was present in the delicate satin when we fled the city. By the time we hit Utah, it was pretty much falling off. My heels were long since abandoned, swallowed up in the streets we left behind. Darragh had silently handed me one of his button downs, but offered nothing else. That left me in nothing but his shirt and my panties. It was truly a testament to how much I was losing it, because it was pretty much the last thing on my mind.

Darragh's phone call was taking an awfully long time.

I shuffled around. The heat was beginning to suffocate me, but I really didn't want to go on the street half-naked, abandoned town or no. My knee bounced up and down, up and down, and I drummed my fingers on the center console. I needed something to do. Something to fidget with. I opened the center console. Maybe the previous owner left something behind. Or rather, rightful owner. I froze.

Darragh's pistol was inside.

No, not Darragh's. This one was black. A revolver. Either it was planted here and Darragh knew to take this car, or someone very suspicious used to own this vehicle.

I glanced up. Darragh's back was turned to me. No, he didn't know this was here.

Hot blood splattering the sidewalk came back in vivid memory. The pool of blood leaking around me and seeping into my skin. Some of it was still crusted between my toes.

He didn't kill me. He said he wouldn't kill me.

I reached for the gun. I've never used one, but I've seen Andrea load and unload them a thousand times in my room. A nervous habit he'd never admit to. Open the chamber, put in the bullets, close the chamber, spin.

I popped it open. All six holes contained a shiny, silver round.

He didn't kill me. It was fact number three.

But he killed a man right in front of me. A man he lied to. A man he said he would spare if he just told the truth. A man whose death would put the biggest fucking target in America on our backs. The hit.

But I was supposed to be the hit.

I was supposed to be dead.

I opened the door and stepped onto the sidewalk. The heat hit like a brick wall, drying up the very moisture from my lungs. My bare feet burned on the cement as a hellish breeze swirled the edge of Darragh's dress shirt around my hips.

He didn't turn around. His low voice carried on the wind like a death knell. The bible described the Angel of Death as an unseen force. A spirit drifting from door to door to collect those it claimed. But the book was wrong. The Angel of Death was not an omniscient spirit of the night. He was a violent man with blue eyes and a thick, Irish accent.

I steadied my breath. The burning soles of my feet planted into the ground. Hot wind caressed my legs as I stared into the thick,

3

dark locks over the back of Darragh's head. Rust-colored dust blew around me, scraping the corners of my eyes and springing hot tears to my irises. But I never took my gaze off the Angel.

My arms lifted to eye-level.

The gun went steady in my palms.

My finger wrapped around the trigger.

1

PINA

All my life, I've known two key things: what my family does after dark is not to be questioned, and my life was never my own. The latter was a hard fact from the moment I was born. As not only the youngest child of Don Lorenzo Delarosa, but the only girl, my life was laid-out in neat little steps: I was born, I'd be raised by a few maids whose lives were routinely threatened, and occasionally I'd see my mother. I'd be homeschooled, but instead of science and history I'd learn to be a good wife. And when the time came, I'd be sold off to the highest bidder for the betterment of the *famiglia*. Probably produce a few heirs and then die bitter and alone. And so was the sad, short tale of Giuseppina Delarosa.

I suspected the marriage portion of my timeline was just around the corner. My new bodyguards, two lumbering husks my father hired, escorted me from my room to the forbidden wing of our fortified home in the upper west side. It'd been a long while since I left the quarters I was designated to roam. My portion of the house consisted of my bedroom, a bathroom, and a kitchen and dining hall for my lessons. One hour of outside time was given a day, accompanied by my bodyguards, of course. I glanced at the two hulking figures beside me, wondering how long it'd be until my father got them killed. I never learned their names because they never lasted long enough. Whether it was because of my father's missions or my insufferable nature, the Don never said. A fresh set of silent muscle arrived each week and the cycle repeated.

The Don's office lay behind a set of double doors and four armed guards. Two with uzis, two with sawed-off .22 shotguns. Try as he might, my father couldn't hide everything about the family business from me.

The doors swung open and my father's smiling face greeted me. My brothers sat behind him, their grim faces set in pressed lips and narrowed eyes. My mother was noticeably absent. Probably drunk or high off pills in her room.

"Sit, *topolina*." My eldest brother, Alessandro, snorted at the nickname. *Little mouse.* It was my father's greatest wish I'd appeal to the demure, little pet name. Alessandro thought it was more fitting to call me *la megera*. The shrew.

I couldn't really blame him.

I seated myself in one of the plush, ruby chairs opposite my father. A mahogany desk stretched between us. A barrier. My brothers sat beside him, but me? Across. Because I was separate. Different. The child who would never hold a gun or roam the streets. The child who's only value was how beautiful I was and who was willing to tolerate my behavior.

Three sets of eyes stared back at me, fierce and unblinking: my father, Alessandro, and my other brother, Andrea. I folded my hands in my lap like the lady I was supposed to be. Then, thinking better of it, I crossed my arms.

"Giuseppina," my father said. "Time is short so I will keep this brief. You are a woman now, ready to set-off and fulfill your duties to the Family. Your brothers have taken to their roles and bring honor to the *famiglia*. I now expect you to do the same."

I understood the underlying words. The Don only spoke in circles, pacing around the point he was trying to make with every breath he took. Even his daughter and sons were no exception to that. So when he spoke of my brothers' *honor,* of my duties to the

Family, I knew what he really meant: do what I say or suffer the consequences.

He waited for me to speak, but I had nothing to say.

"It is time for you to marry. I've been putting it off too long, hoping your education would . . . take more." Alessandro snorted again. "But I can delay no longer. As I'm sure you've noticed, the *famiglia* has been stretched thin. The O'Callaghan *bastardos* creep closer every day."

Unsurprisingly, I hadn't noticed. I wasn't sure how he expected me to when my days were spent locked in the house. But the O'Callaghan name I recognized, at least. The only Irish mob in the city had been a pain in my father's side since long before I was born. And as their forces grew, so did the rivalry. Not a day went by I didn't hear my father and brothers toasting to the deaths of the O'Callaghan's through the thin walls of their cigar room.

"We are falling on hard times, *topolina,* but the Rocci Family has made us a generous offer. In exchange for your hand in marriage, Lucien will provide us with the men and weapons we need."

My tongue turned to lead in my mouth. Alessandro smirked, but Andrea cast his eyes to the ground. This . . . this couldn't be real. Not after everything that happened, not after—

"I know you are not happy about this arrangement, but it is your duty to the Family. I expect you to pack your things and be ready to leave tomorrow."

I gripped the arms of my seat. "Tomorrow?"

He nodded, his thick, grey eyebrows touching his hairline. "Will that be a problem, Giuseppina?"

No more *little mouse.* No more being his daughter at all. Because if he could really do it, really send me off to live with that— that animal— he never cared for me at all. Not even a little. He knew what happened with Lucien, down to every disgusting little detail. What he did to me, what he did to Paulina—

I shook my head. "I'm not going. Find someone else, anyone else, but I won't marry Lucien."

7

Alessandro leaned back, his smile stating he was ready for the fireworks.

The Don slammed his fist on the table. "This is not up for debate. And frankly, I have let this behavior of yours go on for far too long. Whatever past grievances you have with Lucien end right here. You will leave tomorrow, you will marry him and *you will serve your family honorably.*"

I stood up. "Fuck—"

My words were cut off with a hard slap.

Bells chimed in my ears as the world came back into focus, my father's furious face swimming before me. Only Andrea looked taken aback.

"Go and pack your things."

Tears welled in my eyes, but I refused to let him see. Refused to cry in front of any of these *bastardos*. For all their talk of honor and family, they never extended it to me. Never protected me. Never wanted me for anything more than their perfect, little bargaining chip, cast aside until it could be used and promptly forgotten again. I hated all of them.

But the words in my father's eyes told me what I already knew: I could fight, I could scream, I could tell him to go fuck himself as many times as I wished. But if they had to drag me to Lucien's themselves, they would. And Lucien would not mind a kicking and screaming bride. He preferred them that way.

I pushed past my bodyguards and ran down the hall. They sped to catch up, but I was faster. It didn't matter though, I was only going to my quarters, my room. It was the one place I could cry in privacy. And I was supposed to do as I was told.

2

DARRAGH

The Delarosa bastard wouldn't know what hit him.

The wind whistled over the grey scarf covering my head. The Richmond Hotel lay beneath me, the cold cement of the roof freezing me even through my clothes. Freezing, misty rain began an hour ago. I'd been here for seven. It took at least one to set up my gear, check my scope and double and triple check my ammo like I was taught to. Then six more for Pietro Delarosa to arrive. He stood at the opening of a titty bar, smoking a cigar with a nameless new Delarosa recruit.

I took a deep breath and lined up the shot. The calm right before the chaos was always my favorite part. There Pietro was, choking on his Cuban and spinning a glass of whiskey in his hand. He probably expected the night off, to go see a couple girls and have a drink with the fresh meat. Talk about the same old stories from his glory days when he actually did something for the mob instead of leech off the Don's funds. He could spend all Lorenzo Delarosa's money, flaunt his Cuban cigars and pressed-grey suit or do whatever the fuck else he wanted. That wasn't why I was here. Word on the streets was Pietro claimed to kill one of our boys, Cillian. The only problem was, Cillian was currently sitting in his high-rise watching this ordeal go down. The Delarosa's were slipping. We knew it and every other faction knew it too. If Pietro wanted to make up pretty stories to show the strength of him Family, then I'd do him a little favor and pull him out of retirement.

I sucked in a deep breath, double checked my shot was lined up, and breathed. *Fire*.

There it was: the chaos. The street exploded with screams, people in the wrong place at the wrong time ducking for cover. The recruit pulled his gun and spun in frantic circles. I put a bullet in his head too.

Done. An easy mission. Too easy. I pulled the scarf back over my head. Police sirens already wailed down the alley, meaning it was time to go. I grabbed my rifle and ran for the hotel service stairs.

Rory was waiting in his shitty sedan, right on time. I threw a cover over the gun in the backseat and settled into the passenger side.

Rory whistled. "Ya make it seem too easy."

"It's not," I grunted. I picked up the car phone and dialed Sean O'Callaghan, my boss, the kingpin of the Irish mob, and the man I only sometimes referred to as *father*.

"It's done."

"Good. Tell your brother I'll kill him myself if he pulls any fancy car shit. We don't need the cops up our arse."

I hung up and leaned back in my seat. "Sean says don't get pulled over."

"No shit."

But even as he said it, he plowed through a red light. I sighed.

"He won't keep bailing you out, ya know."

"I ain't worried. The old bastard can't afford to lose his personal chauffeur."

There wasn't any arguing that. Rory's fire-red hair and glittering eyes weren't the only thing that made him the black sheep of the family. As the third born son of the Kingpin, he somehow ended up in the place of being the forgotten youngest— until I was born. But my three older brothers came to America long before I did. Up until then, Rory was the baby to my Da and I was the only child to my Ma. Then everything went to hell and the rest is history.

Rory punched my arm. "What's my baby brother moping over now? You ever smile?"

I scowled at him.

"Cheer up," he said. A slew of horns sounded as he careened around a semi. "You got your kills and now you'll get some time off. Go to that stupid house ya love."

Rory was the only one who knew of my secret house upstate. Not by choice either— I caught the slippery bastard following me up on my last visit. Rory couldn't shoot a gun, got squeamish at the sight of blood and couldn't run a business to save his arse, but he was a damn good driver. I'd give him that.

I side eyed him. "You haven't told anyone about that, have ya?"

He grinned. "Why, would you kill me if I did?"

I held my stare.

"I didn't tell anyone about your damn hideaway. What kinda brother do ya take me for?"

I took him for a good one. I loved my brother the way you were supposed to: with undying loyalty and a healthy distance. But it didn't mean I always had to like him. Rory had a special way of getting under my skin. He may have been older in years, but he sure as hell was younger in mind. And couldn't find his way around a gun, so someone had to.

The O'Callaghan Hotel left a golden glow on the thickening rain covering the sidewalk. Dark clouds made the short days shorter as late October settled into New York City. The yellow lights blinked back at me as I stood on the sidewalk, pulling a cigarette from my pocket. Sean's boys were already pulling the car away to the nearest chop shop, never to be seen again.

It didn't matter. I didn't give a flying feck what they did with the cars or the guns. There'd be new ones within the hour.

Rory gave the vehicle a gentle wave goodbye though. I'll never understand what goes on in that man's head.

Sean lived in the penthouse, as expected. The boys nodded their respects as Rory and I climbed the service stairwell. After an incident in Vegas, I had no fecking trust for lifts.

He waited for us in his usual suit. Three snifters of whiskey perched on the table in front of him, but Sean was already right and smashed. Pietro's death was a huge victory for us. He was one of the oldest members of the Delarosa clan, and despite being useless with a gun for years, he was a damn good bookie. It'd be a lethal hit to their struggling finances. And once we took Elm Street, we'd have their gun factory too.

Sean opened a box of cigars and held his glass in the air. "To my sons, the dirtiest fecking bastards the world's ever seen."

I clinked my glass against his and took a long sip. Sean didn't cheap out tonight. Time off really was in my future.

"And to Pietro Delarosa. May the bastard burn in hell," Rory said. A second round of clinking ensued.

Sean watched me with glazed eyes, whether from the drink or the cigar smoke, who knew. A puff of smoke slithered it's way over his aging, grey hair.

My Ma told me once I looked just like him when he was young. All dark, black hair and bright, blue eyes.

I clipped my own cigar and popped it between my teeth.

"The boys tell me Pietro went down with one bullet."

I shrugged. "Two would be a waste."

Sean grinned and shook his head. "You get it from your Ma. About the only good damn thing any of ya got from her."

My hand tightened around my glass.

"But business is business, boys. Now that Pietro's gone, the Don will grow more desperate than he already has. I got one more job for you, Darragh, then I want ya to take a nice long trip while the rest of the boys clean house on whatever's left of the Family."

I set my glass on the table. "What kind of job?"

Sean gave Rory the same look he always did. The sprightly red-head was out the door in seconds, but not before grabbing the half-empty whiskey bottle.

Sean shook his head. "I don't know where that boy came from."

I leaned back in my chair. "The job, Da."

"Right." He took a long drag of his cigar. "What do you know about Giuseppina Delarosa?"

I shrugged. "Just about nothing. The Family's kept her locked up since the day she was born."

"Yes," Sean said. "Until now."

I leaned forward.

"Lorenzo's finally putting his best asset to work. Word on the street is the poor lass will be married off to Lucien Rocci."

I couldn't say I was surprised. The Rocci Family remained the other thorn in our goddamn sides. Only difference was, Rocci wasn't scrambling the way Delarosa was. We'd tried a few times to infiltrate, but the Rocci's were airtight. Not to mention, dirty bastards when it came to fighting. We'd lost more to the Rocci's in the past year than the Delarosa's in the past ten.

Which meant Lorenzo was desperate. The two families didn't like each other so much after some incident with a maid. Rumors circled the daughter was involved, but no one knew more than that. But the Delarosa's needed an alliance if they were gonna keep the storm at bay. The storm being my brothers and my Da.

"What's that got to do with me?"

"Marriage means alliance. You know how the Italians are." More smoke billowed from his lips. "I want you to kill the girl. Keep any alliance from forming."

I snuffed my cigar on my boot. "I don't kill ladies, Da."

"She's not a lady. She's a Delarosa." He gave me a withered sigh that only came with a life too long. "And ya know what we do to Delarosa's, boy."

I nodded. That I knew well.

13

"She leaves the compound in the morning. South entrance. The car will be armored so get her on the street. And then get your fecking arse out of there."

I set my glass down. "You got a car ready?"

Sean jerked his chin towards the window. "Already waiting for you."

That was my dismissal. My hand was on the door when his voice rang out once more, "There'll be ten bottles waiting for ya when it's done."

I nodded silently and pushed through the door.

3

PINA

I stared around at my belongings, wondering what I should even take. None of it was important or sentimental to me. Besides the few trinkets my father purchased me over the years, most of it was just clothes or family heirlooms my father thought would look better in my room.

I sat on my bed and looked around. My whole life had been in this room. I was the Delarosa's most coveted secret. They never allowed me outside, never let me see any people besides the family who visited and the staff they brought in. All twenty-two years of my life spent between the same four walls of our upper west side home, watching out the window but never experiencing any of it. They said it was for my safety, my education, but I knew the truth: I was a valuable asset, and they couldn't afford for me to get hurt or corrupted.

A soft knock sounded on my door. I didn't need to ask who it was. I called for him to come in and Andrea quietly snuck through the door.

He shut it behind him and leaned against the wall, arms crossed. We said nothing. There was nothing to say. We knew this day would come, we just didn't expect it to happen the way it did.

He pressed his lips into a flat line. "How are you doing?"

15

I wrung my hands together in my lap. "How do you think?"

He shrugged. "I don't know. I don't want to tell you how to feel."

My brother didn't need to ask me how I felt. We'd been inseparable my entire life, the children born only ten months apart. He knew me better than I even knew myself, and the same went for him. He'd know exactly what I was thinking right now, which was good because honestly, I didn't even know. It was a steady mix of anger, rage, sadness and shock, all swarming together in a way I didn't understand.

He took out his gun and unloaded it, spun the chamber and pieced it back together. A nervous habit he picked up since he first got the damn thing at ten years old. The endless clicking and rolling pounded in my head.

"Did you try and talk him out of it?" I asked.

He at least had the decency to look ashamed. "You know it doesn't work like that, Pina."

I did know, but I hoped my brother would stand up for me. I guess I was wrong.

"If there was any other way—"

"Yeah, I get it," I snapped. I wasn't angry at him. Just everything else.

He took a deep breath and holstered his weapon. "Can I speak freely here?"

I leaned back on my bed, staring at the ceiling. "I'm sure you will even if I say no, so go ahead."

"I know what happened with Lucien was . . ."

He trailed off, so I filled in the gaps for him. "Pure evil? Demonic? So heinous it's vile that father could even consider this?"

He nodded. "Yeah."

Silence filled the room. I rolled my eyes. "Get on with it."

"You're here now, and this is what it's going to be. It's the last thing I wanted for you, but we have to deal with it. You'll marry Lucien and maybe things won't be so bad. You can make the best of it. And you'll stay in New York, so I'll come visit you every day. I know it feels like the end of the world, but it could be worse."

"It couldn't be worse, Andrea." I hated him for even thinking it. Implying that somehow, after everything Lucien did Paulina, I could just learn to forget and fuck the man who killed my only friend.

He sat beside me and laid down, staring at the same white spot on the ceiling. It never changed over the years. The same white ceiling, the same gilded cage. Maybe I should have been grateful all these years; I was about to be sold off to a worse one.

He took my hand in his. "I love you, P. It's going to be okay. You're my little sister and I've always protected you. None of that will change."

Except it would. Andrea got shit our entire lives for our relationship. I heard countless fights through the wall where father beat him bloody, telling him to spend less time with women and start acting like a man. He wouldn't visit me every day because he couldn't, father and Lucien would make sure of it. Also, now that I was getting married, Andrea and Alessandro would be next. As soon as he had a family of his own to take care of, he would forget all about me.

But I couldn't tell him any of that, not now. Andrea was a sensitive soul. Too good for our world. If I told him what I really wanted to say, it would only crush him.

"I believe you," I lied.

He turned to me and smiled. "Good, because I got you a present."

I sat up, plastering a fake smile onto my face. If it was anything wedding related, I might just fall apart.

I waited.

He nodded towards my bedroom window, the bars locked tight over the front. "This morning, someone accidentally picked broke the bars on your window. The guard posted outside also unexpectedly came down with stomach flu. If someone were to, I don't know, leave through it and walk around for a bit, get some fresh air and go out alone for the first time, I don't think anyone would notice."

I blinked, hardly believing what I was hearing. Father would beat him half to death when he found out, and he always found out, but he was giving me this chance. This one opportunity to not feel so . . . trapped.

"Just make sure that person is back by eleven, okay?"

I nodded, not sure what to say. Only Andrea could think of something like this, realize how much it would mean to me. He pressed his palm into mine and something cold and hard bit into my skin. "Just in case, but you won't need it."

I nodded numbly and folded the little knife into the pocket of my nightgown.

"I'll see you in the morning," he said. He was out my door before I even had a chance to say, *goodnight.*

————————

The cold, oppressive rain battered my nightgown as I slipped off the roof of the house. By the time my feet hit the dark, rain-splattered sidewalk below, the gossamer sheath of my gown was transparent and sticking to my legs. I held my arms tightly around myself as I walked down the street, taking it all in.

The knife stuck out like a thorn between my fist, and suddenly I felt so fucking stupid for being here. It was late October in NYC, pouring rain, I was in a see-through nightgown and freezing my ass off . . . armed. A biting laugh escaped me at the ridiculousness of the situation. Even if I needed the knife, it's not like I knew how to use it, and who knew if I could last hours out here in the rain and cold in nothing but my nightgown. Andrea didn't even offer me his suit jacket.

A looping video of a woman dancing in her underwear gleamed in front of me when I halted on the sidewalk. The lights from a nearby shop illuminated the puddle my feet were now sinking into and my teeth shattered against the cold.

I kept walking.

This part of the city was strangely empty. Maybe it was the rain or maybe it was my father's looming home in the background, a warning to anyone walking this way they should turn back. In the distance, I could hear the sound of taxis, people talking, and footsteps splashing into the street, but here it was silent. Andrea offered this to me as a gift, and in any other circumstance it may have been a good one. Now, it just felt cheap.

There was so much of the world at my fingertips. The entire city and everything beyond. A metal grate beneath my feet let out steam, the sound of an underground train whooshing by beneath it, taking people far away. If I was another person or this was another life, I'd be on that train. Maybe I'd be coming home from work or on my way to visit a friend. What would my life have been if I wasn't born Giuseppina Delarosa? Would I have been good at school, been social, worked a dead-end job, would I have had hobbies?

A fat tear slipped from my eye, mixing with the rain splattering my cheek. Those lives were nonexistent. I had this one. I never got to go to school. I never got to attend university. I never got to work a crappy job. So many people complained about their mundane, normal lives, but what I wouldn't give for a second of feeling utterly plain. I wanted to make bad choices. I wanted to make good choices. I wanted a life that wasn't predestined for me from the moment I was born.

I didn't feel like walking anymore. My skin pebbled with hundreds of little goosebumps and turned a strange shade of blue. I ducked into a forgotten alley behind a shut-down bar and settled into the asphalt. The grainy rocks stuck into my bare legs and the brick wall I leaned against was cold. It smelled like stale beer and garbage, but it was real. This was real. It wasn't the plush carpets of the mansion, the smooth wallpaper lining the halls. My first breath of freedom and it would end all too soon.

19

My family betrayed me. That was a fact. I always knew what my sole purpose in life was, but this felt different. They could have married me to the young, new Don of the Chicago Outfit, or even Boston. I could have met one of our distant allies and gotten the opportunity to know them, maybe even chosen a husband myself from the selection provided for me. My cousin had that choice and she was happy. Instead, they gave me up to the one person I could never care for. The one person who destroyed me by taking away what mattered most. They used me for one purpose only, never taking into consideration I was a human and not just a pawn. If they could really do this, then maybe they never cared for me at all.

I would marry Lucien Rocci. That was also a fact. With the deaths of so many Delarosa's, my father was scared. He never once admitted weakness of the *famiglia* to me, but this rushed marriage to Rocci meant he had no other choice. Without this marriage, the Delarosa's would be at risk. Maybe even fall apart, our one-hundred-year reign coming to an end. So, there would be no discussions, no debates, and no alternatives. It was the same for my mother and it would be the same for me.

But there was one more fact to deal with, the most important one: I could never marry Lucien. I could never marry the man who forced himself on my closest friend. The man who killed Paulina and took her away from me. I could try to run away, hop on that underground train and pray it took me far, far away. Though even if I could escape, they would find me. They'd go to the ends of the Earth to make sure their precious asset wasn't lost. So, there would be no train ticket for me, no negotiations with my Don, and no pleading for mercy from the family who turned their backs on me. But there was one last option of escape, one last choice to keep me from becoming Lucien Rocci's forever.

I eyed the little knife in my hand and took a deep breath.

4

DARRAGH

The rain came down in thick sheets now, but it wouldn't stop what I'd been ordered to do. I settled on a rooftop several blocks away from the house and broke out my long-range scope. I wanted to be as far away from the place as possible when shit went down.

I cursed against the rain filling my brand-new suit with polluted water. The rotten stink of NYC would take days to wash off when I went to the villa upstate. Rory made fun of me for it, but it was the only place on this fecking planet I felt like I could take a deep breath. Somewhere that was my own without all the bullshit and chaos of the city. There'd been enough times I considered going up there and just staying forever, but that was never an option either. Something about this life, my dedication to my family, would always keep me coming back. Even if it meant spending my night freezing my ass off on a rooftop, getting ready to kill a girl I'd never met. All for a man who'd probably kill me without a second thought.

I'd just gotten the scope ready when something flickered in the alley below. I dropped down to my stomach and crawled to the edge of the building. No one knew about this plan but me and Sean, so there was no way someone was here to intercept. But that glint

21

didn't lie. Even in the rain, the neon lights of the bars illuminated that glint into the rain.

When I peered over, it was not what I expected at all.

A young woman, maybe twenty or so, huddled against the piss-stained stones. Her knees shook against her chest and a nightgown not meant for the weather clung to her bluing skin. I imagined that skin held a nice, golden tan when not doused in autumn rain.

The glint came from a tiny pocketknife she held in a tinier, slim hand. That tiny hand shook a single moment before she dragged the steel across her wrists. She collapsed against the soaked stone wall, blood pouring from the wounds in rain-doused streams.

That same moment, sound exploded up the street. The lights from the compound flickered and Delarosa's men poured into the street. I glanced between the dying girl in the alley and the frantic pounding from the house. It only took a second to put two and two together. Giuseppina Delarosa just killed herself ten feet away from me.

A shuddered laugh escaped me. Talk about fecking irony there. Many jobs accidentally went wrong. None had ever gone accidentally right.

Better to just leave her and let the Delarosa's find her. No blood on my hands and a job well done.

I started packing my shit when a muffled groan came from below. The Delarosa's must have been idiots, because the whole swarm of them went in the complete opposite direction. The street was quiet, save for the rain splashing the road and the quiet groans floating up from the alleyway.

Glancing over the edge again, I saw Giuseppina rolling her head against the wall. She was shaking like a leaf in a storm and blood pooled around her like a halo. Best to go put the poor lass out of her misery.

I took the stairs two at a time and emerged in the alleyway. Her eyes were closed, but her whole body clenched as I approached.

A paper-dry tongue licked her rain-soaked lips as she whispered, "Andrea?"

I could only assume the Andrea she spoke of was the bastard second son of the Don. Didn't matter though. I wasn't him.

I pulled out my gun.

"I'm sorry," she whispered.

My gun shuddered in my hand. *I'm sorry.* Only one other woman had ever said that to me before moving onto the next life. Only one other woman truly meant it. A chord struck in my chest, but I shoved it down. That woman was long dead and Giuseppina Delarosa wasn't her.

I held my gun back up and pointed it at her head. I'd make it quick.

Against my will, a memory came back to me. I wasn't in the alley anymore, but a cold, dark room. A woman with fiery red hair leaned next to me, crying. There was so much blood. Maybe it was time that tainted the memory, because there was no way one person could bleed that much.

I shook my head, wrapping my finger around the trigger. I couldn't go there, not now.

Something stopped me. I was being a fecking idiot. Noise clamored down the street: the thick-headed morons of the Delarosa clan finally decided to head this way. I had minutes before they found me here with their princess, pointing a gun to her head. But each time I went to pull the trigger, the same image filled my mind. A woman in a similar position, forced into a position she didn't want to be in and choosing another way out instead. The image that had haunted my dreams since I was ten years old. The image of my mother dying beside me.

Her lips were turning blue, whether from the cold or blood loss, who knew. Her little shakes and gasps were turning violent now. She wouldn't have long. Even if the Delarosa's found her, there'd be a good chance she wouldn't survive the night. Most likely, she wouldn't.

I put the gun away. She did this to herself. I didn't need to be the one to end things.

I turned away, but another shuddered groan escaped her, and again, that image of my mother filled my mind. Her soft, red hair caressing my shoulder as she whispered those words over and over again: *I'm sorry, Darragh. I'm sorry, I'm sorry. I'm sorry.*

I watched Giuseppina and ran a hand through my hair. She was young, beautiful if I was going to be completely fecking honest. She was dying. And for the first time in god knows how long, I couldn't do it. I couldn't finish the hit.

There would be hell to pay, but maybe it didn't matter. I lived in hell already.

5

PINA

Everything was on fire: my head, my skin, but mostly my wrists. I opened my eyes to white ceilings and walls. The little room had nothing in it but a small, wooden dresser, a bed, and me.

I tried to sit up, only to realize I was strapped to the bed. White bondages held me down by my arms and ankles. Sweat trickled across my forehead as heat filled my face and chest. The nightgown I wore, now coated in dirt and smelling something fierce, clung wet and dirty to my skin.

I tried sitting again when a low voice calmly said, "I wouldn't do that."

I landed back on the mattress and the air whooshed from my lungs. I didn't recognize the voice. Least of all, I didn't recognize the thick Irish accent tainting each word it said.

I swallowed. "Where am I?"

The disembodied voice only grunted. I let out a sigh through my nose. I couldn't see him, but now that I knew he was here his presence burned through the room. I suddenly became aware of each little creak, shuffle or scrape that echoed around the walls. The drapes were drawn, so it was hard to tell if it was night or day. The only light came from an ancient, dimmed lamp beside my bed. I felt alive, the pain definitely made sure of that, but I couldn't be sure. Maybe this was Hell. I was dead and it was the devil speaking to me from the corner of my bed.

"How are you feeling?" The voice asked instead.

I snorted. How was I feeling? Fucking great, how about you? I'm only bleeding and strapped down to a stranger's bed. Before that, I was freezing in an alley because I tried to . . . I tried—

"You answer mine and I'll answer yours," he said.

I lifted my head, enough to get a peek of the man sitting in the corner of the room. Only his gray,-suit covered legs were visible. So was the very large, very loaded gun lying across his lap.

I swallowed the bile rising in my throat. "I'm fine. A little hot, but fine."

"I'll turn down the heat."

Heat. In my fog-addled brain, I knew that was a clue. We were still up north, likely still in New York. It was the end of October and it was cold. I couldn't imagine anyone would get far with me in my condition, but it was still a relief to have it almost confirmed.

But then again, why was it a relief? I was close to my family— maybe— but so what? Hadn't I just tried to kill myself to escape them? Escape Lucien?

"You're in my house."

An answer, but not. "Where is your house?"

"In the woods," He replied. My blood boiled in my veins as he said, "Now my turn. What happened in that alley?"

"My wrists were slashed," I said, answering his non-answer with one of my own.

The pump-action rifle he held made a sound that set my teeth on edge. "A real answer."

"You first," I spat.

We sat in heavy, unyielding silence.

"I'm going to make this very easy for you," he said. The gun rifle clicked once more and his foot methodically tapped on the hardwood. "You are tied to my guest bed and I have a gun. I was willing to give you some answers in a show of hospitality, but if you

26

don't want to play then we'll do things my way. You answer my questions or you get to eat lead."

A laugh escaped me, echoing into the room. "Wow, what a gentleman you are."

"I'm a lot of things, *Pina*. A gentleman is not one of them."

The nickname set me on edge. Only my family called me that.

Who was this stranger, and what did he know about me?

"Who are you?" I asked instead.

"Why did you run away?"

I could answer. Or I could not. If I was truthful with myself, it didn't matter either way. There were only two options for me: this stranger got his information, released me, and sent me home. Father would never beat me but make the maids do it instead. My brother's sneer would follow me through the halls until Lucien came to collect his bride and I was sold away. If that option didn't occur, that only left option two: this stranger got what he wanted and killed me anyway.

I preferred option two.

Lucien took everything from me. The little I had in my best friend, in my peace, he ripped it away like it was nothing but an old, bloody band aid, ready to be torn and tossed away. He would do the same to me.

There were things much worse than a bullet to the head.

I closed my eyes, ignoring the annoyed grunts of my captor. He shifted in his seat, waiting for a reply, but none came. I had nothing to say to him. Not out of loyalty to my family or the clan, but because there was no point. My life ended here, now, whether by bullet or by the alternative. So I didn't care.

Please, just make it quick.

"Did you hear me?" He asked.

I closed my eyes, taking a long breath through my nose. "Loud and clear, leprechaun."

He waited. And waited. I was beginning to wonder if I was already dead when he stood and crossed the room.

The soft click of the door echoed across the space. "My name is Darragh." He shut the door.

Darragh,

Darragh O'Callaghan.

How many nights? How many nights did I hear the toast to his death? The one-sided phone calls of another man falling to the bloody hands of the O'Callaghan's assassin. The forgotten brother. The last one.

I was right. This was hell, and the devil stood beside my bed.

6

DARRAGH

What in the ever loving feck was I doing?

I slumped down on the other side of the guest room door, rifle across my lap. The dark glow of my secret, upstate home echoed back at me. The sky outside held an ugly, dark gray tinted in blue as the sun went down and the impending storm blew in. This far north, it'd be snow.

I had no clue what I was thinking. I had one job. One fecking job and I let *her* get into my mind. Giuseppina Delarosa had nothing to do with my own shit, but I still let it break me.

Sean was going to have my ass when he found out. Son or no. I still had no way to know what exactly went down in the city. The second I made my choice I hopped in the getaway, yelling at the newbie recruit to get the feck out and throwing Giuseppina in the backseat. It was either a miracle or the devil at fecking work that she made it the whole car ride to the Adirondacks. Even more divine work was at play considering my shitty stitch job kept the bleeding at bay and she woke up. Three days later, but still.

It was a moment of weakness to save her. A moment of weakness I'd be paying for dearly because Darragh O'Callaghan didn't get fecking weak.

I should have killed her in that room. Been done with it. But part of me couldn't do that either.

She wanted me too. I'd seen enough men die slowly, begging for death either with their words or with their actions. Whatever drove her to do what she did lingered, and she wanted nothing more than for me to finish the job.

It shouldn't have been different. I gladly obliged to kill any of my family's enemies who asked for death. But not her.

Loud ringing came from the kitchen, the phone on the hook rattling against the wall. I already knew who it'd be. He'd want explanations and I had none.

Feck.

It'd be worse if I didn't answer it. But god, I didn't want to.

I squared my shoulders and picked up the phone. "Da?"

"You gonna tell me what in fecking hell happened out there?"

My gaze cut back to the locked guest room door. Locked from the outside, that was. "The hit had . . . some problems."

"No shit, boy. I have Delarosa's all over my ass, a missing mob princess and I've gone the past three days not knowing if my youngest son is dead. So tell me what in god's fecking name happened."

The lie spun in my head, mixed easily into bits of truth so it appeared believable. It was a talent I'd acquired over the years with my Da. There were some things better left unsaid to Sean. God knew he thought the same about me. His assassin son who he kept on a very, very short leash.

Everyone said Rory was the unlucky one. The lanky, awkward brother who could barely hold a gun. Sometimes I thought he dodged a bullet.

I lowered my voice, even though there was no way the girl could hear me through the thickly insulated walls. Or the painkillers I'd been pumping her with the past few days.

"The Delarosa girl ran from the compound the night before the hit. Don't know why, don't know what the plan was, but

I found her in an alley half-dead. The clan was looking for her so I grabbed her alive and ran. Figured we'd have more problems on our hands if they found their princess two blocks away with one of our bullets in her head. They're paying off police to patrol the neighborhood after the Pietro killing."

Only the cops had been a direct lie. The Delarosa's were too prideful to ask for help from the pigs. Even the dirty ones.

Glass shattered in the background, and he muttered, "What a fecking mess." I wouldn't mind breaking a thing or two either. Maybe it'd screw my head on straight for once in the past fecking week.

"Where is she now?"

Again, my eyes were drawn to that closed door. "My safe house."

Even Sean didn't know where it was. No one but Rory. It was safer that way, and besides Rory, we each had one.

"We need her dead and we need her out of New York." A beat of silence passed "I have another job for you."

What a fecking surprise. Vacation time my arse.

"When? Where?"

"We have a rat. Some rookie cop who thought he'd be a hot shot for infiltrating the family. Didn't get far before we discovered him, but he's got info we can't leak to the pigs. One of the boys scared him half to the grave and he fled to Vegas until witness protection can pick him up. Last I heard he was posing as a dealer at a casino on main. I need him taken care of, and I need it fast."

My free hand balled into a fist. "You want me to kill a cop?"

"I wouldn't ask if I didn't have to."

Ah. So that's where I got my good sense of lying from.

"Send me details. What do you want me to do with the girl?"

"Bring her with you."

I blinked, wondering if I'd heard that correctly. "What?"

31

"Bring her with you. Pin the cop's murder on the girl. Make it look like a lover's spat or some shit. Get creative with it. I don't care. Just make sure it gets pinned on the Delarosa's."

Smart move. Kill two birds with one stone and bring the law down on the clan. It was dirty, even for Sean, but he'd always cared more about effectiveness than playing fair. Our side of the world usually did. The alternative was a one-way ticket to hell.

All I had to do was convince the girl tied up in my spare room to come quietly.

"Pat will meet you at the airport on Wednesday. Don't feck this up."

Two days. Two days to heal up Pina and get her back to the city. Quietly and without a fight. Pat would handle the rest— he could make passports so clean they passed any customs line. I just had to figure out the hard part.

"I'll contact you when the job is done."

He hung up without a goodbye. Fatherly love and all that shit.

Perfect timing too, because a muffled groan echoed through the doorway I'd been trying to avoid.

I grabbed the rifle and pushed through the locks.

Giuseppina Delarosa sat up in bed, the bandages at her wrists soaked through with hot, sticky blood. She'd managed to gnaw through one of the bondages with her teeth, but the shitty stitch job had suffered for it. She froze like a deer in headlights, wide eyes roaming over me as I flicked my gaze up and down the scene. I raised an eyebrow. I'd give the princess one thing, she had balls.

"You might not want to do that, love."

The bondage fell from her blood-stained teeth as her mouth parted. "Why?"

I pulled a knife from my hip. She flinched, but relaxed when I only cut the bonds. I pulled out the clean gauze I'd stuffed in my pocket and threw it on the bed.

"Because we're going to Vegas."

She licked her soft lips. "My family will find me."

32

Time to put those lies to the test once more. I gave her a vicious smile. "I wouldn't count on that. According to the Delarosa's, you are very, very dead." I patted the doorframe before exiting. "Clean up. We have shit to do."

7

PINA

My family thought I was dead.

Somehow, that fact didn't disturb me nearly as much as it should of. That didn't stop it from echoing in my mind though. I sat at Darragh's— Darragh O'fucking Callaghan's to be exact— kitchen counter. Three pristine bar stools lined a sand-colored, marble countertop. Deep mahogany cabinets set with stained glass curved over a massive stove and state-of-the art oven. Even the faucets and handles were made of glowing brass. Everything about the open kitchen screamed money, class, and nothing at all of what I expected from a man who made his living in torture.

The Angel of Death himself stood at the stovetop, cooking bacon and eggs. In a totally screwed up way, it was kind of hilarious. Darragh didn't look like a killer —but the way his body tensed each time I shifted, the way his eyes darted back and forth like he was waiting for an army —certainly made him act like one. And here he was, making breakfast.

Watery sunlight peeked through the blinds Darragh drew tight the moment I stepped out of the guest room. At some point while I was asleep, he left a clean pair of pants, a t-shirt and flannel for me on the nightstand. There was pretty much nothing weirder than wearing Darragh O'Callaghan's clothes, but I wasn't about to strut around in my dirty, sheer nightgown either. He hadn't bothered to lock the door last night, so I assumed I wasn't confined to the room and wandered to the kitchen this morning. I thought that made him either incredibly cocky or incredibly dumb until I took the time to observe his house. Alarms were everywhere, anything sharp was noticeably absent from the kitchen and any real weapons were tucked into locked cases. Those cases made up the majority of the living room decor, burning a hole in my back as I stared at Darragh's.

His broad back was definitely something to stare at. In my head, I always pictured him as the ugly creature my brothers and father described him to be. That image was far from the truth. His black hair gleamed under the kitchen lights, so dark it was nearly blue. His skin held a warm glow despite his Irish roots and he had the bluest eyes I'd ever seen. Thick corded muscles screamed to break free of the tight black tee he wore. He looked more like an model than a hitman. Then again, maybe that's what made him so dangerous.

"Feel better?" he asked. Even his voice was smooth and silky, like the expensive brandy Paulina snuck to my room once. I wondered if he, too, smelled like oak and musk.

"No," I said, only because it would piss him off. It was the truth, anyway. The crude stitches in my wrists were no doubt the handiwork of the Mr. Serial Killer. It was also hot as hell in here, despite him saying he'd turn down the heat. A thin layer of snow covered what little grass I could see through the closed kitchen drapes.

He grunted, throwing a few pieces of bacon and scrambled eggs onto a plate. I was starving. Even just smelling the food had my stomach clawing at my rib cage, but I'd rather eat glass than risk whatever was in the meal he laid down in front of me.

Darragh fixed me with an annoyed glare, sighed, and took a huge bite of my eggs with his fork. He shoved a piece of bacon in his mouth for good measure too.

I still didn't touch it.

He stared down at me and I squirmed in my seat. If he hadn't already violated me by stitching my wounds, giving me his clothes, and dragging me off to . . . wherever we were, then his eyes were doing the rest. He'd said nothing since I rose this morning besides, *Feel better?*, therefore I had no fucking clue where I was or why. I figured the evil villain monologue would come over breakfast, but he hadn't said a damn word.

"Why aren't you eating?"

I crossed my arms and leaned back. "Could be poisoned."

His eyebrow flicked up, accentuating a vein fluttering in his neck. "I just ate it in front of you."

"But what if you have a resistance to it?"

The vein stopped fluttering and his jaw slackened. "What?"

"Like, you built-up a resistance to the poison." I waved my hands in the air. "*Princess Bride,* hello? Ever seen it?"

His jaw clenched again. "No, I've never seen it."

"Well, basically, this guy tricks his enemy into drinking poisoned wine by—"

"I really don't care." I pursed my lips. "The food isn't poisoned. One, that's not my weapon of choice. Two, in case you haven't noticed, there are about fifty other objects within ten feet of you that could kill you much, much quicker so I wouldn't have to listen to this shit. So, eat."

I drummed my fingers on the table, centimeters away from the fork. "Speaking of that, why haven't you killed me? That's kind of your job, right?"

He only grunted. I was about two seconds away from clawing the sound out of his throat. After interrupting my escape mission yesterday, he'd spent the better part of the night fixing my stitches and grunting. Always the grunt. No explanations, no threats, nothing. I almost wished he'd just threaten to tear my limbs off or some something.

"I need you," was all he said.

I picked up the fork and pushed my food around the plate. "Why?"

"You don't need to know why. You need to eat." He pointed his own fork at my completely untouched food.

I crossed my arms and gave him my best haughty glare. He tossed his fork down, entering my staring match. He was definitely winning.

"What?" he growled.

I swallowed the lump forming in my throat. Fear clawed its way up for the first time since finding myself here. Darragh kept me alive, but who knew why or for what purpose. Or how long he intended to keep me that way. The Angel of Death didn't let anyone slip him by.

Even though I'd almost completed the job for him anyway, things were different now. I had a few days to clear my head. Literally, because I was comatose for most of it, but there was also that other little thing Darragh said: *your family thinks you're dead.*

If they thought I was dead, they wouldn't look for me. They wouldn't find me if I was as far away from New York, and anyone associated with the mob as possible. Which meant I could be free.

I spent my whole life behind the barbed-wired walls of our home. I had no clue how to survive in the world, but I could figure it out if I was a dead woman. Nobody hunted down the dead.

Darragh still stared at me.

I lifted my fork. "Tell you what. If you answer one of my questions, I'll take a bite."

He crossed his own arms and if it was somehow possible, glared harder. "You're not in the position to be making demands."

No, no I was not. But here I was anyway. Pina, you're off to a great start, aren't you?

"Where am I?"

He didn't move. Not a single muscle twitched. To my surprise, he answered anyway. "My house upstate. We're in the mountains."

I took a bite.

He was still carved from stone when I fired off my next question, "Why did you take me here?"

37

This one took him longer to answer. Much longer.

"We have plans for ya."

"We?"

He nodded toward my plate. I swallowed as fast as I could. "My family."

Darragh's family. The O'Callaghan's. My family's sworn enemy since before I was even born. I had a feeling their *plans* for me weren't anything I'd want to stick around for.

I continued my breakfast in silence. I still wasn't completely sure about the food, but if it was poisoned, I was already screwed anyway. And I was really damn hungry. Almost dying does that, I guess. Darragh looked on with an expression like I was the most unsettling thing in the world, which in turn only made me feel like he was. Unsettling, that is.

And terrifying. And strange. And completely not what I expected, which only made the rest scarier.

"No more questions?" He asked.

I shrugged. "It's not like you'll tell me what your plans are. I figure I should save my breath."

Save my breath and use that energy to think of ways to escape. I had no clue what security measures Darragh had rigged in this place, but I seriously doubted it was your average mountain villa. And that wasn't even including the fact a literal murderer lived here. Outside of any hidden alarms, traps or whatever else, there was the teeny detail every weapon in this place was locked up tight. Darragh had even taken the liberty of removing every single steak knife from the wooden block beside the stove. *Bastardo.*

So that left exactly one option for a weapon: the little pistol glued to Darragh's hip. Even if I could somehow wrestle it away from him— and one look at his thick, corded arms told me that was a fat chance— I had no clue if it was even loaded. For all I knew, he wore it only to scare me. As if I needed any help there.

My eyes scanned over the kitchen, landing on the heavy, cast-iron frying pan on the stove.

Darragh didn't notice the split-second pause. I averted my gaze from that side of the kitchen, focusing in on the drapes instead.

"Did it snow last night?"

He nodded, following my gaze. "It starts early in the year here."

I continued sweeping my gaze over the open kitchen and connecting living room, swiveling in my chair. "If I'm going to be stuck here for a while, can you at least show me where everything is?"

It was a trick. He knew it. He said we were going to Vegas, but not why. If it really was just a trip, then it was safe to assume we'd come back here afterwards to hide, but it was far more likely it'd be a one-way trip for me.

Darragh was smart enough to leave me in the dark, so he took the bait. He pushed off the counter and gestured for me to follow him.

"If you're looking for escape routes, don't bother."

I smiled sweetly. "Wasn't planning on it."

He fixed me with a stare that said, *yes, you were*, but took me through the living room anyway. Besides a bare leather couch, a small TV hovering over the fireplace and the gun cases littered everywhere, it was bare. The room I stayed in lay behind an oak door off the open kitchen, but he didn't bother showing me that.

From there, we took a set of double French doors to a hallway lined with more nothing. The dark, hardwood floors creaked beneath our feet, but all else was silent. A winding set of stairs led to the second floor, where a second, smaller living room lay. Here, an entire wall was made from nothing but a spanning glass window. Two armchairs and a coffee table stood in front of it, facing out. My breath stole out of me as I took in the view.

We really were in the mountains. The snow-capped peaks dotted the rolling forest below, stretching as far as the eye could see. We were in the only house for miles. How the hell did this place even have electric?

My hopes of escape dwindled the longer I looked. Not a single home, building, or any sign of civilization. Except—

A puff of smoke curled upwards in the distance, only a mile or two away.

I pressed my lips together as Darragh tugged me along, saying the last door up here was his room, which I was strictly forbidden from entering.

We made our way back down the stairs and to the kitchen. I ran my hand over the counter, really trying hard not to stare at the frying pan. I drummed my fingers on the counter to hide their shaking.

"Can you show me where everything is in the kitchen?"

He frowned, accenting his smooth, pink lips. His blue eyes crinkled above them. "Why?"

I sighed, rolling my eyes. "Are you planning on cooking all my meals for me?"

My point was made. The frown never disintegrated, but he pulled open a few drawers and cabinets, explaining what was inside. I edged my way towards the stovetop, only pausing when Darragh turned to open a large pantry door.

"I don't care what you make, just clean up after yourself. Clear?"

I gripped the handle of the pan in both hands. "Clear."

His eyes widened a split second before the iron collided with his head.

8

PINA

Holy shit, that actually worked.

I wasn't about to waste time celebrating. Darragh was a crumpled, silent heap on the floor. A nasty gash gleamed red through his black hair. Wait . . . did I kill him? No, I didn't have time to think about that. When— if, whatever— he woke up, I needed to be as far from here as possible.

There was nothing in the living room and I didn't have time to search for a closet. I pulled off Darragh's massive, leather boots and tied them as tightly to my feet as I could. A coat was nowhere to be seen, so my flannel— Darragh's flannel— would have to do. I grabbed the gun from the holster at his hip, careful not to step into the blood dripping onto the kitchen floor. I couldn't leave tracks.

The gun was actually loaded. I popped open the chamber like I'd seen Andrea do a hundred times. Only one bullet out of six remained, but it was good enough. I whipped back the drapes and pulled at the heavy, frozen sliding door leading to a snow-covered backyard. An alarm blared above me, but I ignored it and dove for the tree line.

Branches snapped at my face and hair. The cold hit like a brick wall, making my eyes tear instantly. I had no clue what that puff of smoke was, but unless it was another murder dungeon in the woods, I'd say my odds were better than staying with Darragh. Puffy, dark clouds drifted overhead, turning the sunlight on and off and on and off as they passed. My breath came out in thick clouds in front of me, but that was good. The frozen snow gusted in an icy wind, covering my tracks. It wasn't wet enough to pack down and leave footprints.

My lungs screamed in agony, but I kept pushing, kept running. The bulky shoes were near impossible to move quickly in, but at least the snow covered the sound. It didn't make up for the continuous snap of broken twigs and branches, but I couldn't think of that. I a crested a hill and that puff of smoke became visible over the tree line.

Except . . . the smoke was moving.

I halted, throwing my hands over my ears as a blaring sound cut through the silent woods. The trees shook little patches of snow from their branches with the sound wave. I'd only heard that sound in movies, but I knew exactly what it was.

A train.

The smoke was from a train. And that train was moving away from me.

The odds of me catching up to the train were slim to goddamn none, but my options were kind of limited. I picked up the pace, tripping over my own feet as I raced down the hill. I cut my path to the left, trying to follow that drifting cloud of smoke.

Something moved in the trees. I was only halfway down the hill, but the winter-bare branches of the forest allowed a peek at the racing piece of freedom dead ahead. Train cars painted in bright blue swooshed past, faster than light, when something hit me from me behind.

A heavy weight bore down and sent me rolling down the hill. Thick hands held onto me and a set of icy, blue eyes flickered in and out with each roll. The sky danced above and the snow melted through my thin flannel. All while the train got further and further away.

I landed on top of Darragh at the bottom, inches away from a bush filled with thorns. A trail of blood drops scattered down the hill and now seeped into the snow from his busted head. A look of pure fury crossed his face and his hands latched onto my hips. The train echoed again, farther away now. In a few more minutes, it'd be gone forever.

Something cold and hard poked into my stomach from the waistband of my pants. The gun.

I whipped it out, but Darragh knocked it from my hands and sent it skidding across the patch of ice we laid on. I fell forward, catching myself on his chest, as he went back to holding my hips in place. Heavy breaths panted out of us, but nothing could be heard over the sound of the train, my one chance at freedom, blaring its horn and rolling away.

I sat on top of his stomach, straddling his rock-hard sides with my thighs. His body heat seeped through my wet pants and hands still planted on his chest.

I had no other weapons. He was stronger than me and clearly a hell of a lot faster. The train was rolling away and I was out of fucking time.

Something changed in his face when he noticed our position. His body tightened beneath mine, but the fury leaked out of his eyes and lips and something else, something more . . . primal came over.

I still had one more weapon.

I kissed him.

He went stiller than death. My lips brushed against his, filling my mouth with the taste of blood and sweat and snow. But there was something else too, a hint of oak, just like the brandy Paulina snuck me, just like I imagined.

I pushed my hands further up his chest. His mouth parted for me and began to move with mine. His warm, intoxicating scent filled me, overshadowing everything else. The smoke, the snow, the train . . . it all fled from my thoughts as he took my lower lip between his teeth and passed his tongue over mine.

The hands at my hips tightened and the hips beneath me rolled. A little moan escaped me and I grinded down, not entirely sure what the feeling was but knowing it fueled the heat burning between my thighs. Those hands slid up my back, setting fire along my spine. I pushed my hips down again, letting that fire ignite further, losing myself in the warm taste of musk and iron on my lips. Something hard pressed at my aching core. The kiss deepened. A shuddering breath escaped me, and this time, Darragh's moan echoed back across my lips.

Darragh's moan.

Darragh.

This was Darragh O'Callaghan.

Escape—

I froze above him, but he didn't stop. He gripped me fiercely, pulling me tighter against him. An angry grunt echoed from him and he took my mouth with his. Harder. Frenzied. I kissed him back, dipping my tongue into his mouth and brushing it across the surface. He groaned again and rolled his hips against mine, but that fire was gone. I slid my hands up his neck and dug my fingers into his hair. He already had that head wound and we laid on a thick patch of ice. All it would take was one hit. Throwing all my power into one stroke of slamming his head into the ground. I tugged at the thick, black strands at his head. My breath came in heavy pants but if it was from the kiss or from the fear, I didn't know.

All it would take was—

Darragh stopped.

His lips froze a hair away from mine. He closed his eyes, taking breaths through his mouth that cascaded over my cheeks. Time stopped, both of us freezing with it. Only the heavy up-and-down of his chest beneath mine told me this was still real.

"Go back to the house," he whispered.

His eyes were still closed. My hands were still in his hair. I tried to shove him away but he rolled on top of me.

I screamed and clawed at his face. He trapped my wrists against the ground, the ice so cold it burned along my skin. A feral

44

growl escaped him, but I wasn't giving up. I threw my knee up between his legs, but he only pinned my ankles down with his feet. I thrashed beneath him, screaming and screaming, praying to god or whoever else was listening in these woods.

"Shut up," Darragh growled.

I screamed louder.

"Stop."

My voice died in my throat and hot tears sprang to my eyes. "Stop screaming," he growled.

I spit in his face.

The air brushed cool death against my cheek as he pulled us up. The trees spun upside down. I only had a moment to think before I was thrown over his shoulder.

I pounded my fists into his back, screaming over and over again. Hot blood itched at the back of my throat, and it wasn't Darragh's this time. But it didn't matter. I could scream all I want, punch him all I want, try to kill him as many times as I fucking wanted to. It was over.

My screams turned into whimpers. Those turned into silent sobs. I shook against his back, but Darragh didn't say a word. The forest grew silent around us and the Angel of Death carried me back to hell.

9

DARRAGH

My head was fecking pounding.

I paced back and forth across my bathroom, opening and slamming shut drawers. Where in the ever loving feck did I put that gauze? I had it last night to fix Giuseppina's stitches and now it was gone. And blood was getting all over my hardwood. Mother of fecking shit.

Giuseppina's eyes followed me the entire time, rimmed with red. She hadn't stopped fecking crying since the woods and it was taking everything I had not to finish this right now. At least she stopped screaming. I couldn't deal with screaming broads.

I took a moment to watch her— make sure she didn't have any more bloody brilliant escape plans. Her hands laid in her lap, tied up. Ankles tied up too. In the twenty minutes I'd been searching the cabinets she hadn't moved a single inch from where I propped her against the clawfoot tub.

I held my face in my hands and took a moment to breathe. To think. My Ma always said it was biggest flaw, getting frustrated too fast and blowing everything to hell instead of just taking a moment to calm the hell down.

But I wasn't calm.

I underestimated her. Badly. The sheltered mafia princess didn't know a damn thing about the outside world, but she sure as hell had fight. Men twice her size hadn't fought like that, and they definitely didn't have her brains. I hid every goddamn weapon in this place but left out a fecking frying pan.

At this point, I wasn't sure if I was mad about the escape or mad because of the begrudging respect I had for it.

If I was gonna be honest, I even felt a little bad about tying her up, but there was no way in hell I was leaving her out of sight and I couldn't hold her down every two minutes either.

Just because the devil wanted to feck with me a little more today, my phone's been blowing up with non-stop calls from Sean. Details of this Vegas hit I was supposed to do. With Giuseppina. Tomorrow.

I took another deep breath and searched under the sink one more time. There. Gauze, needles and medical thread, just where I left it.

She'd done a number on my head. Granted, most of the blow came from the fact that pan weighed more than her, but I was shocked her thin, little arms could even lift it. Adrenaline's a bitch.

Three towels full of blood later and I'd stopped bleeding enough to stitch it. As I threaded the needle thoughts of the woods crashed back into my brain. Thoughts I'd been too angry to even dwell on.

A thousand lifetimes wouldn't be enough to understand what happened back there. The best I could do was chalk it up to a brief moment of losing my goddamn mind. On any given day, women were just about the last thought I had. When I was younger, fucking and killing were my two favorite specialties. Lately, it'd just been killing.

Women, they never stuck around long when they found out what my real job was.

So, it was insanity and going too long without getting my rocks off, the only rational explanation for why I did what I did. Good thing we were going to Vegas.

I glanced at Giuseppina's reflection in the mirror. She wasn't looking at me anymore. She turned herself to the window, watching the frozen, little snowflakes that started an hour ago. It was the kind of snow that crossed from the ethereal to the strange. When the woods were more silent than death and the air froze around you. Back in Ireland, as a child, my Ma told me those little snowflakes were winter spirits coming to Earth.

That little story from my childhood did nothing for me now. I grunted and faced my own reflection again. After downing enough whiskey to kill a horse and pouring the rest on my head, I pushed through the first stitch.

I hated this shit. You'd think it gets easier, but that's just what you tell yourself each time you're done. I grunted against the next three stitches and felt numb by the fourth, but the cut went too far behind my head and I couldn't reach the damn thing anymore. Ten minutes went by and the fifth stitch still remained in the needle.

I cursed and threw the needle in the sink. Giuseppina shifted behind me, but I had no patience for her shit either.

Her tiny voice murmured behind me, "Let me do it."

I broke out laughing. "Why, so you can stick a needle in my eye?"

A fresh round of tears welled up in her eyes. Brown eyes, big and round and innocent. She took a shaky breath and shook her head. "You did mine. I owe you."

I eyed her through the mirror. Tears were trickling down her face now. I didn't blame her for the escape. As said, I even kind of respected it. But I sure as hell didn't trust her.

"If you're going to keep me here, just let me do something." She sniffled, and I decided it wasn't just about getting my rocks off. I was well and losing it, because I cut through her zip ties and pulled a chair over in front of the mirror. If I was seriously letting her use a needle on my head, I'd at least watch her reflection while she did it.

She stood behind the chair and met my gaze in the mirror. The needle looked huge in her hand compared to near nothing in mine. Hell, even sitting in the chair still had me nearly at her height.

"I don't know what to do."

"Just push the needle through and tie off the thread. It doesn't have to be pretty."

She frowned but did it. I grabbed a second bottle of whiskey off the counter and started chugging.

She worked in silence. Her tiny fingers looped through the thread, expertly pulling at the knots and beginning the next stitch.

48

She didn't know how to do stitches, but the girl could fecking sew. A small blessing there.

The minutes ticked by when she finally said, "What happens to me in Vegas?"

I took another swig of whiskey. It was definitely starting to go to my head, because I asked, "Do you want the easy answer or do you want the truth?"

She'd fully worked through another stitch before she answered, "The truth."

The truth couldn't hurt at this point. She wasn't dumb. She knew there was some real shit in store for her, so there was no point in trying to lie. "My father's sending me there to take out a dirty cop. I'm ordered to kill you and make it look like a couple's fight gone wrong."

Maybe I should've waited to tell her because her hands began shaking. With the needle still in my head. "Why would you do that?"

I took another hit of the bottle. What the hell, she was a dead woman walking anyway. "To pin a cop's death on the Delarosa's and prevent that alliance from happening with Lucien. Two birds, one stone."

She nodded like that made perfect sense. She was crying again and her hands shook harder, but she was nodding. Again, that begrudging respect surged. Enough that I was tempted to tell her I was kidding and everything would be fine.

"So," she said. Her voice shook around the word. "What happens if I run away? Or get help?"

I met her eyes in the glass. She wouldn't stop fighting. I knew it. She knew it. But we both knew something else: there was no fecking point.

I've never killed a lady. And kids were completely off the table. It didn't make me the epitome of moral or anything, but I only took out those who were involved. Those who knew the risks and stuck with the life anyway. But this girl, she didn't have that choice. She was just unfortunate enough to be born with the wrong last name.

She shook her head. "Never mind."

I gripped her wrist. She flinched, which only made me feel more like shit. Then I felt like shit for even thinking I deserved to feel like shit. I just told this young girl I planned to kill her, not in the nicest way either.

What the hell was wrong with me?

I held the whiskey bottle over my head. "We call it liquid courage."

A shaky laugh breathed out of her. "I think I could use some of that." Then she took the longest goddamn swig I'd ever seen a lady take.

She went to hand me back the bottle, but I shook my head. "All yours."

She finished stitching. Even covered the wound in some antibiotic shit I didn't know I owned and covered the rest with gauze. When all was said and done, both of us stayed rooted to the spot.

"I have one request," she said.

I nodded at her reflection.

She wrung her hands together, taking a deep breath. "I've never . . . never gone out. In my whole life. I was always stuck in the house—"

She looked up and blinked away more tears. Brave. Brave and smart. It was a hell of a combination.

"Yeah?" I prompted.

"So I want one good night. I want to go to the movies, or drink at a bar, or go dancing or whatever. I want to go with one night where I actually enjoyed life." She blinked back more tears. "And another request, actually. Don't tell me when you do it."

I nodded. "Yeah, sure."

She glanced around the bathroom. There was no more shaking. No more crying. But she definitely wanted to get the hell out of here. Away from me.

"That's it," she said. She stepped away. "I'm going to lie down."

"Yeah, you do that," I told her. It was a bad idea, letting her wander on her own, but I was suddenly too tired to even care.

10

———

DARRAGH

The closest airport was a five-hour drive and Giuseppina didn't speak for a single minute of it. All that bravado she showed at first was completely drained. Because of me.

I wouldn't let myself feel guilt, though. That was a death sentence for people like me. So, I took her silence as a small blessing and blasted the radio instead.

Traffic built up the closer we got to NYC. When the cars were lined bumper to bumper, I took the chance to look at her.

I hadn't really paid attention before. You never did when you knew you were ending someone's life. So, I hadn't noticed the way her long legs curved out of petite little hips. She rested her feet up on the dashboard, red toenails winking back at me. I followed those legs down again, over the curve of her stomach and up to her face, hovering on her full, pink lips a little too long. Other than those, her hair, skin and eyes were all the same soft, caramel shade. Like god only used one color when he painted her to life.

She was gorgeous. Anyone with a set of eyes could see that.

I didn't look at her again.

Weakness got men killed, and weakness came in many forms. It didn't matter if it was a faulty gun, a sudden sense of guilt or a pair of long, golden legs.

Pat was waiting for us, right on time. With each encounter we had, the man seemed to grow older. His newspaper cap covered up most of his greying hair, but nothing could fix the sores on his hands and face. Cancer and time, both a bitch.

"How's it going, Darragh?" He tipped his hat at me.

I nodded. "You got everything?"

He grinned. "Just like your Da." He handed me a yellow envelope that'd clearly been used and reused a thousand times. Cheap bastard. Inside were licenses and passports, a set for me with the name Eamon Connelly, and a set for Giuseppina, who was now known as Lacey Connelly.

Giuseppina frowned at the matching last names.

Pat tipped his hat again. "Be safe and have fun."

Giuseppina glared. "I won't."

Pat's smile faltered, but he had the good wits to just walk away.

JFK was a shithole filled with an endless stream of people, as usual. I had enough of airports for a lifetime, but Giuseppina was more than intrigued. Her doe eyes followed all the people, the flashing lights, even the fecking fast food court caught her gaze.

I dragged her to the gate before she could ask me for anything.

Her legs bounced in her plastic, blue seat. Despite the purpose for the trip, she actually seemed excited.

I was just counting down the seconds until all of this was done. Then it was back to the safe house. I'll have a whole fecking case of whiskey delivered.

"Giuseppina." Her leg wouldn't stop bouncing and she was paying me no attention. I planted a hand on her knee to keep her foot on the ground.

"Pina," she said.

I sighed. "What?"

"Pina," she murmured, eyes still darting in every fecking direction but me. "I like to be called Pina. That's part of my 'happy last days' request."

"You get a day."

She turned on me. "I get whatever I want."

The heat drained from her eyes and she planted a fake smile on her face as a flight attendant walked by.

"Fine, Pina." I held her knee down when she tried to bounce it again. She drummed her nails on the seat instead. "For the flight, for the hotel, for anything from here on out, I do all the talking. Are we understood?"

"Crystal fucking clear," she drawled. So, her bite was back. Wonderful.

We boarded. Everything we brought with us was already checked in and stored beneath the plane. I don't know how he did it, but the FBI clearance Pat swung made the process a hell of a lot easier. Legally checking a gun and sound equipment onto aircraft was no fecking joke nowadays.

Of course, all the flight attendants were aware "Special Agent Connelly" was on board. They gave us a wide berth.

"Oh no," she said. A tiny frown formed on her lips.

I gripped her arms, trying to pull her back through the single file line. "What?"

"I didn't get a window seat."

I breathed out a sigh of relief. "One, 'Oh no's' and anything like it are only reserved for real problems. Two, Pat's a cheap bastard. Sorry."

Her face crumpled, but she nodded, bite gone again.

The asshole in the window seat bumped along to headphones plugged into a Walkman. Pina sat in the middle. Me, the aisle.

She tapped the lad on his shoulder.

I gripped her knee in warning, but it was too late. She gave him a dazzling smile as he glared and pulled a padded headphone from his ear.

"Hi, this is my first time on a plane. Like, ever. And I know you got the window seat, but I'd really appreciate it if I could sit there."

The guy watched her, nodding along to every word, only to follow-up with, "Sorry, I like the window."

Her smile cracked, but she kept going. "I know this is really strange and personal, but I'm actually dying. I'll never get another chance to go on a plane, so I'd really appreciate it if—"

The asshole let go of his headphone, letting it snap back to his ear and drown her out.

Pina turned to me with a tear-stained smile. She shrugged, trying to play it off, but was failing miserably.

Feck.

"Go to the bathroom," I told her.

She tried to keep smiling, but it wasn't working. "What?"

"Go to the bathroom and calm down." I handed her a tissue from my pocket. She stared at it.

"Pina."

She grabbed the tissue and walked down the aisle.

I slid into the middle seat and tapped the bastard on his shoulder. He had the fecking balls to roll his eyes and pushed his headphones to his neck. "Look—"

"You, look," I leaned in close, dropping my voice to a whisper. "You're gonna give your seat to the lady, or I'm gonna rip your fecking eyes from your head and shove them down your throat."

Pina arrived a moment later, smiling like a kid at the now empty window seat. The asshole flinched when she climbed over him, now on my right, to get to it.

"What happened?" she whispered.

I shrugged. "He just changed his mind, don't know."

She glued her face to the glass, only pausing to grab the armrests in a death grip during take-off. Again, I found myself watching her. Like an idiot.

Her brilliant smile never went away. In the most fecked up, twisted way I could think of things, it was kind of because of something I did. I couldn't remember the last time I'd made someone smile like that. Probably never.

I jerked my chin towards the glass as we flew over desert. "Keep your eyes open. The first time you see Vegas from a plane is something you never forget."

She practically vibrated in her seat. "I just can't wrap my mind around how tiny everything looks."

I nodded along, not sure what to say. The thrill of it all was lost on me. The first time I'd been on a plane was the flight from Ireland to America, right after everything went to hell. It always kind of ruined the experience.

"Very small," I finally supplied.

To my disappointment, Pina clapped when the plane landed. Louder than anyone else.

The hotel Pat booked was right next to the casino where the cop was hiding out. I'm sure it killed Pat. The place was right on the main strip and was definitely not within Pat's normal budget. Pina was still acting like a bloody golden retriever as we entered the hotel and took the stairs, at my insistence and Pina's annoyance, to the penthouse. High viewpoint, and all that.

Her face turned to complete shock when we walked in. Even I had to admit it was fecking nice.

While she got ready, I used the hotel phone to check in with Sean. All he said was, "Call me when it's done," before hanging up.

According to our info, the cop worked his shift tomorrow night. Somewhere between today and tomorrow it was off with Pina, tomorrow the cop, then by this time Wednesday I'd be heading home. The first thing I'd do when I got back is forget this shit ever happened.

Thankfully, the full bar was stocked. I downed a half a bottle of whiskey before Pina came out.

Wearing . . . that.

"You're wearing my clothes."

She shrugged, red crawling up her neck. "I don't have any of my own."

I sighed. "Come on. We'll find you something."

56

The dress Pina wanted was going to be a problem.

She walked out of the fitting room in a red gown that'd make a porn star blush. She was a small girl, but apparently her tits didn't get the memo because the thick curve of them taunted me through a V cut deeper than the black pit of my heart. The rest of the fabric clung in all the right places, hugging her gentle curves and exposing one, perfectly golden leg through a slit high enough to be dangerous.

Every guy in the place stopped shopping while the salesgirl clapped and squealed along with Pina. She did several turns in the mirror, either completely ignoring or completely ignorant to every guy within ten feet's jaw hitting the floor.

I gripped the armrest. "No."

Pina stopped her twirl. A caramel eyebrow arched sky high. "No?"

The store went silent. They tried to cover it up, but there was suddenly a lot more shoppers at the racks closest to us..

"It's just a little," I waved my hand, looking for a word that wouldn't activate Pina's claws. "Flashy."

"Flashy?"

"Flashy."

The salesgirl looked between us and laughed. "Get it, sweetheart. Your husband is just a *little* jealous. Trust me, you'll be thanking me later." The last part was directed at me. The husband.

Pina's gaze of death never left me. "Is that right, *honey?* Are you *jealous?*"

Jealous wasn't the right word for it. Homicidal, maybe.

I caught the eyes of every guy peeking at her through the mirrors. All their gazes flicked to the floor. I didn't have the right. Not even a little, but that didn't stop me.

Pina flipped her hair over her shoulder and twirled back to the mirror. "I'm getting it."

The irrational part of my brain flared to life. "Find something else."

She shrugged, pursing her lips at her reflection. "I like this one."

The salesgirl looked between us.

"No."

"Yes."

"Pina. *No*."

Twenty minutes and three hundred dollars later, we left with the dress. As well as heels, a purse (clutch? I don't even know), and earrings the salesgirl claimed Pina "absolutely had to have." There must have been some girl code shit going on because they both gave me bitchy glares right after that was said.

Pina's perfect night continued with her showing off the dress. In public. She made me walk the strip four times before deciding she wanted to see a burlesque show. From there, it was a casino (she lost eight hundred dollars), then back to the strip (she won ten bucks from some random street game). Then dinner. Then a rooftop bar for Pina's first ever cocktail. And second. And third.

Anyone who called New York the city that never sleeps had clearly never been here. My watch gleamed back at me, 3:05, but people were still everywhere. It was damn near impossible to hear anything over the live music and sounds of the bar, but Pina's whispered words made it to me anyway.

She took a long sip of her Pina Colada and stared out into the distance. Her face barely moved as she asked, "Do you like it?"

I downed another shot of whiskey. The bartender gave me a look reserved for people who didn't know who the feck they were talking to. "Like what?"

"Your . . . job."

Right now? No. But I couldn't say that to her. I shouldn't have even been saying it to myself. Vegas had never been my scene. New York really wasn't either, but we couldn't run our operations from the wilderness. But I still found myself enjoying tonight. I couldn't give a feck about the shows or the casinos, but it made Pina happy, so it was nice. To make her happy.

Which only made this whole thing more fecked up. I'd done a lot of things with my hits before finishing the job. I played their friend, their ally, I lied, but I never put a hit in a red evening gown and took them out on the town. I never promised them "one perfect night" before putting a bullet in their head. People looked at this life and said I was sick, but none of them men I've killed before were innocent.

This— this was sick. I was sick in the head right now.

"I do what I have to do. Same as my Da. Same as my brothers. It never bothered me before."

As if reading my mind, she asked, "And now?"

I had nothing to say to that, so I downed another shot instead. Then told the bartender to just leave the bottle.

Pina was right and smashed by the time we stumbled back from the bar. I couldn't say what possessed her to buy heels that high when she'd never worn them before, but long story short, I spent the last half of the walk carrying her in my arms. I crashed through the door of our hotel room and threw the stupid, little shoes in the trash before tossing her onto the bed.

The penthouse had way nicer beds than this one, but she insisted it would be her room. Part of me wanted to say it was just a comfort thing, maybe like her bed back home or something, but I knew it was just to defy me. Tell me no. Have some sense of control over a situation she had no fecking control over. A whole life she had no control over.

Once, I knew another woman just like that.

She was half asleep by the time I pulled off my shoes. I threw the cover over her and sat at the edge of her bed, waiting for her to be fully asleep. She was drunk and in bed. She asked me not to tell her when, and I was more than happy to oblige. Killing someone in a penthouse was a ridiculous mess, but if I didn't do this now, I didn't think I could.

I stood to grab my gun when her arm reached out from the covers. "What are you doing?" she mumbled, eyes still closed.

I shut my eyes, drawing a deep breath. "Just go to sleep, Pina."

"Stay," she murmured.

My eyes snapped open, but she hadn't moved. Her little form huddled under the blanket.

"Stay," she said again.

"I have my own bed," I told her.

Her caramel throat bobbed up and down. "I've never slept next to someone before. I want to try it . . . once . . ." Her voice drifted off, replaced by soft breathing a moment later.

Feck. Feck this. Feck Pina. Feck this fecking hit.

The world was tipping sideways but that didn't stop me from grabbing the last of the liquor in the fridge. It wasn't strong enough. Nothing would be fecking strong enough for this.

My gun was on the counter, already loaded. I sat on one of the high-tops and pressed my forehead to the counter, trying to even my breaths. Trying not to get frustrated so I could get the job fecking done.

You've done this a hundred times before.

This is not different.

She is not special.

This is a job.

I repeated those words until they almost rang true. I lifted my head from the granite, grabbed the gun, and went back to Pina's room.

I sat on the edge of her bed.

I tried to whisper her name, but my voice was gone. The second time, I actually made a sound. "Pina?"

Nothing.

"Pina, you asleep?"

Still nothing, save for her soft breath against the sheets.

I pointed the gun at her head.

Do it.

Just do it, ya weak bastard.

I sat like that until my arm went numb and dropped to the bed.

This was different. It was different because she didn't choose this. It was different because she'd already tried to hurt herself and like an idiot, I saved her. It was different because it was one thing to kill dirty mobsters and another to hurt an innocent woman who just wanted a chance at having a life.

I couldn't do it. Again. And this time, it wasn't because she reminded me of my Ma.

No, it was because for the first time, I felt like a complete fecking animal.

I threw the gun on the ground and kicked it away.

Sean wanted her dead and he wanted it bad. I couldn't blame him. The Delarosa's and the Rocci's were ganging up on us and my brother's head would be next on the line. Rory's head. So, Pina needed to die. If I didn't do it, Sean would just send someone else to finish the job. Right after beating my arse and getting creative enough with I never questioned him again. If he didn't just kill me outright for disobeying him.

I could spin something up to explain why we had no body, but Pina would have to disappear. Forever.

Before I could talk some sense into myself, I dialed Pat's number.

"Boy, do ya have any fecking idea what time—"

"I need something."

Pat's voice drained to a whisper. "You in trouble, Darragh?"

My eyes drifted over Pina, still sleeping soundly. "You could say that."

"What do you need?"

"A European passport, a license, five grand in cash and absolute silence. By Wednesday."

He sighed through the phone. "Well, why don't you just ask for the Queen of England while you're fecking at it?"

"No pictures on the passport and make the name female."
I thought for a moment. "Greek. Greek and female."

"Darragh, that's gonna take some ti—"

"Please." I closed my eyes against the sudden pounding in my head. "Pat, I've never asked you for anything personal before. Just . . . please."

"This have to do with the Delarosa girl?"

My jaw clenched. I could lie, but Pat's been alive long enough to sniff bullshit a mile away. "Yes."

"Your Da—"

"I'll give you anything you want."

He was silent a long moment. "Someone else could handle this, you know. You're not the only gunny boy we got."

I sighed, pinching the bridge of my nose. "Just trust me on me this, Pat. Please."

"I trust ya with my life. Same for your Da and brother. Your Ma and other brothers too, god rest their souls." Another long moment of silence passed. "She asked me to take care of you. She knew what this life can do, so she made me promise. I went to Ireland to get ya myself because of that promise. I swore my life on it."

I nodded. The pounding in my head turned to a hammer. "I know, Pat."

"So I'll do this for you, but you're gonna tell me why. Not now, not tomorrow, but I'm gonna fulfill that promise to your Ma before I die. So don't think you're getting off too easy."

A humorless smile pulled at my lips. "Wouldn't dream of it."

"I'll have it on Wednesday when you get off the plane."

"And this stays between us?"

"On your mother's soul and the lord above. Just me and you."

After discussing a few more details, Pat went back to bed. I went back to being a complete fecking creep and watching Pina sleep.

I couldn't believe I was doing this.

But I couldn't dwell on it now. I had a hit tomorrow. That was priority. That's what I came here to do.

She'd have questions. Questions I didn't have the time or the answers for. So, I'd tell her tomorrow night, right before we left and when the real hit was done. There wouldn't be a ton of time between the kill and getting the hell out of the city. She could talk all she wanted on the ten-minute ride to the airport. I'd get her arse on the flight and by the time we hit JFK she'd be twelve hours away from her new life in Greece. If the Delarosa's found her and killed her for running away, at least I tried. End of story. Never to be thought about again.

I found the room furthest away from hers and collapsed into the bed. She had a whole lifetime to find someone else to sleep next to.

11

PINA

Darragh didn't kill me in the night.

The kiss in the woods was only the start of the new plan forming in my head. For all the terror Darragh imposed on my family, he was still human. More importantly, he was still a man. Made Men were more than happy to raise a fist to a woman, to manipulate us, and to sleep with us. But no men, not even my cold-hearted brother or father, were happy to kill a woman. They preferred us on the outskirts, pretty little fuck toys to warm their beds and hang onto their arms, but we weren't supposed to be involved in business. After everything, I had a feeling Darragh was the same.

So, I played the part well. I sobbed about the end of my life, I forced him to analyze every detail of this job and I made him uncomfortable with everything he was planning to do. Last night would have been the perfect opportunity, but he didn't take it. Grown men could beg for their lives, but women had something so much stronger: the power of a pussy and a whole lot of tears. There was no doubt in my mind he still planned to kill me— he was Darragh O'Callaghan, after all— but I made him hesitate. And if I could keep him hesitating until tonight, then I could attempt to get the hell out of here.

Unsurprisingly, Darragh was already awake when I rose from bed. I wondered if he ever slept. He was fiddling with some equipment I couldn't even begin to name as I entered the kitchen. "Breakfast?"

His eyebrow shot up, but he said nothing. I placed my hands on my hips and met his stare.

I left my room wearing one of his dress shirts, which was so large it basically functioned as a dress. My only clothes were the red dress he bought yesterday which left me with few other options. His eyes followed me the whole walk from my doorway, around the island and to the stove in front him.

I leaned against the counter and faced him, planting my hands on the countertop behind me. I wasn't terribly shy. It was hard to be, when men leered at me my entire life no matter how much clothing I wore. Darragh's gaze burrowed into me though, starting at my feet and making an endlessly slow ascent to land on my face, taking a whole lot more time than necessary on my bare legs.

"You should get dressed," he said.

I tilted my head to the side. "You should have bought me more clothes."

Without a word, he walked to his suite and arrived back with a pair of his dress pants. He tossed them at me over the island. They landed at my feet.

I gave him a withering glare and bent down, slowly, to pick them up. His hard swallow was the only audible sound in the room.

I pulled the pants on, rolling up the cuffs no less than five times so they didn't drag all over the floor.

When I turned back to the stove, he sighed. "What are you doing?"

"What?" I asked innocently. Thankfully, the fridge was stocked. I pulled out eggs, cheese and a pepper, placing them on the counter while I dug for a pan.

"I'm not going to fuck you."

I jumped at the implication, whirling around. "I never asked you too."

His eyes turned into slits.

I prowled toward the island and leaned on the countertop. Despite himself, his eyes never hovered higher than my collarbones.

"What would make you think for even a second I could stomach the thought of sleeping with you?" I whispered.

His eyes pulled up to meet mine, darker than before. His whole body tensed around that gaze.

"Desperation," he finally said.

My nostrils flared through the hot breath I exhaled. "I'd rather die with dignity."

I couldn't read the expression he wore. I turned away from him, realizing instantly putting my back to the mass murderer in the room wasn't smart, but I didn't want to see his face.

I cracked the first egg into the pan when he said behind me, "I'm not going to kill you."

My hands froze around the two halves of an eggshell, the yolk slowly dripping out while I wondered if I heard that correctly. The hiss of it hitting the frying pan was the only thing that filled the room.

"What?" I asked, my voice so quiet it was a wonder he heard me at all.

"There's been another change of plans," he said.

Too good to be true. I learned the hard way that anything that sounded as such usually was. This was just another way to keep me tame while he did what he had to do. He couldn't take me on the job with him, so he needed to make sure I wouldn't try to pull anything while he was busy with the hit. I'd be as good as a sitting duck if I listened.

"What changes?" I asked. I didn't think he would tell me, but it'd look suspicious if I didn't ask. I didn't want him to think I was onto him.

"I'll explain tomorrow," he said. And that was that.

I nodded, trying to hurry up cooking my breakfast so I could go hide. I originally planned to make some for him too as a part of my guilt mission, but I didn't think I could handle an extra minute with him only three feet away.

I ate my breakfast in bed and spent the rest of the day in my room, alternating between staring mindlessly at the TV and thinking of every possible way I could sneak out of the room while Darragh was gone. He snipped the phone lines before we left yesterday, so straight up just calling the police was out. I also didn't think Darragh would be dumb enough to leave the front door unbarricaded.

I approached the window in my room, fiddling with the lock. Like most high windows in Vegas, this one didn't open. But if I could find a way to shatter it, maybe I could climb to the roof. We were on the top floor, so it wouldn't be too far.

I searched around the room, looking for anything sharp enough or heavy enough. The thick, wooden bed frame wouldn't break glass— I already tried that trick enough times in my bedroom at home before my father finally put bars on my windows. The old-fashioned rotary phone on the nightstand was useless for making calls, but the thick metal may do the trick with enough force behind it.

Now, there was nothing to do but wait.

I sat on my bed, bouncing my knee up and down on the floor while the hours ticked by. The clock beside my bed read 10:38, which meant Darragh had to be leaving soon. I twitched with each little movement heard through my closed door, waiting for the sound of the front one to snick shut. Instead, Darragh came into my room a little after eleven.

We stared at one another in a long moment of tense silent, so thick you could almost pluck it from the air.

"Put your dress on," he finally said.

My mouth dried out. No . . . that wasn't part of the plan.

I crossed my arms. "Why?"

His eyes darted to the window, like he could already sense my ridiculous plan. "Just do it," he said, shutting the door behind him.

———————

Half an hour later we were checked out of the penthouse and heading for the casino. My red dress swished behind me and my hair and makeup were done to perfection. Some skills from my childhood were useful, after all.

Right before the doors, Darragh pulled me to a stop. He was armed to the teeth, but you could never tell. His gun holster was artfully hidden under his suit, along with knives along his ankles, forearms and hips. His dark eyes searched mine and terror filled me. I let it show, but that did nothing to tame the wild look in his eyes.

The plan was simple: I went inside and sat at the cop's table. I played until his shift ended at midnight and asked him for a drink at the bar. After that, I not-so-discreetly suggested we go to a nearby motel for a night of continued fun. The entire time an earpiece would be strapped to my breast with Darragh listening in. I'd let the cop choose the motel to not raise suspicion, Darragh would hear and then he'd meet us there. He didn't say, but I assumed the next step was killing both me and the cop.

His grip tightened on my upper arm as he pulled me close. His other wrapped around my waist. To anyone else, it only looked like he whispered something dirty to me before saying goodbye.

"You follow the plan. And if you do anything else— If you try *anything*— I'll kill Andrea next."

The blood drained my face. How did he know—

"I heard you whispering his name in your sleep. We wouldn't want to drag your favorite brother into this, would we?" He released me and stood back.

Tears welled in my eyes, but I had no time to rethink plans now. I'd figure out how to warn Andrea later. One step at a time. I needed to take this one step at a time.

"You disgust me," I said. I didn't have to pretend anything this time.

I couldn't see his face as he pulled away and backed down the street. It was time.

The first thing I did was run for the back of the room. After sweetly asking the bartender for a pen and paper, I scribbled my note.

This is a set-up. The Irish mob is holding me hostage.

When you get off your shift, have one drink at the bar with me and pretend we're going to a hotel.

Call your friends in witness protection and meet me in the back alley after.

I'm wearing a wire.

The target dealt at a blackjack table on the far side of the room. No windows and no close escape routes, but that worked for me. The less Darragh could see, the better.

I sat down at an open seat and took the cards he handed to me. The cop barely paid me any attention. He seemed to be around the same age as Darragh, late twenties to early thirties. His stark blonde hair glowed in the thick casino lights and his dark eyes remained fixed on the table. I took a peek at my cards. I had no idea how to play, but it didn't matter. His shift ended in eight minutes.

After losing two hundred dollars in a matter of seconds, a new dealer came over and relieved the target of his shift. I stood up hastily, causing a few glances from the people my way, but nothing more. I bee-lined for the dealer.

"Hey," I said, flashing him a smile. He watched me warily and nodded. He didn't stop his walk towards the casino exit.

"Would you like to have a drink?" I asked, speeding up.

His shoulders hunched forward as he shrugged on a jacket. "I can't get you your money back and I have to get home. I'm sure you can find another nice guy in here though."

69

I bristled and reached for his hand. Anger crossed his face, replaced by confusion as I slipped the note into his palm. As he unfolded it, I continued in the sexiest voice I could muster. "I know . . . it's just that my husband left me here all alone and I'm lonely. I could really use a nice guy to talk to. Maybe you can teach me how to play better?"

He gave me a confused look before skimming the note. His eyes widened and the paper crushed into a ball in his fist. His eyes darted around, looking for something he wouldn't see. I gave him an urgent stare and cocked my head towards the bar.

"Uh . . . yeah, sure. Why not. What do you like to drink?"

I grimaced. It wasn't exactly convincing, but hopefully it was enough to deter Darragh from busting inside and finishing the job with witnesses, consequences be damned. I slung my arm through his and walked toward the bar. I reached up in a fluid movement and pulled the V of my dress slightly down, revealing the wire. The cop nodded and pulled me along faster.

I sat at one of the high-tops and smiled at the bartender. "I'll have a martini."

The cop waved his hand when the bartender looked his way. "Nothing for me."

I squinted at him.

"Actually, pour me a Stella. Thanks."

The cop sat at the stool beside me.

He nodded. "So, what's your name?"

"Lacey. And you?"

"Jim." It wasn't his real name, but it didn't matter.

"So . . . what's it like to work in a casino?"

I took another napkin off the bar and gestured for a pen from the bartender. I scribbled out a second message and slid it across the wood. *Make it convincing.*

The tense small talk continued for some time. I made "Jim" order three more drinks, each of which I only took a sip of before dumping in a nearby plant. I wasn't sure if our conversation was enough to convince Darragh I'd wooed the target, but it was getting

70

late and it had to be good enough. I laid a hand on top of his knee and gave him a coy smile. It was overkill, but there was still a chance Darragh was watching.

"What do you say we get out of here? My husband is upstairs, but maybe we could go to another hotel?"

Jim nodded, wringing his sweaty hands together. "Yeah, I'd like that."

"I'd like something discreet." I pouted. "You know how it is, right?"

He nodded.

The smile I wore was practically breaking my face. "Do you have any suggestions? A motel or something on the outside of town?"

He nodded. "Yeah, I know a place."

I squinted again.

"It's, uh, called The Desert Inn."

I smiled. "Great. I'll go outside and call a taxi while you pay the tab."

Jim nodded and I stood to leave.

I walked out the front first. I wasn't sure how sensitive the wire was, but Darragh needed to hear the busy street to be convinced. I let the sounds soak in. I mumbled to myself a few times about how damn hard it was to flag down a taxi, all while doing nothing but standing against the glass windows of the casino. The bouncers gave me a few strange looks before I strode for the alley beside the casino and made my way to the dumpsters behind the building.

Jim waited for me. I smiled and pointed at the wire. "Sorry, I'm still having trouble finding a cab."

He nodded. "We can take my car." At the same time, he handed me a new note. *I called witness protection. They're sending people over now.*

I bounced on the balls of my feet, trying to even my breathing. This was all going according to plan. Just a few more minutes and I'd be free.

Jim scanned the alley and pulled back his jacket, revealing a gun at his hip. I had a feeling the casino he worked for didn't know he carried. I was almost tempted to tell him to put it away. If Darragh found us, a little handgun would do just about nothing.

We started up our small talk for the wire when something echoed down the alley. I squinted in the dim lights, but there was nothing but shadows. I took another shuddering breath and closed my eyes. I was being paranoid.

Something dropped.

Jim put a hand on my shoulder. "Stay here."

Before I could stop him, he shimmied down the wall of the casino to the end.

I paced back and forth under the light. Ten minutes had passed. Witness Protection should have been here by now.

I froze as a presence sidled up behind me, casting a shadow on the pavement. Before I could scream a large arm wrapped around me and a hand covered my mouth.

A thick Irish accent whispered in my ear, "Quiet now, love."

12

―――――

PINA

I screamed.

It was muffled against Darragh's thick hand over my lips, but it did the trick. Jim's pounding footsteps echoed back down the alley while I thrashed against Darragh's hold. He bit down a curse but held me in place. *How did he know—*

Jim stepped into the light, his pistol shaking in both hands. But he didn't point it at Darragh. He pointed it at me.

Darragh took out his own gun and held it in front of me. My eyes widened as he flicked off the safety and pointed it back at the cop.

Darragh crushed my back into his chest, never taking his hand off my mouth. "I'd put that away, lad."

Jim's darting eyes flashed between the two of us, the gun wavering between both our heads.

Darragh tensed. "Let's be smart, now. We wouldn't want to injure an innocent woman, would we?"

Jim swallowed, a hysterical laugh bubbling up from his throat. "Innocent girl? None of you people are fucking innocent."

Darragh cocked his head to the side, making his cheek brush against the top of my head. I shivered. "Like she told you. She's a hostage of the Irish mob."

Ice settled in the veins at the words. He couldn't have known. That message, only Jim had seen it. Only Jim and . . . and the bartender.

Jim shook his head, eyes still wider than dinner plates. "That's not what he said. He just wanted me to kill the girl, man. Kill the girl and all this would go away."

Darragh cocked his gun. "Who said?"

Jim shook his again, looking to me now. "It's nothing personal."

A shot fired. I screamed and jerked back against Darragh. A heavy ringing sounded in my ears, cutting out everything. Darragh must have been speaking, but I could only tell by the heavy vibration of his chest against my back. Nothing hurt, but Andrea once told me it never did. Adrenaline covered up the pain until much, much later.

73

Darragh dragged me closer to Jim. I thrashed against him, wondering if one of us was hit, but it was Jim lying on the ground with blood pooling around him. Smoke whisped from Darragh's gun.

Sounds slowly filtered back in, most of all, Jim's guttural screams. He clutched the arm that previously held his gun and stared at me with bloodshot eyes. "I'll kill you, Delarosa bitch."

Darragh tossed me to the side. I hit the ground with a heavy smack. Tears welled in my eyes, but not from the rocks digging into my palms and knees. He was one step ahead, always. And now he would finish the job. I'd die in a pool of blood next to a man who wanted me just as dead.

Darragh squatted beside Jim and pushed his thumb into the bullet wound. Jim cried out and angry tears welled in his eyes. He spit at me, but just missed.

"Tell me," Darragh said. He shoved his thumb deeper into the wound. "Tell me who ordered her dead."

Jim laughed. The kind of laugh that made you take a step back and wonder exactly what kind of danger you'd gotten yourself into. He grinned at me. "I thought you were supposed to be good at this job, Darragh. We've done just about everything to bring you in."

"Don't look at her," Darragh spat. Jim didn't move. He grabbed his face and wrenched his chin closer to Darragh's face. So close spit flew across his cheeks as Darragh whispered, "You're talking to me, lad."

"Fuck you," Jim whispered, but it had lost all its bravado. Darragh threw him back into the ground. He stood, pointing his gun—

"Stop," I panted.

They both looked at me.

I stood on shaky legs, gripping my red dress in each fist. I would not cower. I wouldn't be that little girl anymore, the one who hid in her room while the men talked business around her. I would die on my feet and I'd die when I wanted. Giuseppina Delarosa did not die huddled on the ground.

I bit down on my cheek so hard it drew blood. "If you're gonna do it, kill me first. I don't need to watch this shit."

A dumbfounded look settled over Darragh's face. For some unholy reason, Jim didn't look too far behind.

"Just do it," I said. A sob ached to break free from my chest, but I pushed it down. I would not die a coward. I would not die a little girl.

Darragh just shook his head. "I already told you."

A siren echoed in the distance. Darragh swiveled around, but they weren't here yet. Maybe if I could stall for just a few more moments there'd be time.

"Told me?" I asked.

He shook his head, turning his attention back to Jim. The latter cowered under the barrel of the gun. "One last chance. I may even consider letting you go."

Jim gave him a frantic look. "Sean. It was Sean. He told me to make sure the girl was dead. If you didn't do it yourself, I was ordered to take you down too."

A half-grin tugged at Darragh's lips. "Thanks for the tip." His gun fired again.

I screamed. My back hit the warm cement of the building behind me. But before I had time to process, Darragh pulled me against him and dragged me down the alley. Blue and red light flickered at the other end just before we disappeared into darkness.

———————

It was morning by the time I stopped shaking. I barely remembered our last moment in Vegas beyond Darragh hot-wiring a car and getting us out of the city. Just when the city lights twinkled into the distance, he switched the plates on another car we found at a junkyard and jumped that one too. The smell of stale cigarettes wafted up from the seats for the next few hours. By the time the sun rose, I smelled nothing at all. Maybe I'd gotten used to it. Or maybe it was just the cold numbness that settled in the longer we drove.

Nothing but open desert and hot sun yawned before us. The last town we drove past was fifty miles behind us, the last car we passed, twenty. There was nothing but cacti and dried, hard earth in every direction.

Neither of us said a single word. You'd think ten hours of silence would be enough to process some of what had happened, but apparently not. Because I still had no goddamn clue what just happened.

So far, I had only three facts down:

One, Darragh somehow knew I tried to double-cross him. Most likely, the bartender worked for him and saw the message I scribbled for Jim.

Two, Jim was still working for the mob when I found him. For some reason, he wanted both of us dead.

Three, and this was the fact that puzzled me the most, Darragh actually kept me alive.

I hugged my arms closer to myself and laid my head between my knees. Paulina once told me that's what you were supposed to do if you were aboard a plane going down. This was a rusted Honda and I was already on the ground, but I couldn't help the feeling that everything was about to crash and burn.

Nothing, and I mean *nothing*, made sense right now.

An hour later we rolled up on a town that looked abandoned for decades. Weathered wooden stores groaned in the hot, desert wind beside dusty, old cars. Not another human was in sight. Darragh pulled the car to the curb. Besides the haunted storefronts, there was nothing but an old payphone erected from the sidewalk, bleached white from the sun.

"I'll be right back," he said. He stepped out with the car still running. Then, thinking better of it, took the keys out of the ignition and strode for the payphone.

76

I watched in empty silence as he dialed and started speaking to someone through the phone.

I took a deep breath and slowly uncurled by arms from my waist. The car was empty when we found it. Now, Darragh's duffle and my destroyed, red dress lay in the backseat. I don't remember how it got ruined, but a rip was present in the delicate satin when we fled the city. By the time we got the second car, it was pretty much falling off. My shoes were abandoned in the mad dash out of Vegas, too. Darragh had silently handed me one of his button-downs, but offered nothing else. That left me in nothing but his shirt and my panties, but somehow, I was too tired to care.

Darragh's phone call was taking an awfully long time.

I shuffled around. The heat was beginning to suffocate me, but I really didn't want to go on the street half-naked, abandoned town or no. My knee bounced up and down, up and down, and I drummed my fingers on the center console. I needed something to do. Something to fidget with. I opened the center console. Maybe the previous owner left something behind. I froze.

Darragh's pistol was inside.

No, not Darragh's. This one was black. A revolver. Either it was planted here and Darragh knew to take this car, or someone very suspicious used to own this vehicle.

I glanced up. Darragh's back was turned to me. No, he didn't know this was in here.

Jim's brains splattering on the sidewalk came back in vivid memory. The pool of blood leaking around him. Some of it was still crusted between my toes.

He didn't kill me. He said he wouldn't kill me, and he meant it.

I reached for the gun. I never used one, but I'd seen Andrea load and unload them enough times in my room. A nervous habit he'd never admit to. Open the chamber, put in the bullets, close the chamber, spin.

I popped it open. All six chambers contained a shiny, silver bullet.

He didn't kill me.

But he killed Jim. Jim, who he said he would spare if he told him the truth. Jim, the cop in witness protection whose death would put the biggest fucking target in America on his back. Jim, the hit.

I was a hit.

I opened the door and stepped out onto the sidewalk. The heat hit like brick wall, drying up the very moisture from my lungs. My bare feet burned on the sidewalk as a hellish breeze swirled the edge of Darragh's shirt around my hips.

He didn't turn around. His low voice carried on the wind like a death knell. The bible described the Angel of Death as an unseen force. A spirit drifting from door to door to collect those it claimed. But the book was wrong. The Angel of Death was not an omniscient spirit of the night. He was a violent man with blue eyes and a thick, Irish accent.

I steadied my breath like they did in the movies. The burning soles of my feet planted into the ground. Hot wind caressed my legs as I stared into the thick, dark locks on the back of Darragh's head. Rust-colored dust blew around me, scraping the corners of my eyes and springing hot tears to my irises. But I never took my gaze off the Angel.

My arms lifted to eye-level.

The gun went steady in my palms.

My finger wrapped around the trigger.

13

DARRAGH

Was it too much to ask for one goddamn thing to go right? The fecking universe thought so.

It took the whole night for Pina to calm down. She didn't say a single word, which I guessed was a miracle in its own right. The questions I knew she had still had no good answers, and now the whole situation was even more of a fecking mess than I could have thought. I had questions, too. And needed answers some poor bastard would probably die for.

The first town we crossed in hours was an abandoned shithole. We were low on petrol, but I couldn't risk stopping anywhere near Vegas. The plane tickets home rotted in a dump somewhere in Nevada. I'd bet my right hand I was on a no-fly list as of last night. No one thought Sean smart enough to pull off the shit he did, which made him dangerous. If the Italians didn't underestimate the drunken, crass Irishman, they would have stopped our takeover years ago. If the cop knew Sean had sent his son to finish the job, he may still be alive. No one outdid Sean. He ran circles around us all.

And now my Da wanted me dead.

Thankfully, the shithole town still had a payphone. My last lifeline depended on the integrity of a fecking collect call from the middle of hell.

Pina made no effort to follow me from the car and by some fecking miracle, the phone still worked. It only rang once before quiet breathing echoed across the line.

"Da?"

"Where are you?"

I smiled, despite myself. The fecking nerve.

"I wish I could tell you, but there ain't much to go off of in the desert."

Sean chuckled. Ice hitting the bottom of a glass followed it in the background.

"Did you finish it?"

I should've known he'd play the game this way. After all, he had no reason to believe I knew. More than that, Sean knew his youngest son a whole lot more than I'd like to admit. There was no way the cop would take me out. He's been waiting for this call. All he had to do was make sure I actually killed Giuseppina. If not, he'd figure out a more effective way to kill me.

A quick glance told me Pina sat in the passenger seat, still hugging herself. The look in her eyes was one I'd seen a thousand times before. The first grisly murder was always the worst. Or so I've heard. I was too young to remember mine.

"They're both dead," I said.

A long moment of silence passed. "Are they?"

I had about three seconds to think like Sean. There was a reason a poor, Irish immigrant created an empire that put New York in a chokehold. Somehow, he knew there was a chance I'd let Pina walk away. Either Pat ratted me out or it was a rare case of fatherly intuition. He told the cop he'd let him walk if he killed Pina himself. There was no room for weakness in our world. Even from your own son. Especially from your own son.

But he also knew the cop would never get the drop on me. Which left me here, sweating my arse off in the middle of nowhere, wondering if my Da had a bottle of whiskey or a firing squad waiting for me at home.

I pressed my forehead against the metal phone booth.

"The girl was becoming too much of a pain in the arse. I had to kill her in the hotel room. Too much of a risk to get her on the street and the pigs would know she didn't die with the cop. Our old friend was found in the alley behind the casino."

"I already know about the cop. Where's the girl?"

Right now? Shitting herself in the passenger seat of a stolen car.

"My trunk. I'm dumping her somewhere in Utah. Let the birds have her."

More clinking ice. I could see it now, Sean sitting in his ridiculous fecking penthouse, swirling around the ice like the fates of everyone around him. When the kingpin wanted you dead, you died. When you wanted to yank your son's leash, he yielded.

"I'll need proof."

I laughed. "I didn't exactly bring a camera, Da." I also knew damn well Sean was already triangulating the call. I had my doubts there was anyone close enough to reach us before we were far enough away from this shithole, but who knew.

"I got a finger," I said. "And some hair. It'll make a nice gift for the Delarosa's."

"Send them to me."

I nodded. "Yeah, I'll do that." And figure out how the feck to make that happen later.

"In the meantime, lay low. Stay at your safe house and I'll coordinate with you from there. I don't think I need to tell you that you left an absolute fecking mess behind in Vegas. I'm making phone calls every goddamn second trying to clear you with the feds."

"I'll lay low."

"There's been some new developments while you were blowing everything to hell."

I stiffened. "What developments?"

81

"With the girl gone, the Delarosa's blamed it on us. Rocci took the bait and wants revenge for his missing bride. Hell's Kitchen is a fecking bloodbath."

I closed my eyes. "The alliance went on, then?"

"The bastards got a common enemy now."

"I'll take care of it." I had no idea how I'd take care of it, but it was my mess to clean. Two botched hits led to this. My fault. My neck on the line.

"No."

The metal dial shimmered in the heat. A shadow. The car door opened behind me, but I ignored it. I knew she'd get too hot in the car, but I didn't trust her enough to leave it running.

"I have another plan."

"What?" I focused in on the picture reflecting back at me in the warped metal. Pina, in nothing but my shirt, stepping onto the sidewalk.

"This alliance has to end one way or another. The boys are sorting the details, but we'll need you soon. It's time we finish the Italian bastards once and for all. Alone, Delarosa won't be a problem."

Pina shifted behind me, arms behind her back as she stared daggers at my head. "And Rocci?"

Sean laughed. "You're gonna kill him."

I turned my attention from Pina's reflection. "Rocci's untouchable."

"Let's just say he'll have a very interesting New Year's."

Pina's reflection came into focus again. Another glint of light. Metal.

Her arms raised in front of her.

"Got trouble. Bye."

I swiveled and pulled my pistol from the holster.

The scariest part was she didn't shake. They always shook the first time. None ever made the shot. But Pina's eyes honed in on the space between my eyes, the revolver pointing at the same spot. I pointed my gun at that same little point on her own head.

82

She took a deep breath, but didn't move. The hot wind took a swirl of dust across the sidewalk and fluttered the shirt against her hips.

I grinned. "Where'd ya get that, love?"

Her lips pressed into a hard line.

I clicked the safety off my gun. She was smart enough to flinch.

"I'm not playing, Pina. Put it down."

Her face scrunched up. I couldn't tell if she was thinking or about to cry. A lock of silky, caramel hair drifted over her nose, but she didn't move it.

"Look around you," I yelled over the breeze. I gestured my free hand at the desert. "You kill me and you're stranded here. I'd bet my mother's soul you can't drive that car. I'll even bet you don't know how to use that weapon. I doubt that thing's loaded, Pina, so put it down and walk away."

She sucked in an angry breath. Before I could blink, she pointed it at my feet and fired off a shot. I jumped back and the bullet bounced into the dirt.

"I can use it. And it's loaded," she called back. I righted myself, spitting curses as she pointed the damn thing back at my head. "Why didn't you kill me?"

Ah. The million dollar question. Only I didn't expect to answer it with a half-naked broad pointing a gun at my head.

"Put the gun down and we'll talk."

She fired another shot to the left of the phone booth.

I scowled. "*Pina.* Cut the shit, *now.*"

She laughed. Fecking laughed. "What are you? My dad?"

My finger tightened on the trigger. "I don't want to shoot you, but I will. It's your choice, love."

Her smile faded away. "Tell me why."

I laughed. "Why? Here's why. I don't like killing ladies. I even felt a little bad for ya. If you disappeared, it was good as dead, so why have it on my conscious?"

83

She frowned. "So let me get this straight. You, a trained hitman since you were in diapers, all of a sudden had a change of heart and decided to let me go?"

I shrugged. "Something like that."

Her arms wavered, but she never dropped the gun. "Bullshit."

"Not bullshit," I hissed. "Let me give this to you straight. I've dragged you across the country and ever since the cursed fecking day I laid eyes on you you've been nothing but an absolute, monumental pain in my arse. You double-crossed me, got the feds involved, and now I'm in the middle of the desert with your crazy arse and a revolver at my head. If I wanted you dead, you'd be fecking dead, Pina. So, take my kindness as a blessing and move on. As soon as shit is clear I'll have you on the next plane to wherever you want and as long as you stay missing we'll never have to speak again."

That little frown deepened. Nothing but the sound of the wind filled the void. Her arms shook. She was getting tired, and there was only so long she could keep this up. I just hoped for her sake, it was before my patience wore too thin.

I had my arse on the line. Maybe she didn't realize how much, but I still had my limits. I've never killed lady, but I wasn't about to die for one either.

Tears welled up in her eyes. "I don't get it," she finally said.

I grimaced. "You don't have to get it. Just accept it."

A fat tear rolled down her cheek, leaving a stain in the layer of dust covering her skin. "What will happen? I leave forever and that's it? No one comes looking for me? Lucien won't stop looking until he's sure I'm dead. He doesn't take people stealing his property lightly."

I sighed. "You don't have to worry about Rocci."

"You don't get it," she snapped. "Until the day he sees my body he'll think I'm alive. I've spent this whole damn trip planning on how to run away, but it finally clicked into place. He'll search the ends of the earth for me. There's no place I can hide. So, you either finish the job or I end up at his bride."

Jesus Christ. Someone needed to have a long talk with her about conversations you do and don't have with people pointing guns at your head.

"You don't have to worry about Lucien," I said again.

"How do you know?"

I clenched my jaw. "Because I'm going to kill him."

Her mouth froze in a perfect *O*.

"You happy?"

"You're planning a hit on Lucien Rocci?"

I stared into her caramel eyes. "Yes."

She dropped the gun.

Shit. If only I knew to say that ten minutes ago.

I put my gun back in the holster and stalked towards her, just in case she had any ideas. The revolver in her hands went in my free holster and I gripped her arm, dragging her back to the car.

"When?"

"None of your business."

"I want to know."

"Too fecking bad." I opened the passenger door and threw her inside. The second I opened the driver's side, she was on me again.

"Darragh, when is the hit?"

I peeled away from the little town without another word, but the questions just kept coming. *When, where, why?*

I gripped the steering wheel until my knuckles turned white. "I already told you. Family business only. Before you know it, he'll be six feet under and that's all your getting."

The desert raced past us. If Sean decided to test me and send people out, we needed to be as far away as fecking possible.

Pina gripped my arm. "I want in."

I slammed on the brakes.

She must have been joking. That was the only logical explanation, but she sure as shit didn't seem like it. Her eyes

85

widened to saucers, but she never took her hands off my arms. I shook her off.

"I want to kill him," she said.

I raised an eyebrow. "What?"

She leaned back in her seat and crossed her arms. "Drive."

I tensed. "I'm not one of your fecking servants so don't talk to me like one. You're getting nowhere near this hit. End of story."

She gritted her teeth. "I want in."

I clenched the steering wheel. "Let's pretend for one moment you're not one, Italian. And two, a woman. The only reason you're alive is because I say so. The only reason you'll continue to stay alive is getting far away from here. Your family will have you killed. Honor says so. My family will have you killed because they already want you dead. You can shoot a pistol, fecking great. You have no idea how to carry something of this magnitude out and that's if you can even get close enough without being recognized. It's not fecking happening."

"No one knows who I am," she countered. I put the car into gear and hit the gas. "Only my family. Even Lucien has never seen me. My family kept me so locked up my face has never seen the light of day."

She had a point there. God knew I had no fecking clue until I found her in the alley.

"You said so yourself, I can use a pistol. You can teach me what you know. I'm not asking to do this solo, but I want to help."

Train her to be an expert sniper by New Year's. Yeah, I'll just add it to the list.

I shook my head. "Women stay out of this shit for a reason. I'm sorry you got wrapped up in our world, but believe me, you don't want this."

"You don't know me," she snapped. I sighed. "And I didn't get wrapped up in it. I was born into it, same as you."

"What do you want to kill him for anyway? Mad he tried to take you as his bride? Get over it, Pina. Welcome to the fecking mafia. I'm sure you know how we do things around here."

She crossed her arms over his chest and leaned back. "It's none of your business."

I laughed. "So, you want in on mine, but I can't have in on yours?"

Her moody glare turned to the window. "Never mind."

We rode in silence after that.

14

PINA

Darragh planned to kill Lucien Rocci.

I still didn't trust him. I still didn't trust he wouldn't hurt me, but he had his points. If he wanted me dead, I would be. And it was a lot more convenient than anything else he's been doing.

I took two shots at him and he didn't fire back. He didn't know I was aiming for his head, but I wasn't about to tell him either.

Each moment with Darragh only confused me further. He was right about one thing; I did get wrapped up in this world. I was born into the mafia, but in the same way all women were. I was sheltered, seen but not heard, and expected to do nothing but warm my husband's bed. So, this was all new to me. Travelling across the country, witnessing a hit, and getting wrapped up in whatever convoluted mess Darragh was in. I balanced on the edge of everything I've ever known, and everything my family hid me from.

I knew my family did bad things. I knew they killed, plotted and maimed, but I never saw it up close.

I watched Darragh's face flicker in the passing streetlights. He told me we were in southern Colorado, but it made no difference to me. It all looked the same. Desert and more desert.

In the ten hours since the phone booth, we've said nothing. I was starving, had to pee something fierce and hadn't slept since

88

Vegas, but if Darragh had any of the same issues, he didn't say. The closest I got to a response was him saying we were going to pull off for the night.

The desert town he found looked nearly identical to the last one we found ourselves in. The only business open this late was a seedy motel attached to an even seedier bar. I grimaced at the neon lights flashing through the windshield as Darragh stepped out and stretched his arms above his head.

A neon sign of a curvy woman bouncing her leg flickered in the window. "What kind of bar is this?"

Darragh closed his eyes and leaned against the car. "A strip club."

I blanched. "I can't go in."

"Get out."

"I don't have pants."

"Great. You'll fit right in."

He sifted through his duffle bag and threw me a pair of his dress pants, anyway. They were about a foot too long and hung off my waist, but it was better than my underwear. Darragh still wore his suit from Vegas. Judging by this crowd, I had doubts he'd blend in.

I huddled close to his back as he got us a room and pushed through a door that led to the bar. The smell of smoke and sweat stung my eyes the second we stepped through.

Outside of a few strange glances, it was dark enough we pushed through mostly unnoticed. Darragh went straight for the bar and I lingered close behind. Only one girl danced on a dimly lit stage in the back of the room. Country music blasted over the speakers and men twice my age filled the tables. I didn't know what Darragh ordered, but I didn't really care. My eyes glued to the dancing woman, her sparkly bra catching the light and bouncing off the room. She caught my eye across the bar and winked.

Darragh pulled me to a booth in a lonely, dark corner far from the stage and everyone else. He clutched a glass of something brown in his hand.

"I got you a burger. I don't trust much else in a place like this."

Now was probably not the time to admit I'd never eaten a burger in my life. The maids had me on a strict diet since I could walk.

Darragh's bloodshot eyes scanned the room. He sat with his back to the wall, like any Made Man worth their salt would always do.

Unlike most Made Men, Darragh knocked back whiskey after whiskey until our food arrived. After that, he kept going.

I rolled my eyes at the fifth or sixth drink. "You shouldn't get drunk."

His lips pulled into a grin against the lip of his glass. "One, you're not my mother and you're not my wife. So, save it for someone else. Two, I'm Irish. I've been drinking since I was ten and I learned to shoot that way too."

He knocked back the rest of his glass to make his point.

I eyed it. "I must be stressing you out."

Another grim smile. He swirled the little piece of ice in his glass around and around. "You have no goddamn clue."

He set the glass down. "Tell me."

I crossed my arms. "Tell you what?"

"Why do you want him dead?"

I could tell him. It may change his mind, but probably not. Darragh was right, I was only alive because I was dead. He risked enough by doing that. Why risk more?

But none of it mattered anymore anyway, so I looked him in the eyes and said, "He killed my best friend."

His eyebrows pulled together.

"You don't need to know more than that, but she was like a sister to me. The only real friend I ever had. He wanted something from her, so he took it. It didn't end well."

He continued the incessant swirling. "So, you want revenge?"

"I want justice."

The dancer's song ended and the bar clapped and cheered. Darragh waited for the noise to die down to answer, "If you want justice, then it makes no difference who kills him."

"It has to be me."

"Why?"

I clenched my fists under the table. Because she was my friend. Because we were supposed to look out for one another. Because I've been used and thrown away my whole life by men who only used me for a means to an end and nothing more, and I wanted to prove the *bastardos* wrong.

"It's revenge, then," he said.

I scowled. "It's honor."

He chuckled, never taking his eyes off that piece of ice. "Now you sound like you belong to our world."

The glass went back to the wood and he leaned forward, folding his hands on the table. He was staring at me, but I wouldn't meet his eyes. I didn't like the way they looked. Cold as death and so much more terrifying.

There was nothing behind those eyes. Or so it seemed, because he spared my life. It didn't make him any less of a monster, but it made him at least somewhat human. That was the scariest part of all. The worst monsters weren't scary, strange things in the dark. They were handsome men who made you believe they're something that they're not.

"What would I get out of this?"

I met his stare. "What?"

"You come to me with all these demands. Train me, hide me, let me in on the hit. What do I get, love? There's no such thing as one-sided deals in our world. If you want to play with the big kids, then you have to follow the rules."

I took a heated breath. He was patronizing me on purpose. It was all a part of the game. "What do you want?"

His eyes roamed up my breasts in a way that made my skin crawl.

"What information do you have on the Delarosa's?"

I glared. "If I told you, I'd have nothing to bargain with."

He grinned. The grin of a predator. "This isn't a bargain yet, love. You've brought nothing to the table."

Our eyes locked in a heated stare.

"You're playing with me," I finally said.

He leaned forward, so close his warm breath cascaded across my neck. Goosebumps raised across my arms. "Get used to it."

I tried to lean back but he gripped my wrist, locking it to the table. "You have no idea what it would be like if I decided to really play with you."

My teeth gritted against my better judgement. "Do you talk to all potential business partners this way?"

"Let's just say you're special."

"You're drunk," I hissed. "And I'm done." I shimmied out of the booth.

Darragh's presence was a shadow that followed much too close behind. I reached for the door that would take me directly into the motel, but he wrenched my wrist away. The blaring music overshadowed my outraged cry as he flipped me around and pinned me against the wall. To anyone sober enough to watch, we looked like nothing more than a couple about to take advantage of the sketchy, dark corner of the bar.

He pinned my wrists against the wall and pushed his chest flush with mine. He was so tall my breasts only hit just above his navel. Fire crawled up my neck at the closeness, but he didn't pull away. He craned his neck down so his forehead brushed against mine. I squirmed against his grip, but it was utterly useless.

His lips caressed the outer shell of my ear as he whispered, "How far are you willing to go to get what you want?"

I took a deep breath to calm myself. If he tried anything, anything at all, I would scream. Consequences be damned.

"Get off of me."

The sensual undertone dropped this time. "How far?"

I swallowed. Anger rose in my gut and crawled up my throat. "I won't fuck you. You disgust me."

He froze. Every thick muscle froze around me, but he didn't move. "I don't kill ladies, Pina. I don't hurt them either. I told you, even men like me have lines. Just very few of them."

I didn't realize how hard I was breathing until I calmed down. But now I was too calm. The type of calm that was stiller than death and just as dangerous.

Another round of cheering exploded. "He raped her."

"Who?"

"Lucien." I swallowed, bidding the tears at the back of my eyes to go away. "He wanted to get back at my father. They invited him over for a meeting between the *familgias*. Paulina was in my room while I attended classes. I didn't like where they made her sleep. The servant's quarters were terrible, and she was my best friend, so I made her stay in my room."

I took a shaky breath, willing back the tears. I would not cry. I was not a little girl.

"Lucien sought her out. He was looking for me. I don't know what happened. I don't know if she fought. I don't know if she knew what he was really up to, if she thought it was a chance to save me—" I swallowed. "He took her by force. He claimed killing her was an accident. Her head hit the dresser in just the right spot and she bled out before anything could be done."

Darragh pulled away. Not enough to free me, but enough I was no longer pinned against the wall. "He's never seen my face. He has no idea what I look like. Who I am. Anything beyond the night he wanted revenge on my father and mistook me for my maid instead."

Despite my best efforts, a tear broke free. Darragh reached up and brushed it away, but it was as close as he came.

Then he asked the strangest question anyone could. "Do you wish it was you?"

I clenched my jaw and met his eyes. Icy blue. Unreadable and inhuman, just like the rest of them. "Everyday."

His eyes roamed up and down my face. "Killing him won't bring her back."

My hands balled into fists. "Men like him deserve to die."

A half-smile tugged at the corner of his lips. "All men in our world deserve to die."

I smiled back at him. "Then to hell with you all."

I pushed past him for the door. The tired woman at the front desk never looked up from her magazine as I stormed past, Darragh close behind. The door to our room was open, thankfully. I avoided Darragh as much as possible as I climbed into the single bed lying in the center of the room.

In full-suit and all, he climbed in next to me.

I gripped the comforter in both hands. "Get out."

He stretched his arms behind his head and closed his eyes. "I paid for it."

I stood up.

Before my feet even hit the carpet, his voice rang out. "Pina, get back in the fecking bed."

I didn't move. My feet dangled over the side, just a hair's breadth from the floor. I didn't want to sleep next to him. I didn't want to be in the same room as him. I couldn't give a damn if he saved my life, they were all the same. Men used women at their convenience. Men like Darragh used us just for fun.

He didn't rape me in the bar. He didn't get a gold medal for it.

"Get back in bed." He didn't even open his eyes.

Every fiber of my being shook with fury, but I listened. I scooched as far away from him as possible and pulled the covers around me. It didn't matter it was eighty degrees out and the place had no AC. I wanted as much barrier between us as possible.

He reached over my head and flicked the light off beside the table. I held my breath the entire time.

Darkness and stifling heat settled over us. Worse, was the tension. It stole the air from my lungs more than the weather ever could.

"I've killed a lot of people, Pina. I've never saved one."

I swallowed, pulling the covers tighter. "Then why me?"

It took him so long to respond, I thought he fell asleep. "You intrigue me."

He turned on his side, putting his back to me. "I'll think about it."

Moments later, he was fast asleep.

15

PINA

The drive back to New York never seemed to end, even with Darragh refusing to stop more than once a day. We picked up a third car in Kentucky and it'd been non-stop since then. With nothing but the radio to break the silence, I spent most of the car ride gazing out the window.

Desert turned to rocky mountains, then lush, rolling green ones. We curved our way through West Virginia as the world passed me by. In the past few days, I'd seen more of the world than in my entire lifetime. Yet, nothing really changed. I could look but not touch. The whole country at my fingertips behind a thick glass window, racing by as if I never existed at all.

It was ironic compared to how things were faring in New York, where my absence sent the whole city into a bloodbath.

Or so Darragh told me. In the few moments he did speak, it was to come clean. He explained the original hit, the mission in Vegas, and everything that was currently happening back home. I don't know why he told me. I don't think he knew why either. I guess it was better than spending every minute in silence.

When we crossed into New York, Darragh instructed me to put on a blindfold. We were still hours away from his home, but he said it was just a precaution. AKA, he didn't want me to have even a hint of an idea as to where he lived.

The exhaustion must have really worn me down, because moments after my sight was encased in darkness, I fell asleep.

It was dark when I awoke. The quiet thrum of the car nearly put me back to sleep when the passenger side opened and a blast of cool air bit into my legs. I frowned and opened my eyes.

Darragh's face hovered directly above mine. Those blue eyes were still laced with red from the hours of driving and staying awake. He tucked a hand under my knees and lifted me out of the car.

I gripped onto his shirt, my vision spinning the higher I went off the ground. "What are you doing?"

If he wasn't so tired, he may have rolled his eyes. "Don't start swooning. It's snowing and you have no shoes."

It was, in fact, snowing. The pale, white crystals dusted the ground beneath thick, slate colored clouds. The sensor light outside his door came on, reflecting back the little snowflakes sticking to his thick eyelashes.

He set me down inside and wasted no time running upstairs. At the top he peered down, probably wondering if I'd try to kill him again. Luckily for him, I was tired and fresh out of escape ideas.

"I have to make some phone calls. Wait in the living room."

I gave him a fake salute. "Yes, dad."

He rolled his eyes and walked away, mumbling, "Pain in my arse."

While listening to his demands was low on the list of things I felt like doing, there wasn't much else to do in his house. My eyes scanned over the open kitchen and gun-littered living room with fresh eyes. In only a few days, so much had changed. I left this house thinking I was about to die. Now it was my last chance as safety.

If, of course, Darragh was still telling the truth.

I settled into the leather sofa and searched for the TV remote. The last time I watched TV was with Paulina, but I didn't see anything else that would pass the time. Knowing Darragh and his *calls*, I'm sure it'd be a while.

I could go back to sleep. I was certainly tired enough, but there was something still unsettling about passing out among the fifty different ways Darragh could kill me while he debriefed upstairs. I could always go back to the guest room, but I wasn't entirely sure if I was still a guest. Besides, I wanted to know what he planned now that we were back in New York. I had questions.

I flicked on the TV, rolling my eyes at the ten channels Darragh had access to and the lack of anything else. I swear, he was eighty trapped in a thirty-year old's body. Even Alessandro was hooked on *Cheers*, and most of his hobbies included kicking puppies and looking mean.

The only channel that didn't bring in static was the news. A smiling blonde filled the screen as she described a "state-of-the-art" kitchen mixer. My eyes glazed over as she giggled non-stop beside a bored looking chef.

Enough time passed the blonde lady finished her puff pastries and the actual news came on. A helicopter view of a trash-filled alley swarming with cops.

A solemn news anchor appeared beside the footage. His hands folded over one another in the stereotypical, "we're about to say something horrible" pose.

Earlier this week, Las Vegas police responded to the scene of a gruesome murder involving a member of the force. At this time, detectives have not revealed who suspects may be, but sources tell us the murder may be tied to organized crime.

I leaned forward. That alley . . . it looked familiar.

While no information has been released about the primary suspect, police have released footage of a woman who may be involved in the crime. According to witnesses, the victim was seen leaving the casino with the person of interest you are about to see.

The helicopter footage cut away. In its place, a blow-up picture of a casino bar filled the screen. On the right was Jim. On the left was . . . me. It was grainy and almost impossible to distinguish any real features, but it was definitely me.

Fuck.

Fuck. Fuck. Fuck.

If anyone has information on who this woman may be, please contact the anonymous tip line below.

I scrambled for the remote and shut off the TV.

This was bad. This was so bad.

According to Darragh, my family still thought me dead. While my face popping up on national television blew a hole in the story I'm sure they received, there was still a chance they bought into the lie. The footage was godawful. Maybe they wouldn't recognize me at all.

But that was the least of my problems. With my face blasted across the country, there would be no travelling for me anytime soon, grainy footage or no. A trip to the airport was out of the question. Showing my face in public was out of the question. The feds were looking for me. It was just about as damn risky as it got.

And if Darragh decided that risk was too great. That his mercy had a hard limit—

I looked around me. Darragh was a recluse and would be lying low for a while, too. What he didn't know wouldn't hurt me.

I threw the remote on the hardwood with enough force to shatter.

"I already know."

I jumped. Darragh stood at the boundary of the kitchen, arms folded. A thick, black eyebrow arched high onto his face.

I tried to steady my breathing.

He took a step forward. I stepped back. His other eyebrow joined the first at his hairline.

"The radio was on for hours. Don't sleep in the car next time."

I swallowed. "I swear, if something happens, I'd never rat you out."

He snorted and walked into the living room. I tensed, backing away towards the far wall while he settled into the couch. He laid his arms over the back and evaluated me.

A long moment passed in thick silence.

"You are the biggest fecking pain in my arse."

I blinked. "Likewise."

That gained me a half-smirk.

"How many times do I have to tell you?"

I didn't need to ask. I knew what he meant. "Until you prove you're a decent man and let me go."

He shook his head. "Proving anything about my character was never a part of the deal, love."

I had no goddamn clue what to say to that. In a rare moment of self-control, I chose silence instead.

He stood up and reached for my hand. I glanced at the thick, callouses of his fingers. How many people have those hands killed?

He dropped it and gestured toward the kitchen. "Come."

I followed in robotic silence.

He pointed to a bar stool and I sat down. He opted to stand on the other side of the counter, watching me.

If he was searching for the chinks in my armor, I'm sure he found them all. Those eyes didn't miss a single thing. I evened my breathing, trying to tame the fluttering vein in my throat. It was no use. His eyes stared at the tense point on my neck and rounded up to my face. I froze completely when his eyes met mine.

"How far are you willing to go?"

I thought this conversation was done. His "I'll think about it" back in Colorado seemed nothing more than a statement to shut me up for the remaining thirty-hour drive. I'd heard enough similar words in my life to know it was either to console a raging child or shush a nagging woman.

But he looked serious.

"And I don't want you to fuck me, if that's what you're thinking."

It was what I was thinking. Darragh said so himself: I had nothing to bring to the table.

Or maybe he knew that wasn't completely true. A lifetime sharing a wall with the cigar room gave me enough information to sell off to any interested party. But there was only so much I was willing to give. My father, Alessandro, I couldn't give less of a crap about them. They did nothing but use me my entire life. And my mother was nothing but an empty shell these past few years— only the pills and wine kept her alive at all. But there was still Andrea. I would never let anything bad happen to the only true family member I had.

"It depends on what you had in mind."

He unfolded his hands in a gesture I'd seen my father make a thousand times. The universal code for *we're about to make a deal*.

"I have exactly two options for you. You don't have to choose right now. I'd actually prefer you think it over first. But once you choose, there will be no going back. So, make your decision wisely."

I swallowed. My arms folded over my chest instinctively to hide the shaking.

"As of right now, your face is all over national news. Sean O'Callaghan is convinced you're dead on my word and the woman in the footage is an associate, so he isn't concerned. But the second anyone realizes who you actually are my head is on a spike. So, until things calm down, which may take months, I can't allow you to leave this house."

I opened my mouth to object, but he continued. "Your first option is you live here and bide your time. You pay your rent by running the house. No harm will come to you as long as you stay quiet and do your job. When, and only when, I say the coast is clear, you'll be smuggled over the border to Mexico. From there, you can go anywhere in the world, as long as you never come back to the States.

"Option two is this, and I want you to think this over very fecking clearly. As of right now no one knows what you look like.

101

Not even Sean O'Callaghan. The only person who's seen your face in the past week is the man who made our passports, but my sources tell me he died earlier this week. Besides the Delarosa's you are a face without a name. I'll give your family this, it was just about the only damn thing they've done right."

I frowned, but he plowed on.

"I'll teach you to shoot, I'll bring you into the operation and I'll give you exactly one shot at Lucien Rocci. One chance to put a bullet in his head. Your name from here forward will be Annie McCormick. My father already believes you're a freelance associate who aided in the hit. Whether Annie dies next week in an unfortunate accident entirely depends on what you choose."

A chance to kill Rocci. A chance at a new life. One where I was no longer pushed into the shadows. No longer told it wasn't my place in the world as a woman to be involved. Nothing but a weak little girl no longer. I could show my father and brother what happens when my life is threatened by their shit.

It was too good to be true.

"What's the catch?"

He leaned back, contemplating me again. I really wished he'd stop looking at me like that.

"In exchange, you'll be completing a hit for me. Completely on your own and all consequences will be yours. It will put you on the map and I can no longer handle a blood feud with the Italians. Sean's way always ends in blood, but there can be more . . . diplomatic ways to end the fighting. You complete the hit, and at the end, you come clean about who you are and marry me."

My tongue turned to lead in my throat. There was so much to process there I didn't even know where to begin. Marry him? Was he insane?

I saw the way he looked at me, the stares, the eyes roaming up my butt and breasts . . . but that's just what men did. None ever asked me to get married.

I took a deep breath, starting with the obvious hole in his plan. Maybe it would knock some sense into him. "Your father will just kill me when he discovers who I am."

"No he won't."

"Why?"

"Because it's my father you're going to kill."

I choked.

He couldn't be serious.

Goddammit, he looked serious.

I shook my head. "I don't understand."

"You don't need to. Just do what I say and you get what you want."

I slammed my palms on the counter. "I need to know what I'm getting into if I'm going to make that call."

He eyed my hands with annoyance. His hands overlaid mine and pushed them back to my side of the counter.

"Sean is slipping. His bloodbath with the Italians proves that enough. Our men believe him less each day. There is no place for weakness in our family."

I wrenched my hands free of his. "So, you'll just have me kill him then?"

He nodded his head. "Yes, and I'd prefer if you did it before he killed me."

"Why would he kill you?"

"The same reason fathers have killed sons throughout all of history. He has a crown and he's afraid of those who may take it. He already knows I defied his orders once. There's nothing now to stop me from doing it again. He'll use me to finish Rocci and your father. Once all other threats are out of his way, he'll come for me next."

For something so deranged, he looked eerily calmed. "How can you be so sure that's what he plans?"

Darragh reached towards the wall and hit a button beside the phone. A message began to play from voicemail.

"Darragh, I'm sorry. I had to tell him. He threatened the girls. I destroyed the passport before he saw her face, but it's over. I don't know how long I have, but he's coming for you. Your Ma warned about this. She made me promise. Don't trust anything he says. Get as far from here as you can, boy."

Cold dread settled in me. I recognized the voice. It was the old man who met us outside the airport.

I stared blankly at the phone as the message looped. "Was it a passport for me?"

He swiped the phone off the counter. "Yes."

And now that man was dead. Because of me. He was only trying to save my life.

"He told you to run."

Darragh's jaw set in a hard grimace. "I don't run."

Because it wouldn't matter. Because the life caught up to us all.

That made the options Darragh gave me very slim.

"Why not just kill him yourself?"

He frowned. "He's paranoid. Watching me too closely. It'll be hard to get close to him without witnesses, and with witnesses, politics come into play."

I didn't point out his father had good reason to be paranoid.

"Even if I could somehow kill him . . . your father—" I took a shaky breath. "—my family will never accept a truce. They'll claim me as a traitor and the blood feud will continue. They'll come full force if they knew your family was responsible for taking me."

A grim smile appeared on his face. "Not if we're married. You Italians live and die by your codes, no? Marriage and honor would make us family. They'd have no choice. The *familgias* in Chicago and Boston will hold them to that standard whether they want to or not."

I shook my head. "Only if you held the crown, but you have an older brother."

"My brother won't be in charge."

I bristled. "Why? Am I supposed to kill him too?"

Fire flared in his eyes. "No, Rory stays out of this. Just as he's always done."

In the past two weeks, it was the most human thing I'd heard him say. The killer cared for his brother. That would be something to keep in mind.

"Don't even let the thought cross your mind."

I looked to Darragh. The fire burned hotter. So much the ice in his eyes almost melted away.

"Your brother stays out of it as long as you leave out mine."

He nodded. "That will be a condition of option two."

So that only left one last thing to be settled: the conditions of our marriage. It was so completely fucked I almost had to laugh. Saved from one marriage deal just to be thrust into another.

Although technically, that wasn't true. I still had option one, for what it was worth. Darragh didn't run. I already admitted to him, neither could I. Even if my family somehow never discovered I was alive, even if we managed to kill Rocci, Darragh would always know, and he didn't strike me as the type of man to leave loose ends. He offered me escape with a boatload of conditions attached. He never said what the circumstances would be should I mess up a single one of them.

Maybe I could start a new life. I've barely lived this one, so there was nothing I'd be leaving behind. But I would live my life in fear. On the run. Anyone I ever met, anyone I so much as spoke to would live with a target on their back. I risked leaving a trail of innocent bodies in my wake, either so my father could find me or so Darragh could make sure I stayed "dead."

"I don't want to marry you," I said. "Take that out of the deal and I'll choose option two."

He smiled at me. "I'm not here to bargain, love."

He just bargained for his brother's safety, but I wasn't about to point that out. "All this just to end the blood feud? Be honest with yourself, you don't want to be stuck with me either. Or have I somehow charmed you?"

105

He crossed his arms. "I don't like you, Giuseppina. You're temperamental, never know when to shut your mouth, you tried to hand me over to the feds and you've put a target on my back. You're rude, way more violent than any woman should ever be and you'll make a horrible wife."

I breathed out through my nose. "Wow, a very convincing argument you're making."

"But no marriage in our world is ever made for love. And all those qualities may be the only thing that keeps either of us alive. We can end the fighting between our families. Your brother, Andrea? He'll be safe. You'll never have to worry if his next walk through Hell's Kitchen will be his last. I could kill the Delarosa's with Rocci gone, but that would be a waste. The Russians just raised their flag in Brooklyn and the Chicago Outfit creeps closer every day. The fighting will never end. It's just a matter of who I'm killing."

I let those words sink in.

"The happy life with a white picket fence was never an option for you. I've given you two. Run, or stay. It's your choice."

He walked around the counter and squeezed my shoulder. I flinched against his touch.

"Think about it."

16

DARRAGH

I laid in bed, eyes drifting over the glaring monitors hooked up to my security cameras. Blue and white light fell over the bed as I watched Pina pace around the kitchen. I wasn't trying to be a creep, I just still had my doubts she wouldn't try to kill me again. If I was completely honest, it was kind of a turn on.

Nothing but snow fell on the outside cameras and Pina never left the room. I knew I should sleep, but even being awake for the past two days wasn't enough to get me there.

I had my reasons for everything I did. Sean taught me well to calculate every step I made. Unfortunately for him, it wouldn't work out too well in his favor.

I didn't want to think about Pat. About the role I had to play in his untimely end. So, I watched the monitors instead.

I already knew what Pina would choose, but letting her think it over and work it all out herself was just another part of the plan. Let her think she actually had some kind of choice here. She had to know deep down that there would be no actual escape. Maybe it was a possibility before Vegas, but with her face all over TV there was no way her family would think her dead. Maybe they would if I provided the proof Sean wanted so badly. A finger and some of her hair would be enough for all of them . . . I hoped, especially with Sean. He was usually ten steps ahead, but he had no reason to think I'd risk bringing her into the fold.

I wasn't lying when I said I didn't like her. I respected her. As far as looks went, she'd make any man be over the goddamn moon. And she definitely had a will to survive beyond most of the women I've seen. She cried too much, but at least she did it with a gun in her hand.

There were no such thing as happy endings in our world. Besides, even if I could find someone who looked past all the bullshit, they'd be a target for the rest of their lives. Marriages were alliances. Love was nonexistent.

The mafia always had their views on how women should act. I'm sure Pina spent her whole life preparing to do nothing but wait in the wings. Seen but not heard and all that bullshit. Let the man handle things. But she wouldn't last a day like that if my plan worked, and I couldn't spend the rest of my life trying to protect her while running the business. She had balls and she wanted in, so it was enough for me. A wife who could survive and provide me an alliance. A two for one deal.

She paced back and forth some more before finally sitting back on the stool, head in hands. It was like watching the five stages of grief happen in real-time.

I didn't really want to watch her anymore either.

There was nothing I wanted on my mind right now, so I hit the whiskey bottle instead.

An hour later I was still awake. Worse, I was drunk. Pina hadn't moved from her position in the kitchen. Two miserable people. We were already off to a great start.

If she actually chose option two, I had to propose.

I never thought I'd get married, so I never thought about it. If it did happen, it was always under the assumption Sean would choose who he needed me to get with, we'd meet, and that would be it. So far anyone he considered always fell through, and there was no shot in hell of getting Rory tied down to a woman. The prospect of it died years ago.

My eyes drifted to the box on my dresser. The one I always tried to avoid.

It must have been the whiskey talking, because I found myself in front of it, slowly lifting the cover. Three objects stared back at me from the velvet lining. I picked up the first, a photograph.

My eyes drifted over the smiling face of my mother. Beside her, my own smile gleamed, only six years old and still completely clueless to everything. Back in the days when it was just the two of us. When I didn't even know Sean's name. When I had no clue I had three brothers in the United States, two already dead and one just a year older than me.

"What would you do?" I asked. I wasn't sure if I was talking to the six-year old or the ghost of my Ma. It didn't matter though. Both the people in that picture were long dead.

The second item was a medal, a little token from my years in the military. The third was my Ma's engagement ring.

I rolled the ring between the pointer finger and thumb.

"She's a lot like you. She never shuts up," I told the photograph. Grace O'Callaghan's face just smiled back.

"Maybe that's why I've kept her around so long," I whispered. "I think you would have liked her."

I collapsed onto the bed, bottle of whiskey in one hand and ring in the other. Ma stared back at me from the picture, propped up on the dresser.

"I won't be like Da," I told the ceiling, or maybe the photograph. I was too drunk and exhausted to think much into it. "I'm not Sean."

The phone rang beside my bed.

I closed my eyes, letting it ring. The sound wracked around in my skull until I couldn't take it and picked up the line.

"Darragh." It was Rory.

I flipped the ring up into the air and caught it with my hand. "What do you want?"

He breathed heavy into the line. "You alone?"

I glanced at the monitors. Pina still sat in the kitchen. "Yeah."

"Pat's dead."

"I know."

"What the hell did you get yourself into?"

I flipped the ring again, watching the way the center diamond caught the light of the security screens. "Nothing. Hits are done. Shit got messy, but I'm handling it."

His voice dipped to a lower volume. "I've never seen Sean like this before. He's raving fucking mad."

"Don't worry about Sean," I said. "I'm handling everything. Stick with your cars."

"I'm not worried about Sean, I'm worried about you."

I grinned. "I'm the last thing you should be worrying about."

"I'm coming to you. We've got shit to talk about."

"No."

More silence. I sighed. "You can't come here. Not now. We'll talk soon."

I hung up before he had a chance to say anything. The phone rang again. I ripped the cord from the wall.

Pina finally stood up from the bar stool. Her spine straightened, shoulders squared back. I watched her pass from one monitor to the next, entering the living room, the hall, then climbing the stairs.

I sat up in bed.

My door busted open as she fixed me with a glare harder than metal. She meant fecking business. My whiskey-soaked brain wondered if she had any other thoughts in mind too. Like getting into bed with me.

She looked at me in disgust and crossed her arms. "Option two."

I raised an eyebrow. "You're sure?"

She noticed the light. Her eyes drifted to the wall of screens, putting two and two together as she recognized the kitchen and living room. Her whole body tensed.

"Give me that." She swiped the bottle of whiskey from my hands and took a long sip.

"That's not very ladylike."

She killed the rest of the bottle and slammed it on the dresser. "Get used to it."

I couldn't help it.

I grinned.

17

PINA

I woke up the next day with a horrible headache.

I had no clue how Darragh drank that stuff all day long. A few swigs and I was passing out in bed. Darragh offered the space next to him, but as I'd rather claw my own eyes out, I took the guest bedroom downstairs instead.

Although sometime soon I'd probably have to get used to sleeping in bed with him. He never said when this marriage was supposed to take place. It was also never discussed just how *marital* this marriage would be. I could only hope it was just a front with a legal document to back it. I didn't care if he had other women who attended to his . . . needs. Someone else could have that job.

I sifted through the kitchen cabinets, praying to god Darragh had aspirin or something in here. I shut the kitchen cabinet and jumped when his face appeared behind it.

"Morning."

I stared at him, open-mouthed. "Yeah, good morning."

He sat at the barstool and watched as I looked through a second cabinet. He never asked what I was doing and I didn't want to ask him for help either. Technically, I lived here now anyway.

"It's next to the stove."

My fingers hovered around the handle of a drawer. "What?"

He pointed to the cabinet beside the stove. "Aspirin. There's a bottle in here and a bottle in the bathroom upstairs."

I guess I looked more hungover than I thought. Before I could dwell on Darragh's creepy ability to read my mind, I downed three pills and an entire glass of water.

Before my glass even hit the counter, Darragh was speaking. "We start training later today. I have something I need to handle first."

I stared at him, dumb founded. That sounded a whole lot like, *I'm leaving you here alone.* That was a lot of trust for someone who tried to shoot him two days ago.

"What are you doing?"

He shook his head. "Don't worry about it."

I clenched my jaw. "Well, I will worry about it. Because your business is my business now. So, what are you doing?"

A ghost of a smile crossed his face. Normally when I talked back to men, it was met with glares, silence and the occasional backhand. Somehow, the smile was more terrifying than all the above.

"Sean needs to know for sure you're dead. I promised him a finger and some hair. The former will come from the local morgue."

I glanced out the window to the snow dusted mountains. How local could anything be to here?

My eyes drifted down to my hands, dread settling in my gut. "Will my family see?"

He nodded, the smile gone. "Sean plans to send them a gift, and besides, they need to think you're dead for the time being."

I wrung my hands together as sweat dripped down my hairline. "It won't work."

"Why?"

I took a deep breath. Goddammit. Of course Alessandro still had to make my life a living hell, even when he wasn't around.

I laid my hands on the counter, palms up. The white line of a thin scar ran across all ten fingers. "My brother dared me to touch some electric wire when I was eight. The voltage was too high and gave me a burn. It never healed right."

Darragh's eyes scanned the scar, tracing it from my right pinky to my left, and back again.

"My whole family knows I have it. My mother spent years trying to get it removed. She said it was *unsightly.*"

All of them would know instantly if the finger wasn't mine. And in order for this to work, in order for me to kill Lucien Rocci, they truly had to believe it. Or at least believe something bad had happened to me and I was out of reach for the time being.

I needed Darragh alive long enough to teach me how to shoot. After the hit, all bets were off. Husband or no.

Darragh leaned back in his chair, frowning. I jumped as he reached out and ran a finger over the line across my hands. His eyes lifted, a grimace on his face. For once, I felt exactly the same as him.

I sighed, meeting his stare. "Do you have more whiskey?"

———————

"I may be able to find someone that could do this properly."

Darragh sat beside me on a barstool, three towels, a zippo lighter and a first aid kit in front of him. In front of me were two bottles of Tullamore Dew, one a quarter empty (all me) and one three quarters empty (all Darragh).

There was also the biggest fucking butcher knife I've ever seen.

I took a deep breath as I stared down the blade. Darragh's eyes reflected back at me in the silver.

"We can't trust any of your doctors. They might tell Sean."

"I have people who only work for me."

I shook my head. "It'll take too long. It already looks suspicious you haven't sent it in yet."

That last part was a guess I prayed Darragh would refute. He didn't.

For what it was worth, Darragh looked just about as nervous as me. It was probably one of his psycho killer tactics: make the victim think you're empathetic, or something.

He breathed in and nodded. "Okay, so I'll give you a countdown. Just try to stay still. Don't move until I cauterize it."

I nodded, closing my eyes and shaking my hands, trying to gear myself up. I got this. I can totally lose a pinky. Never needed it to begin with. No big deal. Got this, got this, got this.

I laid my left hand on the counter, fingers splayed. All confidence died the second Darragh grabbed the knife.

He squeezed my wrist. "I promise, it'll be instant. Just don't look, alright?"

I turned my head away and squeezed my eyes shut.

"One—"

"Stop. Stop." I wrenched my hand free.

He frowned. "Do you need more time?"

No, don't worry. I do this once a week. I shook my hands out again, evening my breathing. I could do this. I could do this.

I opened my eyes to my future husband, staring at me with a giant butcher knife in his hand.

My mouth dried out.

"We can wait—"

"Let me do it."

The only time I'd seen him this confused was when I said I wanted to kill Lucien Rocci.

"I don't think—"

"Just let me do it."

I grabbed the handle of the knife from his palm. He obviously wasn't expecting that, because it came to me without a fight. I splayed out my hand and set the knife down long enough to take another giant swig of whiskey.

Darragh tensed beside me. "You shouldn't do this."

I wanted to bust out laughing. I shouldn't be doing what? Faking my death? Planning a hit on the leader of the New York Italian mob? Shacking up with a literal mass murderer? Losing a finger was at least something that happened to normal people too.

Another swig of whiskey. I had to do this myself. I'd feel better if it was me. This was my choice. My fate. I'm turning down this road and never going back. If I can kill a man, I can hurt myself. The Made Men felt nothing. They'd cut off their own finger without so much as a second thought. If I wanted to survive in their world, I had to be like that, too.

I nodded at Darragh. He had no idea what I was talking about, but I said it anyway. "For Paulina."

I brought the knife down.

For a second, I felt nothing at all. Darragh brought the lighter to my hand and I screamed.

He took the fire away, but the pain didn't stop. My vision darkened at the corners, my eyes focusing in on the bloody spot where I'm pretty sure a finger used to be. The light gleamed too bright, the air burned through my chest, and then Darragh was kissing me.

A memory of that morning in the woods drifted into my head. The freezing ice, the snowflakes falling, and a gun in my waistband. My hands wrapped in Darragh's hair while he pushed his hips into mine. The taste of oak and whiskey and salt.

He tasted more like whiskey this time, but the feeling was the same. Enough that I almost forgot what just happened. Enough to dull the pain in my hand with the memory of snow soaking through my knees.

He stroked his tongue across my lips and dug his fingers into my hair. I moaned, falling deeper, until the snip of scissors cut through the air.

The spell broke.

Darragh held a thin lock of my hair in his palm.

I slapped him across his stupid Irish face.

His eyes widened, hand springing open and letting the hair drift to the floor. Hot tears burned the back of my eyes, both from the pain and from how much I truly, endlessly hated him.

I gritted my teeth. "That was low, even for you."

He smirked. "It worked for a minute though, didn't it?"

I raised my hand to slap him again, but he caught my wrist mid-air.

I growled through deep breaths. Red dotted my vision where his *bastardo* face filled it.

"Just get rid of it. Now."

He was either smart enough or tired enough to not snap at me for talking to him like a servant again. Or maybe that just made me the idiot. We were both massive idiots at this point.

I wrapped my hand in a towel and shuffled towards the couch. My couch now. If we were getting married, I wanted this one and he could by his own damn chaise.

He dropped the finger into a bag and tied the hair back together with a ribbon. I avoided eye contact at all costs as he strode for the living room and fell down next to me.

I closed my eyes. "Please, just go away."

I drummed my non-maimed hand on the couch. It didn't give the same satisfying tap marble did. My knee started bouncing too. So much my foot came off the floor.

Darragh laid a hand on my knee, pushing it down.

"For what's worth," he murmured. "That took more strength than half the men who work for me could wish for."

I scowled. "It's not worth much."

He laughed under his breath. There was no limit to how badly the sound made me want to punch him, but the adrenaline was coming down and I didn't feel like cutting my finger off for nothing.

He squeezed my knee. "Then it'll be worth it for Paulina."

My voice came out like daggers. "You know nothing about Paulina. Don't even say her name."

He nodded like that made perfect sense. It didn't to me. I had no idea why I was so angry with him, but it felt like everything from the past two weeks was bubbling over and being directed at the Irishman next to me. I chose this. I could have run, but I chose this. But it was so messed up I didn't know how to comprehend it at all. Two weeks ago I laid in my bed, listening to Andrea talk about girls. Now I was in the middle of nowhere, down one finger and engaged to a psychopath.

But what angered me most of all was the way Darragh made me lose myself against his lips. Every damn time. There had to be something wrong with me too.

I knew the truth. It wouldn't take long at all for me to be just like him. He was a Made Man, same as the rest. Just much better at killing. There was a reason they became the way they did. It wasn't through being normal people, in normal lives.

I was angry at myself for craving it. Not just Lucien Rocci's death, but all of it.

Weak no longer.

Darragh unfurled my hand from the towel and took it in his. It could have been worse. I missed the knuckle, which still left me with half a finger. The lighter stopped the bleeding instantly, so now it just looked red and raw. In time it would heal, but I'd always have it as a reminder. Of what I used to be, but more importantly, of what I am now.

Of what Darragh could give me. Because whether I liked to admit it or not, without him I'd either be dead or tied down to Lucien Rocci's bed.

As bad as this was, there was always worse. I just had to keep telling myself that.

Darragh ran his thumb over my ring finger. I didn't understand the look on his face, but I didn't care either. I was so stuck in my own head, it only now occurred to me how close he was sitting. That he was holding my hand.

He reached into his pocket and pulled out a ring. My stomach bottomed out at the massive diamond.

"This was my mother's," he said. "So there'll be hell to pay if you lose it."

He slid it onto my left ring finger. Right beside the half-missing one.

So, this was it.

This was how the next stage of my life would begin.

Not in the compound, not in my father's office. But with a killer in a safe house, a gruesome wound side by side with a wedding band. A proposal with a threat attached.

The sad, short tale of Giuseppina Delarosa just took a turn for the stranger.

NOVEMBER
1988

18

PINA

It was still dark out when Darragh burst into the guest room and dumped something heavy on my legs.

I snapped into a sitting position and glared bleary-eyed daggers at him. Only his silhouette revealed itself, but I could almost picture the stupid smirk he no doubt wore. His thick, Irish accent cut through the room.

"Get up."

I shoved the covers off, but only made it as far as whatever he dropped on me. It was damn heavy. "Good morning to you too."

"Get dressed, grab that and meet me in the kitchen. We have exactly two months to train. You eat, sleep and breathe weapons now."

I ignored his request and scrambled off the bed. He stalked into the kitchen and I followed close behind. I wore nothing but a t-shirt— I really needed Darragh to buy me some damn clothes— but at this point, I'd given up on trying to look decent. For the few weeks I've known Darragh, he'd seen me in it all.

Not naked, but you know. Mostly there.

I honed in on only one thing he said. *Two months*. "You planned it out already?"

He ignored me and went to the fridge, pulling out a carton of eggs. I had a feeling that's all he knew how to cook.

"Darragh."

"Sean is working on the rest of the details, but yes, we have it mostly planned out."

"Tell me."

He turned on me with the cold glare that usually meant I was talking too much. I matched his gaze and crossed my arms.

"Go get your gun."

My mouth went dry. So that's what the heavy object was. And I left it on the guest bed.

I bit my lip. "At least tell me when."

"New Year's."

New Year's. That seemed risky. Lots of potential witnesses. But then again, maybe that was the idea. There was a reason Darragh got away with every hit until the one in Vegas. Either nobody caught him or someone else took the fall.

I just had to hope he wouldn't go back on his deal. That the person taking the fall wasn't me.

"As for the other target, I'm still working out the details."

Right. The hit where I was supposed to kill Sean. Darragh's father. Just another day in the mob, right?

I ducked back into the guest room— my room now, I guess— and put on thick clothes and grabbed the rifle. It was bulky and heavy, but I needed to prove I could do this, so I lugged it back into the kitchen. Darragh watched in a strange combination of fascination and horror.

I pulled it onto the counter and sat at the barstool. My hand throbbed from the healing wound, but it felt better today. Darragh wrapped it before bed and told me how to keep it clean. Beside it, I still wore his mother's ring. Not because I felt like a blushing bride, but I had nowhere to put it and I was afraid losing it would result in my untimely demise.

I patted the top of the gun affectionately. "Okay, so how do I shoot?"

He gave me a blank stare.

I frowned. "What?"

"You're not shooting it," he said. He put the eggs back in the fridge and grabbed the rifle. A shiver went through me, one I couldn't define. Here was the weapon that would kill Lucien Rocci. The weapon I would use.

I was so fascinated it took a moment for Darragh's words to sink in. "What do you mean I'm not shooting it?"

He sighed. "Weapons 101. You need to know your gun. This here is a standard, military grade M40 sniper rifle with a Thompson scope."

I nodded along like anything he just said made sense. "Yeah, got it."

He raised an eyebrow but said nothing else. He pushed a few buttons and slid some stuff out of place. Before I knew it, the gun was in multiple pieces across the counter.

He reached into a drawer and slammed a thick, spiral bound manual onto the counter.

"Clean it and reassemble it. I'll see you in a few hours."

I stood up. "Wait—where—"

"Back to bed," he said, waving me off. I bristled. "It's five in the morning, love. I need my beauty sleep. If you finish early, do me a favor and have breakfast waiting."

"You *asshole*. You can't just—"

His footsteps pounded up the stairs before I could even finish that sentence.

It was ten before I finally figured it out. I was covered head to toe in sticky, black grease, along with half the kitchen. The second I slid the final piece into place Darragh came pounding down the stairs. I'd bet my remaining pinky finger he was watching me the whole damn time from those creepy security cameras.

I heaved out a breath and held out the gun. He looked it over, nodded and said, "Good job. Now do it again."

I slammed it back down on the counter. "I just spent five hours figuring that out."

He shrugged. "Now spend another five hours perfecting it."

After spending the entire day taking the stupid gun apart and putting it back together, Darragh finally seemed satisfied. He wordlessly handed me a basket of towels and directed me to the shower in his room. I had the sense to snap at him for asking me to put the linens away, until I realized I needed every damn one to get the grease off.

Afterwards, I took the longest shower known to humankind. I wasn't supposed to get my wound wet, but I didn't really care. My arms and hands were sore from an entire day working with them, even if I was just sitting at the counter. I was in the middle of lathering a particularly stubborn grease spot when the door opened.

I shrieked and shrank against the tiled wall. The glass was completely fogged over, but I wasn't taking any risks.

Darragh sighed. "It's just me."

"No shit," I called back. I covered my bare breasts and . . . private area.

I couldn't see what he was doing. The shower was large enough for five people, but I retreated to the corner anyway. The colorful smudge of his clothes walked across the bathroom, barely discernible through the fog. He shifted, from what I could tell, and then the glass door opened.

I shrieked and turned around. That left my bare ass on full display, but it was better than him seeing *everything*. "What are you doing? *Go away.*"

"I need to shower and you're taking fecking forever."

To my horror, his bare footsteps splashed on the tile and the glass door shut behind him.

Darragh was in the shower with me.

Darragh was in the shower with me while I was naked.

Darragh was *naked* in the shower with me while I was naked.

"Go downstairs."

"All my stuff is up here."

"Then I'll give it to you and you can go downstairs."

He sighed. A roil of steam blew my way. "I'm already here. Now are you going to wash that soap off or are you going to stand in the corner for the rest of the night?"

My heart fluttered in my chest. I did not want to turn around. I really didn't want to admit to him I hadn't even washed my hair yet. Therefore, this was about to be an extremely uncomfortable ten minutes.

I gathered my courage and turned around, keeping my eyes firmly above a *certain area* on Darragh's body. He was too busy getting his hair wet to notice, but when he opened his eyes, they honed in on me.

I flushed hot red and it wasn't from the heat.

"It's a thousand degrees in here," he said.

My mouth fell open, then snapped shut. That's what he had to say?

He turned down the heat and scrubbed shampoo into his hair.

My eyes roamed over the hard planes of his stomach. A gleaming six pack roiled under the water flowing down his chest and abs. In the heat and steam, every thick corded muscle of his arms popped each time he ran his hands through his hair.

I swallowed.

"I really don't feel comfortable with this."

"What? Nudity?"

"Yes, but most of all with you."

133

He laughed and shook his head. Tiny water droplets sprayed all over me. Even with the steam, I was getting cold standing on the far side of the shower. Goosebumps broke out on my skin, but I wasn't about to share the stream with Darragh.

He took up, like, all of it.

"One, I'm the last person you should feel uncomfortable getting undressed with." He made a show of pointing his gaze at my empty ring finger, still clenched over my breast. "Two, there are far worse people to be stuck in the shower with than me."

Insufferable *bastardo*.

My hands clenched over my chest, still hiding my assets. "How would you feel if someone just barged into your shower?"

"If it was a woman that looked like you, I wouldn't mind at all. As for men, the military makes you forget about being shy real fast."

There were two things to unpack there. One, his "woman that looked like you" comment. While horrified, I couldn't help the small bit of satisfaction that winded through me. Actually, I hated that satisfaction. Nothing about Darragh finding me appealing should be appealing. He was the worst.

Then there was the second thing.

"You were in the military?"

He scrubbed himself down with a bar of soap. Oak and musk drifted through with the steam. "Yeah. Vietnam."

I frowned. That made no sense. "Vietnam? I thought you were thirty?"

"I am."

"So how—"

"Quit freezing your arse off in the corner and maybe I'll tell you."

I clenched my arms tighter around myself.

I didn't want to go anywhere near him, but I was cold. And intrigued.

Morbid curiosity won out. Call me a masochist, I guess. "Just don't get too close."

He stepped to the side, allowing me space under the steady stream of water.

I inched closer, doing everything in my power not to let my eyes drift down to a certain place on him I really didn't want to think about. Apparently Darragh didn't feel the same, because his eyes drifted up and down every revealing inch of skin on me. I still had everything important covered, which only made him stare harder.

His scent was overwhelming, but the heat felt so good. All my goosebumps retreated the second I went under the water.

But I still wasn't peeling my hands away. A black spot of grease in my hair mocked me. Darragh stared at it pointedly, then back at my hands.

"You should wash that out."

I shrugged. "I'm good."

"Wash it out and I'll tell you what you want to know."

I gritted my teeth. "The deal was you'd tell me if I came under the water."

He smirked. "I said *maybe* I'd tell you, love."

Dirty *bastardo*.

A few seconds passed where I didn't move. Finally, he sighed. "At least let me wash it out."

I shook my head. "It's fine."

He groaned. "Gun grease doesn't come out, Pina. You'll ruin all my damn sheets. I won't touch anything but your hair."

I knew he was right. The five towels in the bathroom covered in the stuff said so. And of course, my own damn curiosity was winning out. I caved. "Nothing but my hair. And you tell me what happened."

He grabbed a bottle of shampoo off the shelf and drifted behind me. At least like this, I didn't have to accidentally worry about seeing something I really didn't want to. His hands raked into my hair and massaged my temple in slow circles, before finally drifting down to the wads of grease buried in the strands. I hated to admit it, but it felt nice.

135

"I came to the states when I was ten. Until then, I didn't know my father or my brothers, it was just me and my Ma. But that's a story for another time, so don't even ask."

My mouth snapped shut around the forming question.

"My Da brought me here through . . . untraditional means. I wasn't born here, so I had no rights. Back in Ireland, my Ma had ties with the IRA, so normal immigration wasn't having it. He pulled a ton of strings with the local politicians to make me a legitimate Yankee. I have a fake birth certificate and stolen social security number. I'm thirty years old, but legally, I'm thirty-three."

I nodded. It was a mess, but a mess that made sense. His fingers combed through my hair, just working through one of the greasy knots. I leaned back into the feeling, closing my eyes. "So, Vietnam?"

"Last draft pick was in seventy-three. According to the U.S. government, I was eighteen."

But in actuality, he was only fifteen. A child. That was . . . horrifying.

"Couldn't your father get you out of it? If he could fake your life, why couldn't he buy you out of the draft?"

Darragh sighed. His fingers worked through another part of my hair. A long moment passed before he answered, "My Da dealt with a lot being an immigrant. A lot more with being on the other side of the law. The feds and the politicians were looking a little too close, so he wanted to prove the O'Callaghan's were a legitimate, American family. Nothing says you're more American than sending your youngest boy off to war."

"And your brother?"

"He went too, but he ain't good with a gun and has two left feet. They stuck him in supplies and he did his service partying in the Mojave."

While his baby brother went across the world. I thought back to when I was fifteen. I spent most days dancing with Paulina to MTV and playing with an *easy bake oven*. I couldn't imagine . . . any of that.

136

And it wasn't exactly like I was born to the most stable, law-abiding family either.

"Was it bad?"

His hands stilled in my hair. I wondered if I asked too much when he said, "Yes. And that's all I'm going to say about it."

He spun me around, hand still fisted in my hair. My eyes widened as his face came into view, much too close. His blue eyes bore into the hand still covering my chest, something hot and violent brewing in them.

"I don't want to talk about my Da or the war."

His hand came down, slowly, before tapering at the end of my hair and drifting a breath away from my butt.

I took a shaky breath. "Then what do you want to talk about?"

His eyes told me the answer. They drifted over my face, my lips, and back down to the hand still covering my breasts. The hand previously in my hair came forward and laced through my fingers, slowly pulling my arm away.

Despite the heat, a shiver wracked through me.

His palm came over my right breast. His hand was so large, it covered it entirely. His thumb tucked under and ran a slow circle around my nipple. My toes curled against the tiled floors.

"What are you doing?" I breathed.

His hand crossed to my other breast and continued the circles. "Talking."

My shaky swallow was followed by another shiver. He was so close I could feel the heat coming off his body, but only his hand touched. The water sluiced over both of us while his thumb continued the tantalizing little circles. He pinched my nipple between his thumb and forefinger. I gasped.

His chest was right in front of me. All hard muscles and golden skin. I followed a little drop of water down between his pecs, over his stomach, and then my eyes followed it to the place I'd been avoiding.

Holy shit.

137

My jaw fell open at the sight. From what I knew about men, I didn't think they were supposed to be that . . . big. I'd only seen one once, from a dirty VHS Paulina stole and played in my room on my eighteenth birthday. She said now that we were both adults, we needed to know what one looked like.

We giggled the entire time, but through it all I watched curiously. Attentively. I didn't know if that was what my future husband expected of me, but it looked . . . intense.

Darragh was looking at me with that same intensity now.

I averted my eyes when his gaze met mine. "We're —um— we're not married yet."

And again, I didn't think the marriage portion of our marriage would be this marriageable. Married-like. Marital. Whatever the term for it was.

He pushed his chest against mine and I squeaked. The feeling of his skin on mine was different, strange but also sent warmth down to my toes. Something hard pressed against my stomach, and my eyes widened when I realized exactly what it was.

He tilted his head down to brush my ear with his lips. "We can fix that."

His hand drifted down my back, featherlight, and ended at my ass. He gave it a hard squeeze and pulled me closer.

I breathed heavy against his chest. Excitement raced through me, pooling lower and lower. A wet heat grew between my thighs. I clenched them together, covering my skin in sticky fluid.

This was wrong. This was completely and utterly wrong. We weren't married yet, and Darragh was bad. A bad man. He killed people. A week ago, we sat in this very bathroom while he described how he would kill me.

He bit down on the soft lobe of my ear, bringing my earring into his mouth. I couldn't hold back the moan that came out of me.

"If we're gonna do this," he whispered. "Then we go all the way. Nobody will buy into the alliance if we don't act like a real married couple."

It was like being dunked in cold water. Of course that was all this was. Get me weak and wet for him so I'd make my family believe he was on our side now.

I tried to pull away, but he kept me locked in place. That hard place on his body twitched against my stomach. "And if I'm going to be married to you, I'd be a dirty liar if I said I didn't want to take advantage of waking up to this every day." His hand squeezed my ass again, harder.

A shuddering breath came out of me. Traitor. My body was a traitor.

I closed my eyes, trying to bring some sense into the situation. "You can have any woman you like, Darragh."

That hand drifted lower and lower, until it was nudging at the tightly squeezed apex of my thighs. I gasped as his finger pushed between them, brushing over the most sensitive part of me.

He nibbled at my ear again. "I like you."

"You told me yesterday, you didn't."

"I lied." His teeth grazed over my jaw, coming dangerously close to my lips.

"Why?"

"I don't like everything about you," he said. "But I like this." His knee came between my legs and nudged them apart, right as his finger ran over my center.

I moaned into his chest.

"And I like that you're a little strange." His lips brushed the corner of mine. "That you have bite." Again, another squeeze of my ass. "And I really like how sexy you looked while you took apart that gun this morning."

I scowled. Creep. "You were watching through the cameras?"

"I was waiting for you to come upstairs and kill me. Kind of a turn on."

"You're a fucking psychopath," I breathed. I meant it, too. Because how could someone go from planning my death, to

139

sending my pinky off to their father, to putting a ring on my finger and feeling me up in the shower?

He hooked his hands under my thighs and hoisted me up. I yelped and grabbed for his shoulders as he wrapped my legs around his waist, hands gripping my ass. The way my arms wrapped around his neck brought his face close. Way too close. Closer than death as he murmured, "I'm a very bad man, Pina."

I nodded, staring dumbly at his face. "We established that."

"Do you know what bad men like to do to their wives?"

I did. Or at least, I thought I did. Which is why this had to stop now, but my traitorous body said otherwise. That wet heat grew even more. At this angle, his hardness was poking at the backside of my thigh. He adjusted our weight so it glided over the wet center of me.

The feeling was making it hard to think, so all I said was, "We're not married yet."

He set me down on the ground.

The water turned off and he got out of the shower, grabbing one of the few clean towels left and wrapping it around himself.

I watched, open-mouthed and just a little confused. I stood naked in the shower, watching him dry off his hair and stride for the door.

When I stepped out, he finally turned around.

"I'll go buy you a dress. Do whatever it is girls do with their hair. I'll be back in a bit."

19

DARRAGH

Town was only twenty minutes away, but Pina still didn't know that. Soon, I'd trust her enough to clue her in, but it was still better to be safe than sorry at this point.

The only clothing store in the area was mostly ski and snowboard gear, but they had their fair share of regular shit too. The salesgirl met me at the front, smacking a piece of gum between her lips. A bored gear repairman sat behind the counter, puffing on a cigarette. His eyes were rimmed red, probably from reefer or some shit.

Bubblegum stared at me with vacant eyes. "We close in an hour."

"Yeah, I'll be quick."

Dopehead behind the counter laughed. "Nice accent, man. Where ya from?"

I gave him a scathing look and turned back to Bubblegum. "I need clothes for my fiancé." I slipped her a hundred-dollar bill. "Pick out whatever girls like, just make sure there's a nice dress in there. Preferably white. That's for you."

Her bubble popped and stuck to her lips and cheeks. She stared up at me in shock. "Uh, well, what's your girl's size?"

I looked her up and down, "Probably the same as you."

She must have made commission or some shit, because by the time I walked out of there, I was significantly less rich. Thankfully, a white dress was included, along with whatever Pina would need for the winter. As much as I liked watching her walk around in my shirts, it was about time she got some of her own clothes. She'd be staying a while, after all.

When I got home, Pina was sitting on the couch, wringing her hands together. I kept telling her stop doing that shit with her wound, but Pina was like a little kid. The more you told her not to do something, the more she did it out of spite.

I dumped the three bags of clothing in front of her and handed her the dress. "I got you some stuff. Go put it upstairs."

She eyed the bags, then me. She did her makeup and hair, but god knows she didn't need to. She could have mascara running down her face with a shaved head and still be more gorgeous than ninety percent of women.

"Why upstairs?"

"We're getting married; you can sleep upstairs from now on."

Her eyes darted to the door of the guest room, a challenge playing on her face. One I was having none of.

"Put it upstairs."

She frowned. "I like my room."

"It's not your room, it's a guest room. Married people sleep together."

"We're not married yet," she countered. Then, realizing that argument was going to hold no weight very soon, countered with, "This is your safe house. No one will come here; we don't have to keep up any impressions."

"No risks," I said, nudging the bags closer to her. "Upstairs and put the dress on."

The Lord above must have been rewarding me, because she actually listened for once.

She hovered at the top of the stairs when she was done. The dress fit her good. A little too good. It was white, but that was just about as close as it got to being a wedding dress. The thin straps hugged her shoulders and pushed up her tits in a way that made me want to go back and kiss Bubblegum right on the lips. The silky fabric flowed over her stomach, hugged her ass and tapered off to flow just below her knees.

She didn't look like a proper bride, but she definitely looked like my bride.

She wrung her hands together and took two tentative steps down. "So . . . where are we doing this?"

"I know a place."

Her eyes flicked out to the dark window beside her. "Is it safe to assume this won't be in a church?"

I laughed. "No."

She nodded, raised her chin and came the rest of the way down. I handed her the brand-new coat and took her arm in mine.

She had nothing to say the entire car ride. I didn't cover her eyes this time. Call it a wedding gift.

The casino was about an hour south, family owned and run. A few of Sean's boys came through when they could, but most of the men were loyal to me. It took me long enough to make sure of that.

Pina made a face of disgust when we pulled into the parking lot but had nothing to say. I didn't trust any outsiders to do this, and since I had no clergymen on my payroll this would just have to do. If it really meant that much, to her, we could do another ceremony later down the line.

Tiny snowflakes fluttered around us as I looped my arm through hers and walked her inside.

The casino was mostly dead. Summers and winters were the money-makers. Even though it was so damn cold up here the mountains were already open, November was still considered the shoulder season. But it was good for us, and it was good for this. The last thing I needed were prying eyes.

Kieran waited for us, right on time. I'd known the skinny lad since we were kids. He was loyal, smart and one of the few people I could really trust. His shock of red hair glowed under the bar lights. His eyes roamed up and down Pina but dropped to the floor the second he saw my warning scowl.

He hopped off the stool and led us to a back, private room. I made Kieran get ordained a few years ago when it became obvious how much people liked to drink, gamble and wake up married the next day. The casino mostly posed as a front for our more illegal and lucrative businesses, but it made damn good money itself. Especially with Kieran running it.

Pina shuffled beside me as we climbed to the "altar" I paid some guys to put together. It was proper gaudy, to say the least. But nothing about our marriage was ceremonious, so who cared?

I took her hands in mine. The wound on her hand was looking better, nothing but a little bit of gauze covering it now. Kieran eyed it but said nothing. As he began the usual spiel, Pina's eyes went just about everywhere that wasn't me.

Meanwhile, all I could think about was how I wished Kieran would hurry this the hell up. All I cared about was screwing my wife without her feeling guilty about it, then waking up tomorrow and skipping her training to do it all again. Assassin life could take a backseat to my needs for once.

He droned on for a bit longer, we exchanged the rings I picked up in town and then it was time to kiss the bride. Pina watched me with the corners of her lips turned down. We stared at each other for entirely too long after Kieran said the words. He glanced back and forth between us, but I kept my eyes fully trained on my brand-new bride. The challenge she held for me. She knew that this was it. After this, there'd be no turning back. Life as she knew it was done.

Before the moment could become anymore awkward, I leaned down and gave her a quick peck on the lips. She was cold and rigid the entire time. Then, that was that. I was a married man.

I told Pina to roam around the casino and get herself a drink while I discussed business with Kieran.

He leaned over a piano in the corner, filling out the rightful paperwork while I lit a cigarette from the bench seat.

"If we're looking to make this legal, I need something from her. It's fine if she came here without the papers. She's an American lass now."

I took a drag off my cigarette and drummed my fingers on the piano keys. Pina was rubbing off on me. "No need to make that one legal. Annie McCormick isn't her real name; I just need the certificate as proof."

Kieran sighed. "What was the point of doing the ceremony, then?"

I tapped my fingers on the papers, right where he put *Annie* in thick, messy script. "To give to Sean. I'll contact you with a real name soon. I want it legalized after the New Year."

He straightened. "Is there something I should know, Darragh?"

I clapped him on the back and stood to leave. "Nothing more than you already know. I'll be in touch soon. Don't forget to send the quarterly reports on time."

He nodded and moved out of the way so I could join Pina at the bar.

I'd been gone no longer than twenty minutes, but in that time she managed to knock back three martinis. For a lass that barely drank her entire life, she really turned into a proper lush.

I put my hand on her back. "We can stay the night or head home. Up to you."

She swirled the toothpick around her glass, spinning the remaining olive in circles. "Whatever you want."

A gentleman would plan something nice for their wedding night, but that, I was not. The longer we were out, the more risk we ran. The feds were still looking for us.

She was silent the whole way out of the casino, the car ride, and the walk to the front door.

"Go upstairs and wash up," I told her. She didn't argue, didn't scowl, didn't say much of anything. The shower turned on overhead while I did my rounds, checking the locks and security feeds like I did every night.

When I arrived upstairs, she laid in bed wearing nothing but the thin, silky nightgown I just bought her. It was the only thing I picked out for her on my own. I was damn proud of myself for it, too.

Her caramel curls splayed across the headboard as she pulled the covers up to her chest.

I sat on the edge of the bed, a bottle of champagne and two flutes I took from the casino in hand. She wordlessly took one of the glasses while I popped the cork. I lifted my glass to hers.

"To my beautiful wife."

She clinked her glass against mine and downed the whole thing. Still, silence. It was so much more unsettling than when she wouldn't shut up, but I didn't care to interpret it. I had other things on my mind.

I took our glasses and laid them on the side table before turning off the light.

The room flooded with darkness. Pina was still tucked in tight under the covers. I kicked my shoes off and shimmied out of my suit before lying beside her under the sheets.

I ran a finger down the side of her face. Her wide eyes were only outlines in the darkness, but I could see enough of what I wanted to: the edges of her slender arms, the dip of her waist and the thick curve of her ass all being hugged by ivory satin.

I dropped my fingers from her face and curled my hand around her hip. I pulled her flush against me and she gasped.

"What are you doing?"

I frowned. Was that not obvious? "It's our wedding night."

She swallowed. It echoed around the quiet room. Did she want music? Candles? I never fecking understood women. The only bright side of Pina was she was normally pretty vocal about whatever she wanted. Or demanded.

She only met me with more of that heavy silence. If she wasn't going to ask, then I wouldn't ask for her. I pulled her close, wrapping my hands through her thick curls and pulling her lips to mine.

Finally, I got something from her. Her body reacted the way I'd hoped, her legs parting to straddle my waist as I brought her down on top of me. I ran my hands down the silk nightgown until I reached the edge and pulled it over her head. Her little tits bounced free and I took one nipple in my mouth, cupping her lacy underwear with my free hands.

She moaned a little, but nothing like when we were in the shower. The movements from a few moments ago all but stopped as she went rigid as a board in my hands. I gripped her tighter, pulling her lace-covered pussy to my erection. I bit at her nipple and kissed down, but she stopped moving altogether.

Something warm dripped onto my arm. A tear.

When I looked up, her face was covered in them. She bit her lip and turned away, but the damage was done. I sighed and fell back to the bed. She still straddled me, crying harder now, but silently, thank god.

"What is it?"

She bit her lip harder and shook her head. Little teardrops were falling nonstop, dripping off the curve of her jaw and running down her chest. Like little snowflakes fluttering to the ground.

"Pina."

She laughed, which I decided was the scariest thing, after all. Much worse than the stark silence.

I gripped her thighs "Pina—"

"I hate you." She smiled, still shaking her head. "I absolutely fucking hate you."

I scowled, moving my hands off her legs to grip the sheets. "And what has garnered your hatred this time?"

She laughed again through another flood of tears. "God . . . you're all animals."

I sat up, bringing us nose to nose. Her smile died, but the tears didn't. She tried to squirm away, but I held her in place. "An animal would have killed you in the city. An animal would have killed you in Vegas and left you to rot in the desert. An animal would take you right now, even with the tears, even with the insults. So, call me what you want, Pina, but this marriage was an alliance to save your life, so maybe be a little fecking grateful."

She growled and shoved at me so hard I slammed back into the bed. "Grateful? *Grateful?*"

I rolled my eyes. "Here we fecking go."

"Shut up," she snapped. "You saved my life so now I have to fuck you? That's what you think?"

"No," I seethed. "All I'm saying is, you entered this marriage of your own accord, love."

"Well, if this marriage is nothing but an *alliance* then why treat it like it's real?"

I sighed. "I already told you—"

"I don't need to fuck you to make this look real. Do you see anyone else in this room?" She spread her arms wide, gesturing to the darkness. "You did this because you want to get off, nothing else. None of this was necessary. Did it ever occur to you I'm a virgin? I messed around with you yesterday and brought up marriage non-stop because *I'm not ready to sleep with you."*

She stole a long, shaky breath. "This marriage is a sham. It's an alliance so we can both get what we need. But if you're going to get additional perks from it, then I need some too."

My jaw set. "Is the idea of sleeping with me so vile it can't be a perk for you too?"

She stared at me, long and hard. "I haven't decided yet."

Silence encapsulated the room. I watched a single, angry tear form at the corner of her eye and slide down her cheek.

"You rushed a ceremony so you could sleep with me. You dragged me to a casino in a thirty-dollar dress and made one of your workers ordain it. I've known you for less than a month, under the most ridiculous circumstances imaginable and I'm not ready for any of this, but all you have on your mind is the *perks* this deal can get you. But I'm not a real wife. I'm your business partner. You're training me to be an equal. So, you will treat me like a goddamn equal and not a naive, blushing bride. Because if all you wanted was a pretty, young girl to fuck, then I was better off with Lucien Rocci."

She pulled her legs off me and grabbed the discarded nightgown off the floor. The three bags of clothes I bought her hadn't been touched. She clutched all three paper handles in her palms and stomped towards the door.

"I'm going back to my room. Move my stuff and I'll shoot you."

She slammed the door behind her.

I laid in the dark, staring at the ceiling, wondering once again where in the ever-loving hell I went wrong.

Pina moved across the security monitors, a little caramel-colored fireball wreaking havoc through my house. When she reached the guest room, she slammed that door, too.

It was a whiskey kind of night.

I reached for the bottle in my nightstand drawer, but even that felt cheap. I pissed her off. She was right, it was my fault. I didn't get to drink away my own mistake.

Instead, I found myself reaching for the wooden box on my dresser. I flipped it open, eyes combing over the little, smiling boy. The person who hadn't been crushed yet.

And beside him, a fiery-haired woman who did everything she could to escape. Someone who knew what Sean was, what he did to people, and exactly what he would do to her son. She knew because he had already broken her to bits, and I promised I wouldn't make that mistake again.

I stared long and hard at the photograph. My mother's smiling face. In this light, she almost looked disappointed. But there was nothing in this room but me, the walls, and the dead.

I stared at her smiling face. "I already fecked up, didn't I?"

20

PINA

I woke up to the smell of bacon and someone softly shaking my shoulder.

I groaned and buried my face in the pillow. "What?"

"Wake up and put something warm on. I made you breakfast; we head out in twenty minutes."

My eyelashes scraped against the pillowcase as I peeled my eyes open. The alarm clock beside my bed read 5:32. I had half a thought to lock my door and go back to sleep, but the food did smell good. I'd barely eaten anything yesterday but martinis, and my stomach felt it.

I pulled on a pair of brand-new jeans, a flannel and dragged my new coat out of the closet. At some point I'd have to put everything away, but I didn't care to right now. It felt a little too much like accepting this was my home. Even if all the clothes were brand-new, just like everything else in my life.

Darragh was right last night. I did choose this willingly. I could have taken option one. But accepting the deal of our sham marriage was still nothing but a business transaction, and I stuck by that. If he wanted a real wife to suck his cock and do his laundry, he was more than able to go find one.

But for all my talk of respect and being equals, there was something else that bothered me, maybe even most of all. Something I'd never admit to Darragh. I was disappointed yesterday, not just because he put a ring on my finger to get in my pants, but also because I never expected it to be like this. I always knew I'd end up in an arranged marriage, but a real wedding, a real husband and real sex were still possibilities. Just because my family chose my spouse for me didn't mean I still couldn't have all the things I dreamed about as a little girl. The closer the deadline loomed, the more I prayed I'd marry someone I could even love.

Then Lucien Rocci was put on the table and that all went to shit. Darragh was better than him, but choosing between the lesser of two evils wasn't exactly my dream scenario.

Getting married in a casino with an hour's notice so my husband could get laid, even less.

It was fine though, because if Darragh wouldn't respect me, I'd respect myself. I had enough dignity to put my foot down and draw the line. If he killed me for it, at least I went down swinging.

I was not a little girl anymore.

I was not helpless anymore.

I repeated those two mantras in my head while shoveling down food. Darragh stood against the stove, arms crossed and staring at me the entire time. It was only then it occurred to me the breakfast may have been a peace offering, but it would take a lot more than scrambled eggs to earn my trust.

Darragh grabbed the gun I'd spent yesterday disassembling and piecing back together. Frigid morning air and twinkling darkness smacked me in the face as he opened the sliding back door.

Thank god he had the foresight to buy me good winter boots.

We trekked deep into the woods and crested a large foothill. By the time we reached the top, I was breathing heavy and peeling layers of warm clothing off myself. Darragh stopped me when I went for the gloves, insisting that my hands would lock up too much.

It would still be hours before sunrise and this deep in the woods, I could barely see my hand in front of my face. It'd finally stopped snowing, and with it, the clouds were gone. But the bright moon and full, twinkling stars weren't nearly enough to see.

I jumped when Darragh grabbed my hands in his and pulled me in front of him. His warm breath cascaded down my cheek as he leaned in and whispered, "Tell me the direction of the wind."

My first thought was to look to the trees, but in the darkness, I could barely make anything out. Even with light, these trees were old and sturdy and the winter took their leaves. They barely moved.

It didn't feel like there was any wind. Maybe because I was still bundled up so tight, but I couldn't detect anything at all. It also could have been that Darragh was entirely too close and it was ridiculously distracting.

I pulled away, but Darragh snatched me back. I yelped as he leaned back in again. "You need to be able to feel it. Even if there's barely any wind, even if you have something blocking you. Tell me the direction of the wind."

He ran his gloved thumb over my ruddy cheek. The fabric burned my frigid, raw skin. "Feel it on your face. Close your eyes and tell me what you feel."

I closed my eyes. At first, I felt nothing, but then a hint of a breeze cooled the left side of my face. Or at least, made it colder.

"It's coming from . . . my left."

"What's your left?"

I opened my eyes. "What do you mean?"

"Your left can mean anything. What's left? Give me a direction."

I frowned. I didn't really know what he wanted from me. I scanned the sky, spotting the North Star. I recognized it from Peter Pan as a kid, but hey, it was something.

"North?" I tried.

He nodded. "Better. Now run down the hill and run back up again."

I stared at him like he had three heads. "What?"

He waved his hand. "Go. Run."

The next two hours passed the exact same: run to the bottom of the hill, run up, check the wind. Run down, run up, check the wind.

I peeled my jacket off as the sun started bridging the horizon. Darragh smoked a cigarette against a tree, watching me with boredom.

"Okay, I'm done now," I huffed. I bent over to put my hands on my knees, heaving in large breaths. "The wind is coming from the fucking south now, you happy?"

He smiled and flicked his cigarette into the snow. "Chipper. Good job, let's go home. I'm freezing my arse off."

My hands balled into sweaty fists. "Go home? I haven't even touched the gun."

He shrugged. "We're done for today. We'll see about the gun tomorrow."

The next day, he didn't ask me to put warm clothes on.

"I'm going to teach you how to adjust the scope." Darragh sat at the kitchen counter, gun in front of him. I didn't like the idea of sitting in close quarters with him all day, but it was better than running sprints in the snow.

I yawned, stretching my arms above my head. "And then you'll teach me to shoot?"

He shrugged. "Let's see about the scope first."

We spent the day adjusting, taking apart, and cleaning the scope. He'd tell me the wind was coming from the north at 5 miles per hour, 10 miles per hour, 20 . . . then make me adjust. We did that so many times I began to find a personal hatred for the cardinal directions.

The next day we were back at the hill. Up, down, direction of the wind. Up, down, direction of the wind and adjust your scope. Up, down, fucking direction of the wind. Adjust the damn scope.

Try not to strangle my husband of less than week when he lights a cigarette and watches me from a tree.

Three more days and nothing changed. The sun had just peeked over the hills, I was sweating through my parka, and I'd just about freaking had it.

"It's east," I snapped before Darragh could even open his mouth. "Do you want me to adjust the scope or are you done torturing me? It's been a week and we've done absolutely nothing but adjust damn scopes so whatever I did to deserve this punishment, here's my goddamn apology."

He walked toward me, slowly. Despite it being ten degrees out, he didn't look chilly at all. He stuffed his hands in his pockets and rocked back on his heels, his eyes darting towards the discarded gun.

I groaned and picked it up. He moved it every time I ran down the hill. This time, it was severely unadjusted. I laid down on my stomach and pointed it at my designated target, a little red flag attached to the train tracks I'd come across my first day up here. What seemed like a lifetime ago.

Darragh moved behind me and kicked my splayed legs open wider. In addition to *direction, scope and running*, I got yelled at every ten minutes about my crappy posture.

When my legs were wide enough and my elbows placed correctly, he leaned down beside me.

And pushed the barrel of a pistol to my head.

"Adjust the scope," he said calmly. He didn't look at me once.

My throat dried out. There was a gun to my head. Darragh was holding a gun to my head.

My voice shook. "What are you—"

"Do it correctly or I'll kill you."

My hands shook violently as I adjusted, even worse than I was used to with all the shaking from the running. Hot tears burned the back of my eyes, but I blinked them back. This made no sense.

I had no idea what game he was playing, but he didn't sound like he was kidding when he threatened my life.

Maybe I'd finally pushed him too far.

I got it as close as I could and moved to the side. He never took the gun away, just peeked through the scope and sighed. "You're several degrees off."

My heart stopped in my chest. He was going to kill me. He was finally over it. I couldn't make a good ally, so he was just going to give me the drop, like he always planned. I shook and wrapped my arms around myself, scrambling to see if I had a weapon. But the sniper rifle was empty, and I never brought anything else.

He sat up and faced me, but instead of pulling the trigger, he dropped the magazine. No bullets came out. Not even one in the chamber.

"Not loaded," he said.

At first there was relief.

Then, there was nothing but blind anger.

I screamed and lunged at him. Only a flicker of surprise crossed his face before I was on top of him, reeling my arm back to punch him.

He caught my fist in mid-air and rolled me onto my back. I thrashed beneath him, trying to claw out his ugly, soulless blue eyes.

"What is wrong with you?"

He didn't say anything. Only pinned down all four of my limbs with his own. I screamed again but he laid down on top of me, crushing all the air from my lungs. I panted through my grit teeth. As soon as he got up, I was killing him. He was absolutely *dead*.

"Shhh," he murmured. He tried to kiss my cheek. I spat on him.

He grinned and rubbed the saliva off on his shoulder. "Are you done yet?"

"You're sick in the head."

His eyebrow flicked up. "Maybe, but it worked."

My breathing slowed down. Darragh let off of me a bit. Not enough to free me from his grip, but he was no longer crushing me.

I took the bait. "What worked?"

He rolled off, lying flat on his back in the snow beside me. "When you run, you shake. When you shake, it's harder to adjust. It's even harder to shoot."

He leaned up on his elbow, resting his cheek in his palm. "But the hardest thing is working through adrenaline. On New Year's something will go wrong. It always does. You may have guns pointed at you. You may only have seconds to take your shot. You may just see Lucien Rocci's disgusting face through that scope and every bad memory comes flooding back, but when the adrenaline comes, so does the shaking. We only have a few months so we're learning the hard way. If you don't want me to threaten your life every morning, then we run."

"You mean *I* run." I scowled.

"This is nothing compared to what Sean made me do," he said quietly. "You only get one shot, so let's make it count. Will you live with yourself if you miss because nerves got the best of you?"

No, I wouldn't.

My silence was answer enough.

He sat up, brushing dusty snow off his sleeves. "Again."

21

PINA

Another week passed with more of the same, but I didn't complain this time. Not when Darragh woke me up early each morning, not on the days he told me to skip breakfast, and not on the days when he made me run one, two, or three miles, check the wind, and adjust.

It became evidently clear that everything was designed to torture me. Not because Darragh was a sadist, but because the worse the conditions, the harder it was to work. But as the days passed I got better, and by the end of that second week, Darragh started loading the rifle with blank rounds.

From there, we settled into a routine. In the mornings, he ran beside me. Then we practiced with the scope. He loaded the empty rounds and taught me how to shoot, balancing a quarter on the barrel of the rifle before I took each shot. If I flinched from the recoil, the quarter dropped. If the quarter dropped, he made me do it five more times.

At night we sat in the kitchen, working through breathing exercises. Inhale on the line-up, exhale on firing. We ate dinner. We played cards for an hour. We went to sleep.

During the third week, our one hour of mundane card games turned into math lessons. No one taught me growing up, but

Darragh said I needed to know long division, at the least. We practiced equations revolving around his ledgers for the casino. He taught me to balance a checkbook. Before I knew it, I was good enough to run the family finances.

In all that time, he never touched me once. Nothing even close to our little shower experience happened again. He was distant, respectful and completely professional. A business partner.

It was exactly what I wanted, so I wasn't sure why a small part of me missed his touch.

I chalked it up to loneliness. With nothing but the snow and Darragh to spend my days with, I found my thoughts drifting back to my family more and more. Mostly Andrea, but even Alessandro and my mother too. My father, I'd rather not think about at all.

I rolled out of bed to the sound of Darragh in the kitchen. He no longer woke me up— I did it all on my own. The training schedule got to me quick.

I threw open my curtains even though the sun hadn't risen yet. Shimmery, white snow gleamed back at me, shimmering in the back porch floodlights.

I frowned and went into the kitchen, pulling my robe tighter around myself. It was freezing.

The smell of bacon and scrambled eggs wafted into my nose. I smirked and sat down, drumming my fingers on the counter. "Can you cook anything else?"

He didn't turn around. "Why would I need to know how to cook anything else?"

I raised an eyebrow. "I don't know, your cholesterol?"

His shoulders shook in silent laughter, before he handed me my daily morning cup of coffee (one sugar and a splash of milk) and my breakfast (three pieces of bacon and two egg whites). He ate in silence across from me.

"So, what are the big plans for today? Math lessons, breathing exercises?"

He finished chewing and washed it down with a huge gulp of coffee. "I was actually thinking we'd begin shooting for real today."

My eyes flickered to the back door, where a heavy gust of snow blew across the porch. "The weather isn't too good."

"That's what I was counting on." He held his coffee mug in his hand, staring at me expectantly.

I could ask him, but that's not what he was teaching me to do these past few weeks. Snipers didn't wait for every little answer from their mentor. They figured it out.

"In case the weather is bad on New Year's?" I sipped my own coffee to cover my grimace. Could I sound any more unsure?

He nodded approvingly. "If you can shoot in this, you can shoot in anything."

I knew he was right, but goddamn did it look cold out there. Like, frostbite cold.

An icy blast of snow splattered against the sliding glass door to prove my point.

While I finished my breakfast, Darragh raided the gun case. I flexed and unflexed my fingers, grimacing at the bloody cracks that started to form in my knuckles. Damn cold weather. The little wounds stung, but in a strange way, I was proud to have them. My whole life I was to keep my hands prim and neat. All blemishes were artfully covered or disguised. I didn't have the hands of a mafia princess anymore. I had the hands of a killer.

A killer who would avenge their best friend. A killer who took no shit from the men around her anymore.

"Here." I jumped as Darragh appeared beside me. A little tin of salve rested in his palm. "I picked it up the other day. Your hands look terrible." He placed the container on the counter.

I stared at the tin, trying not to read too much into the action. Everything Darragh did was logical and calculated. The more busted up my hands were, the worse I'd perform. It wasn't an act of kindness. It never was.

I rubbed the salve into my bleeding knuckles as he loaded up two guns. We only ever took one, but maybe he wanted to play it safe in this weather.

"Put this on," he instructed, handing me a heavy, black vest. The fabric had to be several inches thick.

"What's this for?"

"Protection," he said, saying nothing else. I knew a bulletproof vest when I saw one, but had no clue why I'd need it now. The target flags never shot back.

"Are we . . . going after someone?"

Darragh cocked the rifle in his hand and grinned. "Actually, you'll be shooting me."

I chuckled. "Ha-ha, very funny."

He stared at me dead-on. "I'm serious."

My smile faltered.

He handed me the second rifle. "May the best spouse win."

I refused to take it from him. "Are you out of your goddamn mind? What if I shoot you in the face? What if *you* shoot *me* in the face?"

He shrugged. "I won't."

"*And me?*"

He looked at me like I said the dumbest thing in the world. "I trained you to shoot for the center mass. Just remember what you were taught."

I flailed my hand towards the back door. "There's a fucking blizzard. You didn't train the wind."

He nodded. "Yeah. We covered this. I trained *you.*"

I threw my hands up in the air. "Are you so narcissistic you'll play with your life?"

He considered for a moment. "Yes."

I groaned. *Bastardo.* I'd been living here nearly a month. I don't know why I expected any less.

"Give me a ten-minute head start. I'll see you in the woods."

160

My hands balled into fists. "If, and I say *if* you get a shot off, and it hits anywhere but this vest, let it be known I will haunt your Irish *arse* for the rest of your days. Do you hear me?"

His low chuckle was the last thing I heard before he left. He heard me.

———————

If hell froze over, Darragh's property would be colder.

Even through three layers of clothes, gloves, a hat, face mask and goggles, I still felt the chill down to my core. I wasn't sure how far Darragh could get in ten minutes and this weather, but I never underestimated his uncanny ability to surprise me. Or to survive.

I had no clue where he would go, but I'm sure that was part of this little exercise. He'd want me to think like him. Unfortunately, that still left me with very few ideas and a whole lot of anxiety. He was probably setting up as we spoke, and knowing Darragh, he wouldn't make it easy. I wouldn't put it past him to bury himself in snow for cover.

He couldn't have gotten too far. My best bet was setting up as close to the house as possible and getting high. That only left the problem of cover for myself. Even with the blizzard, anything not white would stick out like a sore thumb.

I glanced back at the house. The slanted roof might make good enough cover. The snow was coming down thick, but not sticking. The black shingles stuck out in the early morning light. My clothes would blend right in.

After going back inside and maneuvering myself out of a second story window, with no less than three near death slips, I clambered onto the roof, tested the wind and set up my scope.

I scanned the landscape, left to right and back, just like Darragh taught. So far, I could see nothing but snow swirling in the wind and trees groaning under the weight of ice. With his house being so far up on the hill, it proved to be the best outpost I could choose. There was no doubt in my mind Darragh purchased this particular piece of property exactly for that reason. It was a lot easier to defend a hill when you were at the top of it.

A movement in the trees caught my sight.

I honed in on the sliver of clothing peeking out from a tree trunk. If it was him, he managed to climb very high, very quickly. But that was exactly the type of position Darragh would take.

I evened my breath and lined up the scope. I'd have to wait for him to move, which could take god knows how long. Of course he had to pick the coldest day imaginable for this.

The minutes ticked by and the wind kept shifting. I adjusted, re-adjusted and adjusted again. Darragh didn't move. I dug deep to think like him. There was only so long we could stay out here without freezing half to death. Darragh had been teaching me that a sniper never moves to their target. The target always moves to them. So, I had to get Darragh to move.

There was little out here to use as a distraction. I could trip the alarms in the house, but I doubted he'd fall for any tricks. He was smarter than that.

I lined up my shot. I couldn't hit him, but I could hit his hideout.

I aimed for the trunk of the tree. The wind howled around me, wind snapped at my face and tiny snowflakes stuck to my lashes. I took a deep breath, blinked, exhaled, *fire*.

The bullet ricocheted off the tree trunk just as intended, but only a huge pile of snow fell from the branches. A flock of crows screeched and dove for the sky as the sound of the shot echoed around the empty woods. The black sliver of clothing wasn't clothing at all, just a shadow I'd been focusing on for well over an hour now.

I groaned. I'd done nothing but waste my time in ten degree weather.

He had to be further into the woods than I thought. If he was anywhere near the house, I'd have seen him by now.

I collected my rifle and walked toward a flat portion of the roof. I needed to reposition.

A flash of light caught my eye.

I fell flat to my stomach and pulled my rifle in front of me. Ahead, in the trees, something large moved. A quick check through my scope told me it was Darragh. Even through the snow, the bright, blue of his eyes flashed back at me. And I'd just given up my position.

I fumbled to line up my shot. He'd come out enough to reveal his heavily guarded torso. The black vest stuck out like a stain on the landscape. Everything adjusted into place. I breathed. My finger wrapped around the trigger, but his blue eyes flashed at me again, and I hesitated.

It was snowing hard. The wind was blasting. There was a chance I'd miss and genuinely hurt him.

I didn't know why that bothered me. We weren't really married. We weren't even friends. But that memory of the shower flashed back, as he rubbed soap into my hair and told me about Vietnam. When he kissed down my neck after revealing that little tidbit of his life to me. Then, an even earlier memory, when his arms encased me at the bar in Colorado. When I cried about Paulina, and instead of pushing it, he let me go.

The blue eyes that revealed absolutely nothing while we played cards each night. That crinkled into a little smile whenever I got another math problem right. That followed me up and down the hill each morning he ran beside me, panting heavily, never pushing me to go farther even though his legs could carry him much faster. The same blue eyes that flashed with desire the night I came downstairs in my wedding dress.

I hesitated.

He didn't.

I didn't feel the moment he shot me. One minute I was in my head, the next I laid flat on my back, gasping for air. Black dotted the corners of my vision, but all I could see was dark, gray sky and little snowflakes fluttering down. From this angle, they seemed to fall faster. Little bits of light zooming down from the sky.

I wasn't sure how long I laid there. My lungs couldn't suck in enough air, and even when I did draw breath, the icy cold did nothing but burn me from the inside out. My heart hammered against my chest, my lungs breathed fire and the world froze around me.

A set of hands looped beneath my arms and carried me towards the edge of the roof. Darragh ripped my vest off and threw it to the ground below. I groaned in pain with each jolting touch. He swore he wouldn't hit anything but the vest, but it felt like the bullet went right through me.

I blacked out while he somehow carried me off the roof and came to in his bathroom. Water flooding the tub echoed in my ears as warm air hit my face. It wasn't enough. My muscles still locked from the freezing air, each chatter of my teeth sending spikes of pain across my chest.

Darragh sat on the floor in front of me and started peeling off my clothes. He still wore everything, even his vest. I didn't care.

"I'm going to haunt you," I mumbled.

He snorted and pulled my jacket off. I winced and doubled over when he tried to lift my shirt.

"I hit the vest, love."

I took a deep breath. "It sure doesn't feel like it."

He rubbed my arms over the thermal and slowed his breathing. I followed his pattern, taking large breaths and slowing my heart rate through the pain.

"The vest will keep you alive, but it won't keep you from getting hurt. Getting shot feels like death, no matter how much protection you got."

I gritted my teeth. "You could have warned me."

He continued rubbing my arms, up and down, slowly with each stroke. My breath kept hitching, so it was a task to match it to his. I focused on the warmth of his hands, the tender feeling of his movements. My breathing slowed.

164

"You needed to know what it would feel like," he finally said. I lifted my gaze to meet his. The cursed blue eyes that got me here in the first place.

His words sunk in. "You didn't think I would win, did you?"

He shook his head, a rueful, little smile on his lips.

I sighed in defeat. "I'll never understand you."

"Very few do." His hands stopped their movement and tugged at the hem of my shirt. "You're still freezing. The bath will help."

My hands balled into fists. "I can do it."

He pulled away. I lifted the edges of my shirt, taking short gasping breaths through the wincing. All my muscles seized up. I only had it half off when Darragh reached for me and pulled it the rest of the way. I didn't fight him this time.

I didn't want him to see me fully naked, but I honestly couldn't get the rest of my clothes off myself. When I got down to my bra and panties, I told him to leave them.

He dropped me into the bath. He was right, the warm water did help. Steam roiled around us, stinging my cheeks where windburn made my skin red and raw. I let my chin drop to look at my chest. An enormous, ugly bruise bloomed purple and black over my sternum. The color leeched in every direction, disappearing underneath the soaking fabric of my bra.

"It's gonna be bad for a day or two."

I wanted to nod, but I didn't really have the strength. My heart still fluttered in my rib cage, but the adrenaline was different now. Darragh was staring at me.

"You can go," I said.

He shook his head. "You got hurt. Won't risk it."

I raised an eyebrow. Again, I tried not to read too deeply into it. He wouldn't get his stupid alliance if I drowned in his bathtub.

"So, are you just going to stare at me all night?"

He shrugged. "I could get in."

My eyes widened. "Don't even think about it."

A smirk tugged at the corner of his lips.

I sighed. "Seriously, Darragh. I have no desire to see you naked right now and even less for your games. Give me a fucking break for once."

The look in his eyes could only be described as a challenge. I stared right back, wondering why the hell I let him distract me so much in the first place. We'd spent a lot of time together, yeah, but he didn't mean anything to me. This was a business deal first and forevermore.

He straightened to his full height and dipped his hand into the water. "Feels nice."

"I swear, I will shoot you."

He grinned. Who the hell grins in response to that? He kicked off his shoes and dropped the vest to the floor. That reminded me, mine was still outside. I couldn't imagine those were cheap and the snow would certainly ruin it. Then again, Darragh seemed to have anything he ever wanted at his disposal. Including money.

He went for the cabinets, which I knew by now had his bathroom stash of whiskey. He held out the bottle to me while I glared at him.

"Liquid pain killer, love."

"Get out."

"Suit yourself."

He took a long swig and stepped into the tub. Fully clothed. My mouth gaped when he plopped down on the other side, his t-shirt filling with water and floating around him.

My bare legs scraped against the soaking denim of his jeans. "You're not serious right now."

"I don't play games." He took another swig and held out the whiskey bottle. "Come on, it'll make ya feel better."

I attempted to cross my arms, but the pain flared back. "You're an idiot."

166

In a rare display of Darragh showing . . . well, anything besides his normal scowl and/or stoic mask, he waggled his eyebrows.

He shook the bottle. "Come on."

He looked ridiculous. The six foot two, fully clothed Irishman drinking in my tub. It was almost enough to make me smile, but I resisted. I set my face back into hard stone, making sure he could see how annoyed I was. He grinned again, and I nearly broke. But not because he was making me laugh. Because he looked so stupid. Definitely because he looked so stupid.

He splashed water at me. Between the red dotting my vision and my mouth falling open, all I could see was his smirk reappearing, playful as ever.

I splashed him back.

He blinked water out of his eyes through genuine surprise. The smile was breaking through. The corner of my lip twitched with resistance when he flicked more water at me.

I gasped and shoved a small wave in his direction.

We went back and forth like that. His grin turned into full on laughter now, but I still held out. It wasn't until he poured some whiskey into his palms and sprinkled it on my head that I finally broke.

I couldn't stop the full belly laughs, even as my chest ached in a way I didn't even know it could. Between the laughter and pain I started losing my breath. Darragh flicked more whiskey into my hair as I gripped the side of the tube, trying to control myself.

"Oh my god, stop making me laugh. It hurts."

He leaned back, a smug smile on his face. My knuckles turned white on the tub's edge. I regained my breathing and reached my hand out for the bottle. "Give me that."

He ran his hands up and down my shins while I took several long swigs. I hated to even think it, but I didn't mind the feeling.

I set the bottle down on the bath edge and leaned back, closing my eyes. The warm water felt good and the feeling of

Darragh's hands, better. I couldn't tell if it was the whiskey or the relaxation, but the pain in my chest subsided a little.

"You know, you did really well."

I snorted. "I don't think aiming at the wrong thing and then getting shot on your roof counts as 'good.'"

"I'm an expert, Pina. The fact you found me at all is impressive."

I snorted again, but it was half-hearted. The compliment swelled inside me and filled me up. Like an infection. A happy, warm infection.

When I opened my eyes, he cupped his cheek in his hand and leaned against the side of the tub. His eyes were different. Light, crisp and very, very blue. It was the way he looked at me when I got the math problems, the way he looked at me on our runs, and the way he looked at me in my white dress all rolled into one.

Don't think too much into it, Pina.

I leaned my head back, choosing to stare at the ceiling instead. Made Men only looked at women one way. Killers did not have soft gazes. They only held lies.

"You don't have to lie to make me feel better."

He flicked more water at me. "You should know by now, I never lie. Especially not to make someone feel better."

That, we could both agree on.

I couldn't think of anything to say, so I ended up with, "The water's getting cold."

The cool mask returned. I didn't know what to think of it, but I didn't really care. None of this mattered. Darragh didn't matter.

He helped me out of the tub and downstairs. He patted me dry over my soaking underwear before I made him leave my room to handle the rest. I stared into my closet, holding every item of clothing I could ever need, but none of it was really mine. This house, this marriage, this life, none of it was real. A pretty, little facade.

I settled on the warmest and ugliest clothes I had. When I emerged in the living room, Darragh sat on the couch, still as stone.

"Are we done for the day?" I asked.

He nodded. "You should rest."

We stared at each other, the only sound the methodical drip, drip, drip of water slipping off my hair and splashing onto the floor.

My eyes roamed over his entertainment stand beside the TV. He had three movies, all of them westerns. I hated westerns, but it was better than nothing.

He followed my gaze. "Want to . . . just . . ."

I nodded. "Yeah, sounds good."

I watched Darragh from the couch while he set up the VHS player. The bright, blue screen bounced off his black hair, bringing out the dark hues while he rewinded the tape.

He sat down beside me as the movie began to play, stiff as a board.

It felt strange to go back to this. The past few weeks were spent close. Close while he taught me to use the rifle. Close while we hovered together, noses touching the ledger book at the kitchen counter. Close when he climbed into my bathtub fully clothed or rubbed precious warmth back into my arms. We hadn't been this far apart since the desert. This stiff.

I opened my mouth but he beat me to it. He shifted closer, wrapping his arm around my shoulders. Gentle, like he was barely even there. Testing the waters. I rested my cheek on his shoulder and the arm grew tighter.

There. That was better.

22

DARRAGH

I was really damn proud of Pina.

The shootout from last week played over in my head the entire ride to the casino. She was right, she didn't find me in the tree line, but I covered myself well. All her shots were excellent despite the wind and the climb to the roof was bloody brilliant. I hadn't even thought of that.

She was taking to the training well. Better than I expected, actually. I took a note not to underestimate any other tiny, Italian lass I happened to come across.

The sun just began to set over the mountains as the casino came into view. Most of my business had been done over the phone these few weeks, but some things required a visit. Pina had begged me to come, but today wasn't the day. I'd be a liar if I said I wasn't a little disappointed at the cold shoulder she gave me the entire hour before I left.

Kieran waited for me in the doorway, smoking a cigarette. He wordlessly handed me one from his pack and jerked his chin to the lobby. "Moe put him in the penthouse."

I scowled around the cigarette. Kieran handed me a match. "You trying to ruin my carpets, lad?"

Kieran grinned. Dirty bastard. I let these idiots run around on their own for too long. If the past few weeks paid off, that wouldn't be a problem anymore soon.

The dirty rat working for my Da had the balls to grin when I walked into the room. Someone took the time to tie him to the chair and screw up his face a bit. Blood pooled onto the floor.

I scowled at the mess. "I liked that rug."

"Hey, don't blame me." Blood bubbled to his lips with each word, coating his teeth and turning his smile red.

I pulled a chair over and swung it around to straddle it. The bastard's smile faltered, but only a moment.

"What did Sean send you to do?"

"Sean? Never heard of him."

I glanced back at Kieran and some gun runner I couldn't remember the name of. Kieran smiled and shrugged.

I flicked my cigarette onto my already destroyed carpet. "What is he trying to find here?"

"I don't work for the micks, alright?"

I took a long drag of the cigarette and blew the smoke into his face. He scowled. "Tell me who you work for, then."

"No one."

The gun runner stepped forward, handing me a stack of photographs from the security camera. "He started coming a few weeks ago. Mostly played craps. We caught him tapping into the phone lines."

I frowned at the photos. The guy was sloppy all around. The wire taps were atrocious, for starters, but getting caught fifty different ways on every camera we had in house was absurd. Sean didn't send sloppy men, especially not when he was covertly trying to keep tabs on his son.

If Sean sent him, he was just a distraction. If not, my next best guess was the Italians, but they had no reason to spy on me. It was Sean they were after.

"Who sent you?"

"I told ya—"

I burned my cigarette into his cheek.

He screamed and spat at me, missing. I grinned and gave the photographs back to the kid. "I don't have a lot of time today, so give me something useful."

"Go to hell."

Kieran stepped forward, cocking his pistol. I held out my hand.

I leaned forward, breathing in the disgusting scent of blood and sweat. He was a small-town idiot. Probably didn't even know who he was working for, but I needed something here.

"You have ten seconds to convince me to keep you alive."

The guy swallowed. His jaw set while molten fury leaked into his eyes. He wasn't going to tell me anything, I already knew. Not a small-town idiot then. Small town idiots didn't hesitate to give people up. So, Sean must have sent him, after all.

"I hear you got a pretty new wife."

I froze. The whole room froze. The people, the air, the sounds, the blood in my veins. I clenched my hands over the top of my chair. "Where'd ya hear that, lad?"

He snorted. "All your boys talk about her. She must be a tight little thing, with the way your own men talking about sticking it up her—"

I shot him in the face.

He toppled back with the blow, splattering blood all over the walls. Kieran jumped behind me as I swung the chair out from beneath my legs and slid it across the tile. The gun runner stared at me with wide eyes, clutching his own pistol in his palm.

Kieran swallowed. "We could have gotten more out of him."

I shrugged. "He was useless." The damn blood splatter put out my cigarette. I nodded to Kieran and he pulled me out a fresh one.

I took a long drag. "Pull up a few more of the boys from Brooklyn. I want around the clock security. Just because I'm in

172

hiding right now doesn't mean you fecking morons can slack off, am I understood?"

"Yes, sir."

I jerked my chin at the gun runner. His wobbly legs shook in his much too expensive boots. They all liked the money. None of them liked the real shit.

"Clean this up. I'd like my rug back, got it?"

He gave me a shaky nod and scurried towards what remained of our little intruder.

Kieran gave me an uneasy glance. "He may have just been a regular customer, boss."

"Keep closer tabs on the gamblers. I don't trust anyone nowadays."

He stuffed his hands in the pockets of his suit jacket while we walked to the elevator. "You gonna tell me what's going on, yet?"

The elevator chimed and we stepped inside. The fancy clothed gun runner gave us a final horrified look while the doors closed on the mess of my penthouse.

I took another drag of my cigarette. "It's a need to know basis, Kieran."

"It'd be a whole lot easier to keep tabs if we knew who to look for."

I frowned. "Need to know."

The elevator doors swung open to a lower level. I had another meeting right now, one I probably should have gone to first before getting brain matter all over my suit. Or, maybe it would help my case. You never knew with politicians.

Kieran hovered outside the door. "Do you need backup?"

I stared at him.

He sighed. "Never mind. I'll be here."

I pushed through the door without knocking. A middle-aged man with cropped, gray hair and the ugliest goddamn suit I'd ever seen sat at a tea table, smoking a cigar. Three dead-eyed bodyguards stood around the room, tensing when I walked in.

Senator Kingsley stood up and held out his hand. His beady eyes crawled all over the blood covering my shirt. "Trouble upstairs?"

I ignored the gesture and sat across from him. "No trouble at all. Did you have time to review my letter?"

Kingsley laughed and sat down. "Straight to business. They warned me you'd be like that."

I lit another cigarette and waved the match in the air. Today was an entire fecking pack kind of fiasco. "Who's talking about me?"

"Everyone with an eye towards the future." He gave me a grin more resembling a shark than a human. "How's your father?"

"I'm not here to talk about Sean. Have you read the damned letters or not?"

His right eye gave a little twitch, but the smile never left. "I did. And I presume you looked over the contract I sent in response. Do we have a deal then?"

I blew a long line of smoke in the direction of bodyguard number three. He wrinkled his nose. I smirked.

I never liked politicians, but Kingsley was as disgusting as they came. It was both a blessing and a curse here, because I fecking hated breathing the same air as the bastard but he was perfect for what I needed done. Kingsley had sway with the feds, and from what I've heard, a whole lot of it. I needed that level of sway to get Pina and I off the watch lists once and for all. The sooner we were off the feds radar, the better. So far Sean had done next to nothing to get our faces cleared. If you want something done right, do it yourself.

Unfortunately, what Kingsley wanted in exchange was going to be a pain in my arse.

"The mayor of Chicago, huh?"

Kingsley held out his hands. "What can I say? It's dirty politics."

I snorted. No. Dirty politics was publishing nudes in the paper, not hiring a hitman.

"There's lots of Italians in Chicago. Italians that have had Harmon on their payroll since he was handing out flyers at college rallies. You're asking a lot here."

Kingsley took a long drag of his cigar. "I think it's a small price to pay for tampering with a federal investigation, is it not?"

"You pay some of your own boys in the east. Why haven't you asked them?"

He shrugged. "Politics. You know how it is."

I leaned back in my seat, assessing him. He didn't have the manpower to pull it off himself, so he was hiring out. That was fine, but I didn't play games with his type. If he thought he could pay me to be his lapdog the same he did with the Italians, he was sorely mistaken.

I folded my hands in my lap. "No deal."

The cigar froze halfway to his mouth. "I think you underestimate the situation you're in with the FBI."

I smiled. The fecking balls on this one. The bodyguards around the room tensed and shuffled their feet. Unfortunately for them, their boss hadn't read the situation clearly enough yet.

"I didn't schedule this meeting so you could tell me how good I am at *estimating*." I stuck my cigarette into the ashtray. "You'll learn I get what I want, senator. I don't make deals in bad faith and I have plenty of other ways to get the job done. If I were you, I'd just hope my next option doesn't end with a bullet in your head instead."

The cigar fell from his trembling fingers to land on the table. I scowled at the scorch mark in the wood. "Don't make threats you can't follow through on, boy. I can have your ass in federal jail by the end of the day."

Time stilled around us. Only I broke the frozen silence but standing, leaning forward and breathing into the senator's shriveled face, "I don't make threats."

Kieran stood up straight as I exited into the hall. "I take it that didn't go well either?"

I shook my head, gesturing for him to follow. "It went fine. Expect to hear from the senator within the next few days. In the meantime, gather as much dirty laundry on him as you can. I want good collateral if I'm going to follow through on this one."

His eyes darted side to side. "What'd he threaten you with?"

I snorted. "Nothing I can't handle with the right photographs and the right testimony. Does he still visit that little blonde from Bushwick?"

He nodded. "Last I heard."

"I want recordings of it. Then, offer her a free one week stay at the casino. President suite."

"Yes, sir."

We stepped onto the elevator. The doors shut, I counted to three, and hit the emergency stop.

For as long as I've known Kieran, it didn't stop his legs from wobbling in his boots as red light washed over us. I folded my arms and leaned against the back railing.

"What is it, boss?"

"Who's talking about Annie?" I asked, giving him Pina's fake name.

It should have been the last thing on my mind, but I couldn't get that piece of shit's words out of my head. It looked bad on me to have my men talking about my own wife like that, but even more than that, it made me want to kill every last one of them. I'd maintained enough control around Pina the past few weeks to earn a fecking trophy. She deserved the respect. She earned it. And now that she was the boss of these feckers, she earned it from them too.

Also, I didn't want anyone thinking about Pina's tight little arse but me.

Kieran shook his head. "I don't know. I haven't heard nothing, but the boys talk when I'm not around. I'll give them a warning."

"No warning," I said, hitting the break button. The lift whirred back to life. "You hear anyone talking about her, put a bullet in their head."

His hands tensed on his pistol. "Sure thing."

The doors slid open to the lobby. With the holidays coming up, the casino flooded with everyone from young families to the lonely drunks with nothing better to do but gamble alone. I ripped the bloody dress shirt off and handed it to Kieran before anyone could see.

He walked me to the front, handing me off one final cigarette before I pushed through the revolving door. His fingers clutched the book of matches as he hesitated to say something.

I swiped them from his hand and lit the cancer stick. "What?"

He blinked. "You gonna tell me your wife's real name yet?"

I shook my head around a grin. "Need to know, Kieran. Need to know."

———————

When I got home my house . . . wasn't my house.

Pina threw a smile at me over her shoulder while hanging up floral curtains I swear I didn't have five hours ago. In fact, I didn't think I had half the shit now occupying my living room. Bright, yellow throw pillows illuminated the couch beside a stained glass lamp and an oil painting of the sunset. A huge potted plant marked the transition from the living room to the kitchen where a little wooden moose held a green spatula on the counter.

I threw my hands up in the air. "What the ever-loving feck, Pina?"

She shrugged as she climbed down from the stool, brushing past me with a haughty look. "This place looked like a serial killer den. It needed a few new touches."

I held up a doily that definitely didn't cover my coffee table this morning. "A few?"

"If I'm going to live here, I want it to feel like home." She put her hands on her hips and surveyed the living room. "I think it needs a few more plants."

"Do I even want to know how you paid for all this?"

She grinned. "Your emergency cash, of course."

I rubbed my temples. Teaching her to drive was a goddamn mistake.

I was so taken aback by all the *decor* I didn't even notice a vital piece of my living room missing. "Where's all the gun cases?"

"The garage!" she chirped from the kitchen. I watched in horror as she folded plaid dish towels on the counter.

"You can't just rearrange all my shit, Pina."

She frowned. "It's my house too."

Yeah, that it was. Another one of my brilliant ideas. Although, the venom at that thought faded real quick when I realized what she was wearing: tight little shorts that coated her legs and arse like a layer of paint.

I shook my head to clear my thoughts. We were leaving for Chicago in a few days. Getting our names off the FBI's radar. That was top priority, no matter how good my fake bride looked in spandex.

"Get some clothes on, we're going out."

Her head snapped up. "Where?"

I snatched the kitchen towels from her and stuffed them in a drawer. God help me. "I'll explain as we walk. Dress warm."

She pouted, but didn't argue. Maybe I'd have to let her raid the nearest home store more often.

For the first time in god knew how long, it wasn't snowing. The bright sun poked out from a single cloud as we trekked deep into the woods, wet snow squelching with each step we took. Without a fresh layer of powder to muffle the gunshots, I wanted to be as far from the house— and civilization— as possible. As we walked, I explained we'd be heading to Chicago soon for a hit.

Pina frowned beside me, her knees practically hitting her chin to walk through the thigh-deep snow. Thigh-deep on her, at least. "But if you told him there was no deal, then why are we still going?"

I held out my hand to help her over a particularly large fallen tree. She huffed as her feet hit the ground, the thick knit hat she wore sliding down to cover her eyes. I smiled to myself a bit before she shoved it back onto her forehead.

"I know how these men work. Tomorrow I'll be getting a phone call with an apology and bonus cash in the bank."

She contemplated. "How can you be sure?"

"Because he doesn't want me to kill him instead."

She stopped, staring at me with wide eyes. "Would you?"

I shrugged. "He threatened me, Pina. Threatened us, actually, because anything he tries to pull with the feds comes back on you too."

She nodded, clutching her sniper rifle closer to her body. What looked like a normal weapon in most men's hands looked absolutely massive in hers. She'd taken a strange liking to the gun, going as far as to name it 'Betsy.' Real snipers had their own weapons though. Maybe I'd get her one for Christmas.

"So, what then?" Her face twisted into a frown as she maneuvered through another patch of downed trees. I grabbed her hands and helped her over. "We go to Chicago, head to this gala or whatever and you just shoot the mayor? Seems high risk."

I smirked. "Actually, you'll be shooting the mayor."

Her jaw dropped. Before she could get a word in, I said. "It'll be easy target practice for the real-deal with Rocci. We have a few more days to get some practice out here and I'll be there the whole time. You'll do fine."

Her eyes cast downward, hand stroking over the barrel of the rifle. It made me fecking sick, but I imagined those little hands stroking something else in that moment.

"You never said I'd be killing anyone else."

I raised an eyebrow. "Does it matter?"

179

She rolled her eyes at me. "Of course it matters. I have . . . history with Rocci. I don't even know this guy. What if he's, like, a good person or something?"

I took her hand in mine and pulled her farther down the path. We were almost at the location I wanted, a good five or six miles from the house. The quicker we got done here the quicker we could begin the trek home. Even with the sun, it was still fecking freezing.

"If it makes you feel any better, I have it on good authority he beats his wife and kids. All the cops are on his payroll, so nothing ever comes of it. I'm sure you'll be doing them a favor."

Fiery anger erupted in her eyes. She picked up the pace.

Pina sat on a rock and combed through her backpack as soon as we hit the river. It was large enough to provide a good, clear shot across the bank and far enough away no one would hear the shots. I leaned against the nearest tree and lit up a cigarette while she took to setting up and loading the gun. Her little hands worked with purpose, running through the checklists I taught her with the speed of an expert.

A strange sense of pride overcame me.

She took to the lessons well. She took to the training well. She took to every goddamn thing well. For someone banned from learning anything besides cooking and cleaning, she was ridiculously smart. More than that, she put every ounce of effort into every task she did. I thought she'd fight me on the math lessons, so I started with playing cards to gauge her abilities. It turned out that was pointless. She was eager to learn and a quick student. There was a lot to be said for someone like that. Most people I've met would accept their shitty hand in life and never fight for anything else. Pina fought for everything, kicking and screaming.

I didn't mind teaching her, either. The weapons, finances, how to drive . . . the time spent with her was surprisingly enjoyable. She was still a massive pain my arse, but in a fecked up way I liked it. When I got in the bathtub with her last week, it was the first time I'd really laughed in years.

Me, laughing. Rory would have a fecking stroke.

"*Dammit.*"

My head snapped up just in time to see a box of ammo drop from Pina's gloves and shatter on the ground. Bullets hit the river bank with a *ting* and scattered across the ice.

I pushed myself off the tree as she stood, spitting curses and grabbing for the nearest bullets on her hands and knees. They slipped from her gloved fingers, rolling farther across the ice to the middle of the frozen river.

She looked up at the sky and groaned. "That was our only box of ammo."

The bullets caught the sun and glinted off the slippery ice, mocking us. Five miles of deep woods trekking for nothing.

I threw my cigarette in the snow. "It's fine. We'll come back tomorrow."

She frowned. "No, we came all the way out here." She sat on the edge of the bank and pressed one fur-lined boot to the ice, testing it.

"What are you doing?"

"It's frozen solid. I'll be right back."

I glanced up at the sun, then down to the dripping icicles slowly melting off each tree branch. "It's not safe."

She waved me off, pressing her other boot to the ice and rocking back and forth. "It's fine."

"*Pina.*" I took a deep breath as her eyes snapped back to me, wider than a doe's. "It's warm today and the river hasn't been frozen that long. It's not worth the risk. Let's go home. Now."

Her mouth set into a hard line. I knew the look all too well. It was the same exact expression she had whenever she was about to tell me to go to fecking hell and did whatever she wanted anyway.

I sprinted for the riverbank, but she was already several feet onto the ice.

I groaned. "Pina, now's not the time."

"I told you, it's fine," she hissed. She took a few more tentative steps while I hopped nervously on the shore. I could run after her, but that would just put more weight on the ice.

I crossed my arms, staring pointedly at every single inch her boots touched. The ice looked solid, but that didn't mean much. "Pina, come back. I'm not fecking kidding."

She gave me the finger.

My hands clenched into fists. The only sound in this part of the woods was the crunching snow beneath her feet. She took each step carefully, pressing down a little before putting her full weight forward. She reached the closest bullets and scooped them up, throwing them in the pocket of her parka.

She continued for a few more minutes, circling a small section of ice and picking up scattered ammo. When half the pile was safely retrieved into her pocket, I yelled from the shore, "Alright, that's good enough. You can come back now."

Her gaze darted between me and the remaining bullets in the middle of the river. I could almost see the gears turning in her head.

"Pina—"

She turned around and huffed, throwing a cloud of steamy breath into the air. Tiny hands clutched tiny hips as she stared me down, a challenge in her eyes.

"The longer you argue, the longer I'm out here."

I grit my teeth so hard the sound bounced in my skull.

She took a step backwards. Then another one. "The river is frozen solid."

"I don't like this."

"Get your panties out of their bunch, damn."

I stared at her open-mouthed, wondering when, exactly, Pina decided I wore panties. And why they were bunched.

She did a little hop. "Perfectly safe."

"Come back."

She jumped again. "Stop being ridiculous."

"Would you knock it off?"

She took another step back, grinning. A sharp crack echoed through the woods, drowning out her next words. Her eyes widened a moment before rushing water filled the air and she fell through the ice.

23

DARRAGH

Pina fell through the ice.
Pina fell through the ice.
Pina fell through the ice.

The thought tripped like a broken record in my brain. There was no room for anything else. No room to contemplate the dangers of running onto the river myself. No time to remember I weighed nearly double she did and the ice was already weakened. No fecking thoughts in my brain at all except she was no longer standing on the river, she only had minutes until she drowned, and she wouldn't be able to pull herself back out of the water.

Solid ground turned to frozen water beneath my feet as I leapt from the shore to the riverbed. Only a few feet in, the ice groaned under my feet. I stretched my arms out and dove across the ice, trying to spread my weight and reach her as fast I could. The longer it took the farther the current carried her, and the less of a chance I had to save her.

Pina was going to die.

I shook the thought from my brain. She wasn't lapping water in the broken section of the river, which meant she was trapped underneath. I waved my arms across the surface like a fecking mad man, brushing snow to the side, but I couldn't see her. No matter where I looked there was nothing but freezing water beneath the surface. A full minute had already passed and I was running out of time.

Something scratched beneath me.

I swiped at the surface until just below, Pina's frantic face stared back at me. Her nails dug into the frozen water, locking her into place, but the river dragged her hair back at a terrifying speed. She wouldn't be able to hold on for long and she was running out of air.

The ice groaned beneath me, but that was what I was hoping for. I scrambled to my feet and stomped down on the ice, over and over again. Pina's eyes widened below the surface before a crack ran through, covering her face. I slammed my boot down again, breaking through the crack and flooding freezing water across my skin.

The hole was just enough to pull her through. I flattened myself again and grabbed for her shaking arms. Water leaked through my stiff gloves as I pulled her to the surface, screaming and spitting curses as the rushing river's flow tried to sweep her back under.

She normally weighed next to nothing, but with all the water soaking her heavy clothes it was a task just to drag her the few feet away from the broken section of ice. It groaned again, getting ready to fracture and break. A swell of adrenaline pumped through my veins as I grabbed her arms and dragged her across the river, my only thoughts getting her to safety as quickly as humanly possible.

We collapsed onto the shore in a heap. I took a heaving breath and turned to her. "*What the hell were you think*—"

Her eyes were closed.

She wasn't breathing.

Her blue lips chapped in the frozen air. Her chest wasn't moving. The only thing moving was a few strands of her caramel hair, lifted off in the breeze.

I dedicated my life to learning how to kill people. How to hurt them. It was what I was most effective at, what I was most trained in. If I could save her— if she could even be saved— I was at a complete loss.

An age-old memory played back to me, a friend of my Ma's doing CPR on one of the members who'd gotten shot. I dug deep into the thought, trying to remember how he placed himself, how he pushed, anything that might work, then slammed my hands into Pina's lifeless chest.

Time may have stopped. I don't know, but the next few minutes felt like an eternity and then some. And for some un-fecking known reason, all I could think of was the image of her shaking in her torn red dress in the side-street of Vegas. The blood covering her bare feet and legs. The way she looked at me in horror, in disgust, in absolute fear, because right then she knew I was a monster. She thought I would kill her. I'd spent the last month doing anything but— earning her trust, becoming a mentor, giving her an opportunity at life she never had. And now, because of me, she was going to die. That fearful girl in the alleyway right.

Water spurted from her mouth and nose. She doubled over, retching into the snow. I grabbed her hair and face in my hands as her body heaved. She shook like a leaf in a bad storm and was cold to the touch, but she was alive and that was all I fecking cared about.

When she was finally done, I turned her to face me, but her eyes were closed again. She was breathing. It was shallow, but she was breathing. She lost consciousness somewhere while vomiting, or maybe never regained it all. I wasn't a fecking doctor, I had no clue. But she was wet and cold and we were quite literally not out of the woods yet. She didn't drown, but there was a chance she'd freeze.

The house was miles away. Even if I managed to sprint the whole distance while carrying her it'd still take hours. She didn't have hours.

She shook so hard I honestly couldn't tell if she was having a seizure. The blue of her lips turned an ugly violet, while any surrounding skin was whiter than the snow.

Everything was fecking soaked out here, but starting a small fire may have been possible. I couldn't even use the gunpowder from the bullets to ignite it, since they were all drenched now too. I had matches, my pack of cigarettes and the backpack Pina wore out here.

I grabbed as much winter grass as I could and set light to the cigarettes. It was enough to get the backpack ignited. The fabric would burn out fast, but it would buy her a little time. I pulled her beside the ridiculous fire and ripped through her soaked clothes. Her bare chest gleamed back at me beneath a layer of frozen cotton. I undid my own jacket and took off my shirt, wrapping us in as much of the material as I could and pushing her chest flush against mine. Body warmth and a makeshift fire. It could be enough. It had to be enough.

Her cheek shuddered against my bare shoulder. I rocked her back and forth, running my fingers through her hair and trying to dry it against the fire. The backpack was fully ablaze now, the heat echoing off and burning the back of my hands where I touched her, but I'd rather her have burns than die of hypothermia.

Nothing but crackling fire and rushing water filled the empty woods. I wanted to say something to her, get her to talk, but she was still unconscious. At least she had stopped shivering so much. Some color even returned to her skin. If I could warm her up enough to get her home, I could deal with the rest then.

I didn't want her to die.

The thought hollowed out my chest. The only person I actually worried for was Rory, but even with two left feet he still managed to handle his own. I never had anyone else to care for. Everyone I once cared about was already dead. That's what happened to us in this world. We either survived and turned into the very thing that shaking girl in the alley feared, or we died at the hands of the survivors.

And weaknesses, they were a one-way ticket to death. *It didn't matter if it was a faulty gun or a golden pair of legs*. I told myself that when I first met Pina. Somehow, somewhere along the line, I let it go too far. Because I cared about her. I cared about my fiery, temperamental, talkative, stubborn, overly emotional and absolutely impossible wife.

The fire dwindled to embers. Her violent shakes died to little shudders. If I ran, if I held her close for body warmth, if, if, if . . .

I didn't give myself time to think. Time was the last thing she had. I knew the path home like the back of my hands. When I bought the house, I spent years surveying these wood understanding every little trail, looking for possible signs of civilization and marking escape routes. There was no faster way home. There were no ranger stations or shelters. I chose this spot well, too fecking well, all things considered. I clutched her close to my chest and pushed through the burning in my lungs, the burning in my muscles, the icy pain in my leg where I soaked my own skin in the river, everything.

She shook violently again by the time we reached the house. The dim winter sun had long fallen beneath the tree line and along with it, the temperature. I shook along with her, barely able to keep my eyes open as I pulled back the sliding door and laid her down on the couch.

The artificial heat burned my skin. I shook out my limbs, trying to regain any feeling at all. My fingers curled stiff and frozen in the position I carried Pina. She still needed to get warm. The five-mile sprint made me want to collapse to the floor, but I needed to do something. I dragged my heavy, swollen feet to the garage and dragged out a bundle of firewood.

When the fireplace burned hot and bright, I threw a bunch of blankets onto the floor beside it. It was a chore to get Pina's remaining clothes off her. By now, they'd frozen stiff to her skin. Glittering ice winked across her bare legs as her breath hitched. I stopped, panic flooding my chest while hers failed to move. But a moment later her breathing started again, shallow, but it was there.

I took off my own clothes and threw everything onto the kitchen floor. I pulled her against me and settled us onto the floor. I couldn't feel much in the foot I slammed into the river, and I was too afraid to look. As cold as I was, she was colder, and her bare freezing skin sent my teeth to chatter. I wrapped the blanket around us and stroked her hair again. When she warmed up, she would wake up. When she woke up, she would be fine. Probably scream some Italian curse words about waking up arse naked with me. Everything would be absolutely fine.

I had to stay awake. If she stopped breathing again, if she seized, I needed to be there. But my own body was hurting. Hours and hours in the snow, freezing half to death myself and the miles of running while carrying her across my chest. I blinked away the darkness edging my vision. Once. Twice. But in the end, I failed to do that right too.

24

PINA

Everything glowed.

Maybe Darragh pulled the sun down into his living room. Most men offered to wrangle the moon, but when had Darragh ever done anything the right way?

My eyelids weighed heavier than stones as I peeled them open, one at a time. The glow wasn't from the sun. In fact, it was pitch black through the window. The normally cold and empty fireplace roared to life, flickering golden light across the floor.

Everything felt heavy. It was the best way to explain it. My body crushed into the soft layer of blankets, like my very skin was made of metal. I wanted to shift— the fire burned way too hot on my face— but I could hardly move. The thick, fur-lined blanket clung wet to my bare skin with sticky sweat.

Something moved behind me.

No, someone.

I wasn't heavy. He was. Darragh's thick arm swam into my blurry vision, hugging my waist tight over the blanket. His breaths, shallow with sleep, ebbed and flowed across my back where his chest pressed against my spine.

Everything burned. Even taking a breath felt like pulling fire into my lungs. It was hot, too hot, which was ironic considering the last thing I remembered was being colder than death. I was standing on the river, annoyed with Darragh for worrying so much. Of course, he had to be right. I remembered cold water, the panic as my hands reached up and felt nothing but the thick ice, and then after that, not much else.

I pushed Darragh's arm off me and threw the blanket back, squirming away to put a few inches between us. He grumbled in protest, but he didn't wake up. The golden light and throes of sleep softened the edges of his face, making him appear much younger than he actually was. I could almost see the scared teenager who was sent off to war. The young man taught to kill and torture at his father's word.

I kicked the blanket off the rest of the way, sending waves of nausea through me. I melted back into the floor, steadying myself and giving my muscles a moment to rest. Maybe under different circumstances I'd be upset about the clothes, but I knew Darragh well enough at this point that he wouldn't do it without reason. Besides, he'd already seen everything. And I felt too much like shit to care.

I turned my head to the side, watching Darragh's nose flare on each breath. He clutched the blanket in his sleep like a lifeline, but enough was pulled back to reveal he didn't wear any clothes either. It was wrong to look. He afforded me the respect of never pushing for anything since our wedding night, hadn't even so much as walked in my room while changing. But maybe there was no harm in looking, just for a moment, while he was still asleep.

His muscular chest lifted with each soft breath, rising and falling in a perfect beat. A smattering of dark hair covered his golden skin and stretched down the plane of his stomach, ending where a set of thick, powerful thighs flexed. I'd only seen him this bare one time before and was too taken aback by his . . . other part to notice the two dark tattoos caressing the tops of his thighs. Both were words, different on each leg, and written in Gaelic.

My gaze just hovered between the dark, looping words when his eyes snapped open.

For a moment, all we did was stare. Red laced through his eyes like spiderwebs, making the bright, icy blues of his irises startlingly sharp. He no longer looked like the soft, young man. He didn't even look human.

He sucked in a deep breath, like he could draw all the power in the room into his lungs. Fierce. Terrifying. Anyone who chose to defy him was either insane or stupid. I didn't know how anyone could look into those eyes and feel anything but pure terror.

I had, but that was different. He never looked at me like this, even in the beginning. Even when he still planned to kill me. It was rage, it was fear, and it was strength. And it terrified me.

"What are you?" I whispered. I hadn't been able to figure him out. Not in the months we've known each other now, and probably not in the years we had to come. The killer who did not kill me. The man who did not strike me. The husband who never demanded my body. The Made Man who never showed mercy, the name that'd been cursed a thousand times in the cigar room on the other side of my bedroom wall, the Angel of Death, the man who taught me to shoot a gun and drive a car, and the only person in my entire life who didn't think I was nothing but a scared little girl or a bride-to-be. The man who saved my life in more ways than I realized.

He was a walking contradiction I couldn't understand, especially when he whispered back, "Your husband."

I gripped the edge of the blanket to steady my hands. I didn't want him to see them shake. Blood pumped harder and faster through my chest, the rushing filling my ears. "What happened?"

"You fell through the ice."

"Then what?"

He blinked. The intensity in his gaze faded. "I got you out, warmed you up."

I stole a shaky breath. "You carried me all the way back?"

I said one thing, but I really meant another. He saved me, he kept me alive and he carried me five miles through deep snow back home. He wrapped me up and started a fire and made sure I

191

was okay. So few people could manage that, even if they wanted to. Many more wouldn't have the drive to save anyone but themselves, strategic alliance or no.

He licked his lips, the intensity draining back into his gaze. "You would have died."

I couldn't read into it.

I wouldn't read into it.

He released the blanket. A shaky hand lifted and brushed a strand of matted hair over my shoulder. My bare breast met open air where it was previously covered. Nothing touched my skin, but it was a different kind of naked I was scared of Darragh seeing.

"I thought you died," he murmured. His hand tightened on the back of my neck, gripping me like I was about to slip away. "You stopped breathing and I didn't know what to do."

I swallowed the lump forming in my throat. Despite every neuron in my brain warning otherwise, I leaned closer into the touch, closer to him. "Whatever you did worked. I'm here."

He tensed again, pulling me closer. I glided across the satiny blanket beneath us, inching towards him like a magnet being pulled home. There was so much in his eyes I didn't even know where to begin: fury, relief, desire, worry . . . they flickered across his face with frightening speed. But nothing was so alarming as the way his body crushed against mine. The feel of his hot skin against my chest. The fingers curled around my neck and gripping into my hair. The way his other hand gripped the back of my thigh and pulled it to rest on his hip. Every point of contact buzzed with heat, with want, with fear.

"You will never do that to me again." The words came low like a warning, heated like an alarm.

I sucked in a deep breath. "Walk on thin ice?"

He shook his head. "Never scare me like that again."

It was too late for me to stop. I read into it.

I tilted my face towards his, searching his eyes for the permission I so desperately wanted. It was a pointless question. Before his gaze could reveal anything, he leaned down, brushing his lips against mine. It was nothing but a faint whisper of a kiss, but it sent chills down my spine. The hands along my neck and hip tightened and he consumed me, filling my mouth with his intoxicating taste.

Heat prickled along my skin. It was overwhelmingly warm, but the fire burning me up came from within. He gripped my hair in his hand and pulled my face to the side, pressing his lips to the corner of my mouth before dragging them down my jaw. I sucked in a breath while his other hand gripped my ass tightly, pulling me against him and pressing his already hard erection between my thighs.

He took my earlobe between his teeth, biting down gently. The hand at my ass slipped down, down, dangerously low. One callused finger dragged over my soaking wet core, achingly slow. I shivered and moaned beneath the touch, wanting more. He pressed another to my neck while his thumb did slow circles around my clit. I jerked forward, pushing his cock between my thighs and against my opening. The resounding moan that came from him made my knees weaker than they already were.

He rocked back and forth, gently, moving his erection between my thighs. He wasn't inside me, but I could feel him at the entrance, so close. He nipped at my jaw, groaning softly when I whimpered in response. The fingers circling my clit slid down, resting between my folds. I grinded my hips against his, needing something, anything from him, but just like our lessons, he was out to torture me. Slow, soft kisses pressed down my jaw, leading back to my mouth. When his lips touched mine, he slipped a finger inside me, swallowing the embarrassingly loud moan I was too filled with need to care about.

His finger pumped in and out of me, hard, fast, angry. Angry for not being careful. Angry for scaring him. Maybe even angry for making him want me the way he did. Part of me resented him for the same. This was supposed to be nothing. We weren't supposed to care, to want each other. Everything about this marriage was a fluke to finish our goals. But something changed along the way, and my body craved him in a way I didn't expect. I dripped wet heat all over his fingers, showing him just how badly I wanted him. The hand in my hair tightened and a second finger slipped inside.

He fucked me with his fingers, while I moaned into his mouth. The heat in my core built higher and higher, ready to explode. With the fire low in my belly and his mouth pressed to mine, it was becoming hard to breathe. Hard to think. I needed him so badly it made my head swim. The fingers weren't enough. I grinded my hips into his hand, trying to get him to go further, deeper. He shuddered beside me, hands yanking me closer and fingers pumping faster. My hips rocked back and forth with his movements, wanting, needing, desperate for more.

"Fuck me," I whispered.

He stopped so suddenly, I wondered if I did something wrong. His fingers froze inside me, palm flattened against my center. The hand in my hair loosened while his lips hovered at the edge of my lips, a breath away from skin. He pulled his fingers out of me, brushing them against the slick wetness between my thighs. I whimpered at the emptiness, needing to feel him inside me again.

He stroked up and down my core, pushing his cock between my thighs again. He placed a row of fluttering kisses up my neck, coming to a stop just below my jaw. His fingers pinched my clit, his words nearly inaudible through my gasp, "Promise me."

I buried my face in the crook of his neck, breathing deep. My chest tightened to the point of pain, but all I could think of was the blind need between my thighs. The way his fingers felt when they fucked me and how much more filling his massive cock would be. I wanted him on top of me, filling me up as he rocked in, and drawing my moans as he rocked out. I wanted my legs wrapped around his waist. I wanted his lips on mine. And I wanted to see exactly what those two little Gaelic words looked like when they crashed against my thighs.

His hand untangled from my hair. He stroked down the side of my face, kissing my neck like it was the most sacred thing to ever touch his lips. "Promise me, Pina."

My thoughts cleared just enough to answer. "Promise what?"

He grabbed my ass and shifted me up, so his tip hovered at my entrance. My hands dug into the muscles of his back. I tried to lower myself down, needing to know what he felt like, but his hand held me in place. He nipped at my ear and murmured, "Promise me you'll never scare me like that again."

My breaths came out fast and hollow. He pressed his tip into me, the thick head of his cock nudged into my opening. I panted, the heat inside me burning so hot I could scream. My vision swam as he pulled out, rocking in just a little more. I needed to feel the rest of him. Needed to feel how every single inch felt as he slid deep inside me.

"Darragh," I breathed. The world tilted strangely. Heat flooded my chest, my brain and took hold of my lungs. The rapid breaths became painful. I no longer felt his arms around me. No longer felt Darragh's lips on my neck. The beat of my heart turned to a dull ache in my chest, a painful *thump thump* that knocked any thoughts from my head.

"Promise me," he said, but it was too late. Darkness caught the edge of my vision and I fell into oblivion.

195

25

DARRAGH

One moment she was breathing my name, the next she was convulsing in my arms.

I froze around her while she shook, large, brown eyes rolling to the back of her head. She was flushed, a fever taking over her body I was too distracted to even notice. The shaking only lasted a minute, but she was back to unconsciousness as soon as it ended. She was burning up, and I'd tried to sleep with her.

It was amazing how in the last day or so, I'd felt more like a helpless little kid than in my entire life. Pina's eyes shut as she breathed soft, shallow breaths. Her dunk in the river must have made her sick. What did you even do for sick people? People who were so fecking sick they started seizing? I pulled on my underwear and carried her upstairs to the bathroom. She was hot. Really fecking hot.

Her eyes opened to little slits as I laid her down on the tile. I ran a hand towel under cold water in the sink. First, she was too cold, now she was too hot. I could throw her in the bath but ice water was how we got here in the first goddamn place. I laid beside her and put the washcloth over her forehead, twirling a piece of her hair around my finger.

She licked her chapped lips and looked at me. "I don't feel right."

I nodded, "Yeah, I know, love."

She sucked in a deep breath. In the silence of the bathroom, every little crackle and hitch reverberated around the walls. "It's hard to breathe."

"It's okay. You'll be fine." I wanted to believe that to be true, but I had no clue. I couldn't take care of her. I thought she would be fine if I got her inside and warmed her up, but once again, I vastly fecked up the situation when it pertained to Pina.

She needed a hospital. Doctors, real medicine. But our names weren't clear until we went to Chicago. I didn't even know how the hell I was going to get there with Pina like this, but one crisis at a time. If I brought her anywhere, we'd both be caught. I could pull my strings and find a way, but if the Delarosa's realized she was alive, she'd be shipped back to them in a heartbeat. After that, Lucien Rocci. If he even still wanted her. That would be best case scenario. Worst, he killed her for spending months on the run with another man. Even if she lied and said nothing ever happened, he'd never believe it.

I knew Pina. She'd rather die of a fever than die at the hands of Rocci, but I wasn't prepared for either of those scenarios. No one loyal to me had any medical experience. I had a doctor under my wing for a few months, but he was taken out last summer by one of Rocci's boys. Anyone else reported directly back to Sean.

Pina's eyes closed again. I squeezed her hand and lifted her back into my arms, leaving her on my bed this time. I was out of options and had very little time to make a choice. There was a chance she'd get better on her own, but it was a massive risk. I wouldn't let her die in my care. In my bed.

I didn't know if she could hear me, but I leaned down to whisper in her ear, anyway, "I'm going downstairs to make a call. I'll be right back."

I sat in the kitchen, phone in one hand and head in the other. I squeezed my eyes shut, building up the courage for this favor I was about to ask. I didn't want him involved in anything, but I had no choice anymore.

The phone rang once, twice, three times. I was about to hang up when Rory's voice tumbled through the line. "I'm ass naked with a model right now, so this better be fucking good."

"I need help."

"Darragh?"

"Yeah."

"Hold on."

Something shuffled around. A woman whined in the background through Rory's heavy breaths and the sound of clothes sliding over skin. He covered the speaker, but his mumbled, "Get out," still came through clear as day.

He laughed softly. "Sorry about that. What'd you fuck up this time?"

I scowled. "Is there a chance anyone's on this line?"

"Not that I know of, no."

"I need a doctor."

A beat of silence passed. "Are you alright?"

"It's not for me." I pinched the bridge of my nose, squeezing my eyes shut tight. "I can't trust anyone working solely for Sean but I'm out of options. I need someone you think can stay quiet, and I need them now. Don't tell anyone what you're doing or where you're going. I'm at the safe house."

Rory released a breath into the line. "Do I get anything more than that?"

"No."

He sighed. "There's one guy . . . he's new, so probably our best bet. It'll be hard to find anyone else at this hour."

"Make it happen." After a moment, I added, "Thank you."

"Ah, that's a first." He laughed. "This sick person must be awfully important."

"See you in a few hours." I hung up before he could ask any more questions. The less he knew, the better.

Back upstairs, Pina was sound asleep. Her chest rose and fell with strain. Sweat soaked into the sheets around her, darkening the fabric. I grabbed another washcloth, a glass of water and some aspirin. It was the best I could do for now; hopefully it was enough.

I brushed a piece of sticky hair off her forehead. "Someone's coming," I told her, but this time I was positive she couldn't hear me.

Maybe I cursed the whole damn situation. I shouldn't have tried to get her to promise, shouldn't have been stupid enough to think that nothing bad could happen to her if we both tried to keep her safe. Nothing was ever safe in this world, and I hadn't even introduced her to the real part yet. This was just the training.

I stared at her long lashes, fluttering on sweat-soaked skin. It was just the beginning. She got hurt. She got sick. She would enter my world with a gun in her hand and a target on her back. If it was anyone else, it'd make no difference, but for the first time in my life, I was genuinely afraid.

DECEMBER

1988

26

DARRAGH

The sun was just coming over the horizon when the headlights to a rusted Ford pulled into my driveway.

The doctor was a skinny, weasel-faced man with thinning, grey hair and two thin lines for lips. Beady eyes scrutinized me behind wire-framed glasses as he lugged a thick, leather case up to my front door, Rory tailing just behind him.

"Your brother hasn't given me any clue as to what we're dealing with, so you better hope what I have is enough."

I scowled at him. In any other circumstance, he wouldn't be talking to me like that. I'd just add it to the long list of sacrifices I seemed to be making lately. Rory pulled out a cigarette and hovered in the doorway, letting all the cold air in.

"She's upstairs. I'll be there in a minute." I directed the doctor to the hall and walked back outside, shutting the door behind me and lighting my own smoke.

Rory's fire-red eyebrow shot to his hairline. "She?"

I shook my head through a puff of smoke. "You've missed a bit."

"I guess I have." A shit-eating grin crossed his face. "Don't tell me I'm about to be an uncle, or something."

I snorted. "Nothing like that. And this stays between us. Da can't know anything, not yet."

The end of his cigarette bobbed between his lips as he spoke. "Does that mean I get to know what the hell is going on yet?"

"What do you want to know?"

He took his cigarette between his fingers and pointed it at the upstairs window. "For starters, who the sick lass in your house is."

I frowned, mumbling around my cigarette, "My wife."

His cigarette froze halfway to his lips. The shit-eating grin only got wider. "Well, congrats then, man. I never took you for the type."

"There were circumstances," I said.

"Does this wife have a name?"

I couldn't tell him yet. I trusted Rory. He was the only person on this whole goddamn planet I could trust, but when it came to this, the less he knew the better. For everyone's safety.

"Annie."

"Annie," he repeated, dragging out the sound like he was testing how it sounded. "I like her already."

"Wait until you meet her to say that."

He threw his half-smoked cigarette into the smoke. "Shall we, then?"

The doctor was setting up a saline bag and an IV when we walked in. Pina laid on the covers, still unconscious, still feverish, still looking like absolute shit. Her raspy breathing had gotten worse the past few hours, with nothing to do but wait for the doctor to come, I sat next to her and prayed each little hitch wasn't her last.

I'd barely slept in two days. All the energy of watching Pina combined with that had me ready to collapse, but I wasn't leaving her alone with someone I didn't know. I didn't want to rest until I knew she'd be okay, at the least. The doctor looked at me as he pulled out a long, thick needle, waiting for permission.

I nodded. "Whatever you have to do."

Rory stepped up to the opposite side of the bed, eyebrows drawing together as he looked at Pina's frail frame. "What happened?"

"She fell in a river yesterday. It took a while to get her out of the cold."

The doctor frowned. "You're lucky hypothermia didn't get her."

I crossed my arms. They couldn't see the way my heart raced while the doctor put in her IV, but it couldn't hurt to hide it. "What's wrong with her now?"

The old man shook his head. "I don't know yet, but with the way she's breathing and her fever, my best guess is pneumonia."

My hands tensed. "Can you help her?"

He peered at me over thin glasses. I wanted to snap them in two and make him eat the glass. "I'll do what I can. If we can get her fever down, her prognosis is much better."

My teeth ground into one another. "She could die?"

The doctor had enough intelligence to look concerned then. His gaze flashed between me and Rory. "I can't say at this time. We'll know in a few hours."

The world filtered away: my room, my bed, my sick wife lying in it. All my rage focused onto the doctor. The moron who was supposed to be able to help and now was saying she may die anyway. Even after I carried her in from the river. Even after I got her warm. Even after she was one fecking breath away from promising everything would be okay.

Rory grabbed my arm, pulling me back. "C'mon. Let him do his thing."

"I'm not fecking leaving," I growled.

"Darragh." The only movement I made was tensing under Rory's grip. "You're not helping her any by getting in his way. She'll be fine if you go downstairs. Let's go."

The exhaustion of the past couple days hit like a brick wall. I didn't want to leave her like this. What if it was the last time I saw her still—

I backed away before the thought could complete itself. The doctor would make her better. He'd do it, because if he didn't, his grave would be dug right next to her's. So she would be fine.

An hour later I found myself sitting across Rory and at the bottom of a bottle. My brother couldn't shoot for shit, but he sure could fecking drink.

He knocked back another shot and leaned against my kitchen counter. "So, how did you meet a little American gun-runner anyway?"

I took my own shot and slammed the glass on the counter. "Doesn't matter."

"Has to matter for something." He lifted up the near empty bottle and frowned, sloshing the remaining liquid around the glass. "I'm assuming Da doesn't know."

"He knows she worked with me in Vegas. That's all."

"But not that you're married." He cocked his head to the side. "How did she feel about you killing the Delarosa girl?"

I shut my eyes and leaned back on my bar stool. "I'm not talking about this, Rory."

"Fine, fine." He surveyed the kitchen and the living room beyond. The floral curtains, little throw pillows and the stupid wooden moose on the countertop. "It looks different in here."

I honed my gaze in on the bright painting Pina hung beside the back door. "Yeah, I didn't have a choice."

Rory nodded like everything finally clicked into place. "So . . . your wife. You've both gotten pretty comfortable here, huh?"

It was a question within a question. Rory would never ask if I actually gave a shit about her because we both knew what that meant. The mafia and the mob didn't just arrange their marriages for politics. This life was a lot easier if your closest family wasn't all that close.

I cared about Pina, that much I was sure of. I didn't know how much of a problem it would be yet. I cared about Rory too, enough to keep him arm's length away from me for most of our lives. My two oldest brothers, the ones I never met, their deaths were hard on him. He never said so, but I could tell. Maybe I'd be the same if I knew more than just their names and how they died. If I didn't spend the first ten years of my life running with my Ma, while the rest of my family suffered at the hands of Sean. Either way I'd never know, so the least I could do now was make sure Rory didn't go through it again.

"It's been fine," I said. It was only kind of a lie. We both knew, but he didn't push it any further.

The phone trilled on the wall beside me, thank fecking god. Kieran's voice echoed on the other side of the line.

"He wants in. I'll have the plans ready and flights booked by tonight."

I grimaced. Not the phone call I wanted. In all this, I'd all but forgotten about the hit in Chicago. The hit that would clear both mine and Pina's names.

I looked up at the ceiling, like I could see right through the sheetrock and into my room. I trusted Rory, but I didn't trust any doctors. Especially not ones new to the mob. Besides that, I made a promise. I was going to take care of her. I couldn't do that from the Midwest and I wouldn't leave my brother in my place to handle her for me.

"Tell him it's off," I said, slowly. I was making a huge goddamn mistake, but there'd be other ways. I wasn't leaving her here.

He paused. "What are you talking about?"

"Something came up."

"Darragh, I don't know what's going on, but you can't just—"

"It's off," I snapped. "Give my apologies to the senator. I can't make it to Chicago."

Kieran released a long breath. "He's going to fuck you over, you know. He has a lot of pull. This is dangerous."

"Let him try."

"But—"

207

I slammed the phone back onto the hook and downed the remaining shot in the bottle.

Rory watched me with genuine concern. "What was that about?"

I slammed the bottle back onto the counter. I either underestimated how pissed I was or how hammered, because the bottom of the bottle shattered against the granite.

We both stared at the broken shards of glass, sticky and reflecting the kitchen lights around the room.

"Someone needed a favor that can't be done at the moment." My attempt at saving face only left Rory more confused.

"I can handle things here, Darragh."

"I'm not going," I barked. "And before you ask me another goddamn question about it, it's none of your business."

He took a step back, confusion and concern melting into a tinge of fear. Fear of me. Same as Pina when we first met, only I've known my brother since I was ten. He didn't have to like me, but he was supposed to trust me.

"I'm going to check on her," I said, pushing away from the counter.

She didn't look any different than when I left her. Her hair splayed out on the pillow, a shock of warm, golden brown against the white sheets. Her breathing had evened out a bit, but she was still pale. The doctor held up his hand for silence as I hovered in the doorway, his stethoscope plunging into his ears and pressed down to her chest. A minute ticked by before he pulled the little piece of metal off her skin and turned to me.

"She still has a fever, but it's gone down significantly. Without proper testing I can't say what's exactly wrong, but it sounds as if she has fluid in her lungs."

I sat on the edge of the bed. "Pneumonia?"

He shrugged. "Most likely." He held up a small bottle and syringe. "I've started giving her antibiotics for the infection. The rest is up to her at this point."

I didn't like the sound of that, but it was better than what he was saying just a few hours ago. I pulled her hand out from beneath the covers and gripped it in mine. Her wedding ring flashed in the midday light. I ran my thumb over the stone, dampening the little rainbows that cast around the room from the rock.

The doctor leaned forward, looking towards her hand in mine. "What happened?"

For a moment, I had no fecking idea what he was talking about. Then it occurred to me, most of his patients had ten fingers, not nine. The healed edge of Pina's wound slipped between my fingers as I dropped her hand back to the sheets.

"Kitchen knife accident." Again, not a complete lie.

He watched me through narrowed eyes, reaching for her hand. "May I?"

I could say no, but there was probably no harm in it. Hopefully. This doctor wouldn't have seen the finger Pina cut off and delivered to Sean, who promptly delivered it to the Delarosa's door. If I said no and left, he'd likely inspect it after I left, anyway. I nodded and moved to the side, allowing him to grab her hand and inspect the scar.

"It must have been one very sharp kitchen knife," he murmured, letting his fingers pass over the shorn knuckle.

A response would have been the normal thing to provide, but I had just about nothing left in me. The doctor continued his inspection, finally turning her hand over and freezing like a deer in headlights.

It was a moment, nothing more, but I didn't miss the brief stroke of his thumb over the thin, white scar crossing all her fingers.

He dropped her hand to the bed and stood. "For now, she should be okay. I'm due back in the city this evening. I'll leave you with the medication and instructions for when to change her saline. If anything changes, give me a call."

Tension thickened between us. I stared, hoping the conclusion I was about to draw about the doctor's knowledge was just coincidence and not fact. That his sudden rush to get back to

Manhattan was just happenstance. He ran a hand through his thinning hair, sweat forming on the edge of his brow.

"Leave everything here," I said. "I'll see you out in a moment."

I raced down to my kitchen. Rory fecked around with my record player while downing another bottle of whiskey. I shoved my hand into his chest and slammed him into the wall. His eyes widened around his, "What the fuck, Darragh?"

"Where did the doctor come from?"

He shook his head. "I don't know, Da got him a few weeks ago."

I ripped the bottle of whiskey from his hand and slammed in on the counter. "Why? We have plenty of doctors?"

"How the fuck should I know?" Rory threw his hands up in the air. "What in the hell has gotten into you, you're acting fucking mad."

"When did he get the doctor?"

Rory stared at me, contempt written all over his face. "I told you, Darragh. A few fucking weeks ago. I think it had something to do with the Delarosa girl. He wanted to know the body parts were legit."

I punched the wall, shoving my hand right through the sheetrock. *"Feck."*

I turned on my heel for the garage.

Rory followed close behind. "What are you doing?"

I ignored him, ripping open the adjoining door to the new location for all my guns. Goddamn Pina and her goddamn decorations.

He tried to block my entry back in, but I shoved him out of the way. "Where are you going?"

I was going back into my house. I was going upstairs. I was going to my room. I was going to solve one more goddamn problem that seemed to pop up every two fecking minutes these days.

The doctor bumped into my chest on his way out the door. He lifted a shaky hand to push his glasses back up his nose. "Darragh, can I—"

I shot him.

I shot him, and the craziest part of all was the only thing I could think was Pina must have been really fecking sick, because I blew a 9mm ten feet away from her and she hardly even moved.

Rory yelped behind me, jumping back to avoid the pool of blood running down my wooden floors. He pressed himself against the hallway wall, staring at me in shock, horror and a few other things I couldn't even start to name right now. "Darragh, what the fuck did you do?"

I dropped the gun to the floor. This was shit. Sean was going to have my motherfecking head for this one. My only saving grace here was he most likely planned to kill me soon anyway.

Rory backed down the hall. I turned and he broke into a run.

I groaned. "Rory."

His voice carried up the stairs, holding an unusually high tone. "I'm leaving, Darragh. You've officially fucking lost it."

"Rory."

I stomped down the stairs after him. My front door swung on its hinges, the beaten up Ford already puffing exhaust into the winter air. Rory fumbled with the keys while I knocked on his window. He jumped in his seat, nearly pulling the keys from the ignition. I pounded on the window until he rolled it down, just an inch.

"I'm not gonna shoot you, you fecking idiot."

He pointed a finger at my front door. "You just killed a doctor."

"I know nothing makes sense right now, but you have to trust me."

Rory laughed. Not just any laugh, like a fecking hyena. He threw his head back, clutching the door handle like a lifeline. "I don't know anything about you anymore, Darragh. You pulled away

211

from me a long fucking time ago and it's been nothing since. Hell, I've spent the last two months not even knowing where you are. Half the time not knowing if you're alive. I didn't even know you got fucking *married.*"

I rolled my eyes and pulled on the door handle. It didn't give. "You sound like a fecking woman. Get out of the car, I need your help."

His smile died to a scowl. "I'm not doing shit for you until you tell me what's going on."

We entered a staring match. The kind of challenge only flesh and blood could give you, because even though you wanted to strangle them, all the threats behind it were empty. My brother could drive off right now and nothing would happen to him. He was probably the only person in the world with that kind of power.

I let go of the door handle, offering a truce. "Get rid of the body and I'll tell you everything."

His eyebrow shot up while he maniacally grinned. "*I* get rid of it? I'm your brother, not your cleaner, dickhead."

I slammed my hand into the side of the car. "I can't leave her alone, Rory, and I need the body far away from here. Last favor, I swear, and I'll tell you everything."

He ripped the keys out of the ignition. "You can tell me everything on the ride to go dump *your* fucking mess."

I clenched my teeth. "I'm not—"

"She'll be fine for a few goddamn hours. Now do you want my help or not?"

I did want his help. I also knew that for all the leniency Rory gave me, I could only push him so far. It was easy to forget he was the older one. Technically, that made him my boss. It also just followed the strange set of rules all siblings seemed to have ingrained in them.

"Thank you," I finally said.

He shook his head. "I don't even want to hear it, Darragh."

212

27

DARRAGH

The empty highway blew past us as Rory did ninety down the interstate. Bare trees filled with nothing but snow and ice became hollow blurs against a dark, gray backdrop and a blotted sun.

I clutched the handle and tapped my foot on the mat. The radio blasted some pop shit while Rory bobbed his head along and whistled to the tune.

"You should probably slow down."

Rory shrugged. "Why? It's not like we got a body in the trunk or anything."

It took all my restraint not to throw him out the driver's side door. It took a solid half hour to drag the doctor's body out the front door and to the trunk of the car. Another to scan the local maps and decide the most remote place to dump the body. All the while, Pina remained unconscious. I checked on her at least three times before we left, switching out her saline bag according to the instructions just in case it took us a while to get back. I debated on leaving her a note on the off chance she woke up soon, but Rory was itching to get this over with quick.

I drummed my fingers on the center console before realizing what I was doing. Pina's nervous habits were getting to me.

"Would you fecking slow down? The last thing I need is to end up on FBI's Most Wanted twice."

Rory scoffed. "Like the FBI cares about one doctor who got his license in Columbia."

I didn't take the time to panic over the fact Pina's doctor got his license below the equator. The exit we planned to take approached and Rory veered off at breakneck speed. Ten minutes later and we reached the long abandoned hiking trail where the doctor would be laid to rest. I pulled out a cigarette while Rory did a check on the car and popped the trunk.

We each took an end of the body bag and began the long, cold trek into the woods. The shovel strapped to my back clanged against my spine. Rory's face turned the color of his hair as he dragged the body farther and farther into the wilderness, never taking a break.

When we finally reached a point we both agreed was good enough, we strayed off the trail. A few miles later, and we dropped the body bag to the earth with a sigh.

Rory leaned against a tree, arm outstretched and trying to catch his breath. I lit a smoke several feet away and watched him heave breaths. After a few minutes he reached his arm out. I handed him a cigarette and a light.

He slumped against the tree and lit the cigarette between his lips. "You owe me more than one, asshole."

I nodded, tensing with each little sound in the woods around us. We were so remote the chance of anyone crossing our path was near nonexistent, but I didn't like taking chances. I also didn't want to have to sell my safe house. It'd grown on me a lot, and Pina seemed to like it, if her decor had anything to say about it.

Rory took a long drag and stared into open space. "So . . . before we begin. What's the fucking deal?"

I took a drag myself. I wished he had something more specific to ask, because I honestly had no fecking idea where to start. Thankfully, Rory picked up on that for me.

"Is her name really Annie?"

I never gave Rory a lot of credit, but I should have. Most would have started with the obvious: what does she do, is she really a gunrunner, etc, etc. Rory either knew me well enough or was smart enough to figure the biggest piece of the puzzle out. I stared into the tree line, wondering just how long it would take us to dig a six foot hole and said, "No."

He chuckled, taking another drag. "Alright, give it to me then."

I didn't know why, but my hand shook around the cigarette. "Giuseppina Delarosa."

He let out a barking laugh. "Ha-ha, hilarious. Seriously, what's her name?"

I stared at him. His joking smile remained another moment or two before melting away into something much more serious.

"You're fucking kidding me, right?"

I shook my head.

In a moment completely un-Rory-like, he slammed his fist against the tree he rested on. "Goddammit, Darragh. There's, like, three billion fucking broads in the world and you had to choose that one."

I closed my eyes and leaned back, drowning out the sounds of the woods. "Like I said, shit got complicated."

He laughed. "Complicated? That's not complicated. That's fucking insane." He chucked his cigarette into the snow. "What in the ever-loving fuck were you thinking?"

I could go into my long-term plan. We both knew Rory didn't want the family business. We both knew Sean was a ticking time bomb. For all the distance Rory gave himself between his life and *the life*, he even knew how beneficial an alliance between us and the Delarosa's would be. How much better everything would be for business with Rocci gone and the Italians on our side. But I knew that even that wouldn't be enough to convince him to the downright fecking insanity I'd put myself through to keep Pina alive and well. And on top of that, everything to become part of her life and train her to kill Rocci. Train her to do math and understand the finances.

Teach her how to drive and fight and take care of herself so she'd make it in this world. Train her to be a killer like no man in the fecking mob had ever seen so my petite, little wife could be just as dangerous as me. It would have taken a month, tops, to get her good enough to take one shot at Rocci. But that wasn't what I wanted.

I didn't know how to explain to him this had all gone way too far.

Nothing but winter birds and a light breeze echoed through the woods. Rory watched me with another expression so uncharacteristic for my brother: complete seriousness. "Do you love her?"

I shook my head and doused my own cigarette in the snow. "No, nothing like that."

He raised an eyebrow at me. I felt the sudden, overwhelming need to punch him.

Instead of pushing it, he said, "I thought you killed her in Vegas."

I shook my head. "I killed the cop but got her out."

He frowned. "And the finger? The hair?"

I shrugged, trying not to let my own guilt at what she had to do overcome me. "I cut off the hair. She cut off her own finger. We had a plan for everything, that was part of it and she agreed."

He blew out a long whistle. "So the little Italian has some fucking balls, then?"

I snorted and shook my head. "Yeah, something like that."

His grew quiet and stared at the ground. "He's gonna kill her, you know."

He didn't need to say who. I knew. The same man who created me, raised me and would likely kill me as well.

I crossed my arms. "I got a plan for that, too."

He pressed his fingers into the snow, playing with the little crystals like a child. "You always do, don't you?"

I had no idea what the hell that was supposed to mean, but I was growing tired of the cold and tired of this conversation. Not to mention, it'd been hours of leaving Pina alone, and she was due for her meds soon.

We could only get the grave a few feet deep with the frozen, packed dirt. We were so far from any civilization there was a slim chance of anyone finding the body, if it didn't completely degrade by the time that may happen, anyway. Stars twinkled in the clear, cold night as we packed out our shovels and began the long trek back to the car. What was only supposed to take a few hours took nearly ten, but better safe than sorry.

The two of us rubbed our frozen hands together and huffed hot air into our palms back in the car. Rory blasted the heat while I lit another cigarette. I'd never been a heavy smoker, but recent circumstances were making it hard to resist.

For whatever reason, Rory decided to do the speed limit the entire way home. When we didn't have a dead man in the trunk anymore.

"Tell me about Rocci."

I gave my brother a sidelong glance. "There isn't much to tell. Da wants then hit done on New Year's."

He frowned. "And you don't know much more than that?"

I shrugged, staring out the window. "I don't think he has all the details worked out himself. I was only told to lay low until end of December and wait for the plans."

Rory drummed his fingers on the steering wheel. "What does Pina have to do with any of it?"

"She wants to kill him herself."

"Jesus Christ." He ran a hand through his hair. "I thought women liked jewelry and getting their hair done and shit."

"Only the women you spend time with."

He laughed. "I'll take shallow over trigger-happy. That's all you, brother."

My hand clenched on the door handle. "She's not trigger-happy. She has her reasons."

He looked at me. "And they are . . . ?"

217

I shook my head. "Her business to tell, not mine. We have an agreement, and part of it was she gets the first shot at Rocci. Da will think her name is Annie McCormick and by the time the truth comes out, the rest won't matter."

He frowned. "Why?"

I couldn't tell him I planned to take out our Da. Rory hated the bastard as much as I did, but this crossed a line. Even if my father was gunning for me first.

"I'm still working on it," I said. I'd told more half-truths in the past forty-eight hours than in my entire life.

The dash said it was past ten when we pulled into my driveway. I disabled the security measures and stepped inside, letting my ears adjust to the silence. I never came home to emptiness anymore. Pina was always cooking, decorating, watching TV, doing something.

I'd check on her as soon as we got the shovels and dirty clothes away. The last thing I needed was to make her more sick by carrying something else into the room. Even unconscious, I was worried about bothering her. I gestured for Rory to be quiet and follow me down the hall to the garage. I moved to flick the light on in the living room when a gunshot went off.

Rory and I both ducked to the ground. All I had on me was my pistol and I had doubts Rory was armed. I reached for the little six-shooter when someone's gasp echoed through the room.

I glanced up, eyes adjusting to the darkness. Pina sat against the far wall with her rifle across her lap.

28

PINA

I woke up in the afternoon. I groaned and rolled onto my side, letting out a sharp hiss at the sting in my arm. I yanked my hand away, a needle attached to a tube buried deep in the crook of my elbow. I followed the cord up, watching the methodical drip of saline from an IV bag positioned above my head.

What in god's name happened?

My head pounded something fierce and I was dripping in sweat. I had no clue what Darragh may have given me already, but I needed something for the pain badly. The throbbing pulse at my temple knocked any sense from my brain. I threw my wobbly legs over the side of the bed and slowly stood. Each inch I dragged my feet took more effort than it should have, but I was determined to make it to the bathroom. Aspirin. I needed aspirin.

An array of little bottles laid across the counter when I finally shuffled in. A piece of paper held scribbled instructions that were barely legible. I didn't recognize the handwriting, but Darragh wouldn't leave this here if it wasn't legit. I painstakingly deciphered the words, line-by-line, before taking three small, white pills marked with the correct number.

The shuffle back to the bedroom was harder now that I wasted all my energy getting to the bathroom. In the doorway to

Darragh's room, I slumped against the jam and leaned my head back on the doorframe. Darragh's security monitors glowed in the corner, flickering blue and white light across the bed.

The longer I watched them, the more my frown deepened. Each room looked exactly the same as yesterday, but missing one vital piece: Darragh wasn't here.

I shook my head. He was probably here, just outside or something. Maybe he ran to the store. Hopefully he'd come back to check on me soon, because I honestly wasn't sure if I had the strength to pull myself up to the bed.

A wracking cough ripped through me. I clutched the cool, tile floor as wave after wave hit my chest. When the tremors in my lungs finally stopped, Darragh still wasn't anywhere to be seen.

I groaned and inched myself back to standing, dragging the little rolly thing the IV bag hung from. It took embarrassingly long to get back into bed, but the soft feel of the sheets against my face melted any of those worries away.

I opened my eyes and froze.

On the floor, in the doorway, a poorly cleaned pool of blood streaked the floor.

Not just a little blood, either. Half the damn room seemed to be covered in it. All the sickly lethargy fled my body as I sat up straight in bed. The dark, red streaks ended at the doorway and began right next to my bed.

And Darragh was nowhere to be seen.

I dug deep into my brain to recall what the hell happened last night. I woke up in the living room with Darragh. He said I fell into the river and he took me home. We were . . . we weren't wearing anything. And I asked him to—

I blinked back the hot wave of embarrassment that flooded me. I wanted it then. Part of me still did, but I couldn't believe I did that. That I said those things to him. I would blame it on the illness when I saw him. If I saw him. The bloody stain on the hardwood sent a pang through my chest.

I didn't remember anything after that. I was hot, my head hurt and then I passed out. It'd make sense if I was sick, but what if I was poisoned or something? What if Lucien or my family found us, knocked me out and killed Darragh, leaving me bed-ridden and sick to be collected at a later time?

The idea seemed ridiculous. I knew that on a logical level, but I had no other answers right now. Darragh was gone, his room was covered in blood, and I couldn't remember shit.

If someone did come back for me, I wasn't going down easy.

The cameras told me the house was empty, along with the immediate periphery of the property. I was completely alone, but that didn't stop the fear clenching my chest. Darragh would have stored my rifle in the garage. It was a far walk from the bedroom like this, but I wasn't hiding in here unarmed.

The painstaking trip downstairs took far longer than it should have. I stopped to catch my breath on the stairs five times and nearly vomited when I hit the bottom. I took a long breath before dragging myself down the hall and shuffling to the garage. Thankfully, Darragh stored my case right next to the door. If not, I may have given up and just dropped dead right there.

The weapon was already loaded, another small mercy. Back in the house, I settled against the back wall of the kitchen, facing the front hall. Anyone who came in would likely go upstairs first. If or when they came down, I'd be ready for them.

The pounding in my head slowly subsided the longer the medication kicked in. Hours passed and no one arrived. At one point my saline bag ran out and I ripped the IV from my arm. Night settled over the house and basked each room in thick darkness. It didn't take long for my eyes to adjust. It would be advantageous to settle with the rifle and use the night scope, but everything was too close range for that. I swore up and down to myself Darragh hadn't taught me to use a pistol yet, not that I even knew where to find one in the sea of gun cases stored in the garage. Or had the energy to get back up and search through all of them.

I started nodding off when headlights flashed through the empty hall. I sat up straight, wrapping my finger around the trigger and became stiller than death. The floodlights on the porch illuminated two figures for a split second before the door shut behind them. Darragh never brought anyone to the safe house. It wasn't him.

Panic clawed at my throat, but I shoved it down. Now was not the time to freak out. I steadied my breath and did my best to aim for the center of the hall through the heat swimming in my brain. One of the men shushed the other and the two stepped softly inside.

They didn't go upstairs. They came down the hall.

The darkened silhouettes tip-toed across the wood. I used my last remaining strength to lift the gun. One of them reached for the light. I fired.

A slew of curses echoed around the room as the two men dropped down. The fog in my brain was hard to get through, but I wasn't dying like this. I wasn't being taken back to Lucien Rocci or anyone else. I wrapped my finger around the trigger again when the first man, the one who reached for the light, glanced up.

It was Darragh.

My mouth went dry. He said nothing, but shock was written all over his face. The man behind him slowly stood, arms in the air. I swiveled the gun at him.

"Who the fuck are you?"

"Pina, put the gun away," Darragh snapped. He pulled himself to his feet. "He's my brother, calm down."

Darragh's brother. I never met him, never knew what he looked like. His name was Rory, I think. That was the most I had. But none of that explained the blood on my floor, and this could still be some strange trick. I didn't lower the gun.

"Pina," Darragh warned, voice low. My arms wavered. "It's fine. I promise. Put it away."

We should have come up with a code word or something. Spies and assassins always did that in the movies. Every horrible possibility ran through my head when another coughing fit took over. The rifle slipped from my hands and clattered to the ground while I doubled over.

Darragh was beside me in a blink, holding me up and rubbing my back. His hand ran over my arms, swearing at the still leaking wound from where I tore the IV. The other man, who I guessed actually was Rory, flicked the light switch. I blinked back thick tears as my eyes adjusted to the golden light flooding the room.

Darragh's brother was ... well, nothing like him. They were about the same height, which was where the similarities ended. A tuft of bright, red hair covered his head around dark freckles and bright, green eyes. Also, he was grinning like a fucking fool.

"Nice to meet ya, sis."

I stared blankly.

Darragh murmured something beside me, but I couldn't hear the low words under his breath. His hands dipped under my legs and back to lift me, but I waved him off.

"I'm fine," I said. I wasn't fine. I felt like I'd been hit by a truck and knocked off a cliff, but I wasn't ready to go lay back in bed alone. Not with this new development in the form of Darragh's fiery-haired, mischievous looking brother.

I met the strange man with my own dangerous grin. Maybe he was more like Darragh than I thought, because that only seemed to delight him more.

Rory knelt down beside me and held out his hand. "Pleased to meet you, Pina."

I frowned, turning to Darragh. He didn't look too happy either. I thought no one was supposed to know who I was until after the hit, family included. Maybe it had to do with the bloodbath upstairs.

"Don't worry, your secret is safe with me," he said. He straightened back to his full height. "Darragh, you got any beer?"

Darragh grumbled next to me, "You drank me dry, Ro."

A smile tugged at my lips. I didn't think drinking Darragh's house dry was even possible. I guess anything is with two O'Callaghan's in the room.

Darragh gripped my arm. "You should go back to bed."

I shook my head, still watching Rory as he whistled and jostled around the kitchen, opening cabinet doors and closing them with a soft swear when they came up empty.

"I'm okay," I lied. Even if I was, I knew it would do nothing to calm Darragh down. Stubborn *bastardo*. My tongue felt like a dried piece of paper in my head and my throat was hoarse. I hadn't eaten or drank anything in god knows how long at this point, so maybe I could use that to my advantage. "I could really use a glass of water. And I'm starving."

Darragh was on his feet and scouring the kitchen before I could register my plan worked.

Rory watched me with that same curious grin. To the normal onlooker, he probably seemed friendly, a little weird, but nothing harmless. Only a trained or paranoid eye could detect the dangerous glint in his. All Made Men had it.

I held out my hand. "If you're doing nothing, help me up."

He snorted, but obliged. "She's perfect for ya, Darragh." I didn't even know how to begin deciphering that. His cool hand wrapped around mine and pulled me to my feet. After helping me settle into one of the bar stools, he plopped into the one beside me.

He kicked his legs like a little kid and swiveled around. "Whatcha making?"

Darragh slammed a pan onto the stove. "Nothing for you."

Rory grinned and jabbed an elbow into my side. "What a great little brother he is, huh?"

My mouth hung open as I waited for a response to come. Nothing did. I took the moment to knock back the glass of water Darragh handed me instead. Lack of experience made it an unfair comparison, but right now, with my dry throat and wavering fever, I swore the ice-cold water was better than sex.

Rory leaned back against the seat, casting Darragh an amused look. "Can you still only cook bacon and eggs?"

I choked on the sip I was taking, splattering water back into the cup. Darragh froze to the spot while Rory howled beside me. "I'll take that as a yes?"

I couldn't help the little grin I wore. "I tried teaching him how to make pancakes for a little variety. It didn't go so well."

Rory leaned forward, cupping his face in his hands. "Now *that's* a story I'd love to hear."

"Save it for another time. Pina's tired," Darragh snapped. I turned on him, glaring daggers. I felt like shit, yeah, but that was for me to decide. He wasn't going to be my keeper just because I was sick. He wasn't going to be my keeper, ever. Even if it meant I plunged feet first into a watery death. At least it was my dumb mistake to make.

He gave me a warning look in response. Neither of us backed down.

Rory glanced between us. "So—"

"What happened upstairs?" I asked, cutting him off. Darragh flinched, so briefly I almost missed it. Rory, on the other hand, wore his heart on his sleeve. A nervous expression dawned on him while he looked anywhere but me.

"Not now."

"What. Happened."

Darragh ran his hand over his face, sighing. "Someone was here that shouldn't have been. It's been handled, and I've had a very long day. I'll explain everything when you're better, but not now. It's done, so please, just leave it."

Icy anger prickled my skin. Rory shrugged beside me, shaking his head. "Don't take it personally. He does the same shit to me."

I crossed my arms, still staring daggers at my husband. Said husband chose to ignore me, becoming unusually focused on perfecting the way to crack an egg into a pan.

"Please tell me he's not always this much of a pain in the ass."

Rory barked out a laugh. "Dar, I might ruin your marriage right now. Have no fear, Pina, it absolutely, undeniably, and irrevocably never, ever gets better. He's the fucking worst."

Laughter bubbled out of me this time. Even Darragh fought a small grin, still staring at the frying pan like it held the secrets of the universe.

I clinked my water glass against his. "Cheers to that."

"Damn right," he said, smashing his glass so hard against mine water sloshed over the edge.

Darragh rolled his eyes at the stove.

"So, there's something I've really been dying to know all these years." Rory watched me with complete seriousness.

I raised an eyebrow.

He leaned in close, hot breath tickling the skin over my neck. "Tell me, love, does Darragh still talk in his sleep?"

He wrapped his arms around himself in a tight embrace, closing his eyes and making fake kissing noises. "Oh, Ms. Fawcett, you feel so good. Ugh, Farrah, *Farrah,* keep doing that thing with your mouth—"

"Alright," Darragh snapped. He reached into a small cabinet and slammed a full bottle of whiskey in front of Rory. "Quit torturing my wife."

Rory threw his hands up in the air, giving a girlish squeal. "Yay!" He popped the cap and clinked the full bottle against my glass, giving me a devilish wink before downing at least three shots straight from the source.

I decided I liked Rory after all.

I traced little circles on the granite, my skin too sore from illness for my normal tapping. "No sleep-talking, from what I've heard. He snores like the devil though."

Rory grimaced. "It's in the O'Callaghan genes. My deepest condolences, sweetheart."

226

I chuckled, continuing my little circles. I noticed something strange about Rory's voice before, but it didn't hit me until now. "But the accent isn't? You sound American."

Rory laid his hand over his heart, puffing his chest out proudly. "I am American. Unlike the rest of my family, Darragh here included."

I looked between them. "Are you a lot older? I thought you were all born in Ireland."

"I was born here, Darragh in the motherland. And yes, I am older, ten whole months to be precise. Irish brothers and Irish twins." He winked and took another swig from the bottle.

I frowned. Darragh had mentioned something about not coming to the states until he was ten. I knew he never met his eldest brothers who passed a long time ago, but if him and Rory were so close in age, that didn't make much sense. "But—"

"That's also a story for another time, love," Darragh interjected. There was no bite to his voice. Just sadness.

Even Rory's goofy look turned solemn. Darragh turned away and Rory gently patted my knee. "He'll tell ya when he's ready," he whispered.

I knew there were still secrets between us, but I didn't know just how deep it went. I knew about Vietnam, about his relationship with Sean, the hidden sadness for the brothers he never met, even the basics of the mysterious and shadowed first ten years of his life. We didn't talk about him much anymore. I knew it was purposeful, which is why I never pushed it, but I still couldn't help the small twinge of hurt at being left in the dark on something so obviously important.

Darragh's vulnerable gaze met mine across the counter. Pain, he was showing me pain. I couldn't be completely sure, but I highly doubted he allowed much of anyone to see him like that.

Like a light being flicked to darkness, his face settled back into the cool emptiness I was used to.

After a few minutes of Darragh cooking silently, me, staring at the countertop, and Rory, happily humming to himself while getting drunk, Darragh laid down two heaping plates of bacon and eggs on the counter.

Rory feigned shock, pointing to himself and loudly whispering, "For me?"

Darragh rolled his eyes. "Don't push it, dickhead." He chucked a fork at his brother and gently slid a second one towards me.

I glanced between them, smirking. I never expected Darragh's relationship with his brother to be so . . . normal. It made me miss my own brother. I hadn't thought about him in weeks, but the loss suddenly hit like a ton.

I pushed my eggs around the plate, not so hungry anymore.

Rory elbowed me. "Why the long face?"

I gave him a watery smile, trying not to think about what Andrea was up to now, if he was safe. Darragh hadn't updated me on the fighting in the city in a while, but it was safe to assume the streets were still running with blood, especially now that my family knew for certain I was harmed. Even if Sean didn't claim my "death," they'd search for whoever did. Andrea would be in the direct line of fire.

I blinked back my tears and focused on my plate. "Nothing, I just miss my brother, sometimes."

Rory pondered that. "You have two, right?"

I nodded. "Alessandro and Andrea."

"You close with them?"

"Um, well, Alessandro is . . ." I broke out in a nervous laugh. "He is what he is. Andrea and I were always the closest."

Rory nodded along like I just said the most profound thing in the world. "Do you trust him?"

My hand clenched around my fork. "He's the only person I've ever been able to trust."

I didn't meet Darragh's eyes as I said it, but his body tensed in my peripheral.

"Maybe I can find out how he's doing for yo—"

228

"Rory." Both our heads snapped to Darragh. He grit his teeth, shaking his head slowly at his brother.

I pushed my plate to the edge of the counter. "I'm tired," I declared. I was more angry and hurt than anything, but I wouldn't admit that in front of these two. It was strike two for Darragh tonight. I said I trusted my brother, but apparently Darragh didn't trust me. My word was good. If I said Andrea wasn't a threat, he should listen.

Darragh gripped my wrist, stopping my descent off the bar stool. "You need to eat."

I cut him a glare so intense, for once, he actually backed down. His hand slipped away as I slipped the rest of the way off the stool.

"I usually sleep in the guest room, but it's all yours," I told Rory. I didn't really want to sleep beside Darragh, but it made more sense than making the two large men cuddle. All my meds were upstairs anyway.

A flicker of confusion crossed Rory's face, but I didn't feel like explaining why we slept in separate rooms. That this wasn't a real marriage. That I wasn't even entirely sure if I liked Darragh as a person or not. It varied day to day. Today, it was worse.

"Goodnight," I called, dragging myself up the stairs before either O'Callaghan could protest.

29

_____

PINA

I was still awake when Darragh came in an hour later, but he was either too tired or too drunk to notice. Judging by the whiskey breath, I'd say Rory got to him before exhaustion did.

He stood on the side of the bed and prodded at my shoulder. If he was going for "gently waking me up" he failed on epic proportions. I flipped onto my side and glared at him. "What?"

"I need to put your IV back in."

My rage ticked down a notch. "I already did it."

His face twisted into a cross of confusion and surprise. "But—"

I held up my arm for him, showing the needle I had just finished jamming in about two minutes ago. I was going to have an unbelievable bruise, but it was done. Who would have thought cutting off your finger would be easier? "It's taken care of."

He frowned. "Did you take your pills?"

"Done."

"Drink water?"

"Yeah."

"I think there was something I had to—"

"It's done." I took a deep breath. "Let's just go to bed."

He lingered a moment more, ending the standoff with a sigh and retreating to the bathroom. The shower turned on. With each passing second steam drifted into the room, my anger grew more, but there was nothing to say and lying here raging in my own head was pointless. Neither of us would ever budge, so I was better off going to sleep. I fucking needed it.

I was just drifting off when Darragh came back into the room and fell onto the opposite side of the bed, nothing but a thin towel wrapped around his waist. He slung his arm over his forehead, breathing softly.

I opened one eye, watching him. "Are you gonna put clothes on?"

He shrugged. "Probably not."

I took a breath to steady myself. It was just another thing I really didn't feel like dealing with at the moment. I turned on my side, trying to ignore the fact I was only six inches away from a completely naked Darragh.

"You're mad at me," he whispered.

I clutched my pillow. Yes, I was mad, but there was no point. He didn't fully trust me, and no amount of arguing would change that. Those things took time. If I was honest, I didn't completely trust him either, but in my defense he was supposed to kill me. Not put a ring on my finger.

"It doesn't matter," I murmured. Just to drive home the point home I really didn't feel like doing this right now, I added. "I'm tired."

"But you're still awake."

"Darragh." I flipped onto my side, meeting his wide, blue eyes. "Drop it, for the love of god."

He ran a finger down the side of my cheek, slow and spreading warmth across my skin. The memory of last night came back in a flash, just how close we were to doing something maybe both of us would have regretted. Everything happening here was already so complicated. I told myself this would be nothing but a partnership— a marriage of convenience— but even that didn't seem quite so true anymore. We spent every waking moment together, so some relationship was to be expected, but I never anticipated the way my mind would flood with want when he touched me like that.

"I'm sorry about last night," he said.

All the warm and fuzzy feelings flooding my brain fizzled. I wasn't sure if I regretted it just yet, but apparently Darragh did.

"I didn't realize how sick you were. I wouldn't have done anything if I knew."

I nodded. Okay . . . so, maybe not regret. At least not in the way I thought. It was clear this was more of Darragh's "mob speak," coming out, asking a question without really framing it as one. It would be easy enough to wiggle my way out of this. I had the easiest excuse in the world. But it wasn't entirely true, and though I was ashamed of the way my breath hitched when he moved closer, I didn't want to stop it either.

"It's okay," I said.

He cupped my cheek in his hand, searching my eyes. The smell of oak and whiskey washed over me like a toxin. "Is it?"

I nodded, eyes wide. Nothing would happen right now. Darragh was trashed and I had an IV in my arm for god's sake, so this was safe. A safe situation to test the waters.

He ran his thumb over my lips and I shuddered.

"How tired are you?"

My mouth went dry at the implication. I couldn't find any words in that moment, so I shrugged instead.

The corner of his lips tipped up into a smirk. He ran his thumb over my mouth again and pressed a soft kiss to my lips. All the annoyance and anger I felt before dissipated completely with the taste of him. It was nothing like the previous times, so careful and soft. I didn't think he was capable of handling anyone so lightly.

He ran his hand down the front of my chest but didn't take anything off. I had a feeling if the IV wasn't firmly rooted in my arm, it'd be a different story. His lips trailed away from mine and brushed across my jaw. The string of little touches continued down my neck to the edge of my nightgown.

He shifted on the bed, dropping the towel from his hips as he came on top of me. I couldn't help but stare at him, heat prickling across my skin at the sight of his bare body hovering above mine.

He lowered himself onto me. It was strange still being completely covered while he was not, but it definitely didn't bother him. The sight of his rock-hard erection between the Gaelic tattoos said so.

He pressed a kiss to the cool satin over my stomach. "I can help you get to sleep," he murmured against my navel.

I bit my lip. This was dangerous. This was crossing a line. Each time we found ourselves in this scenario, there was some excuse to write it off, but this felt too intentional. Even a bit drunk, Darragh knew what he was doing. And so did I.

He caressed my upper thigh with his hand, running his thumb over the scalloped edge of my gown. He pressed another satin-soft skin to my inner thigh. "Do you want some help, Pina?"

I groaned at the way my name sounded on his lips. He watched me with hooded eyes, tinged with lust but also waiting for permission. He wouldn't give me the option of making another excuse. Either I told him what I wanted, or we both went to sleep unsatisfied.

The fogginess from his touch was dulling all my thoughts, especially the reasonable ones. "Yes," I rasped.

He smiled, breaking our gaze to focus his attention back to the soft spot on my thigh. He nudged the edge of my nightdress higher and higher, until the fabric ended just above my hip bones rather than mid-thigh. A growl of approval came out of him when he realized I wasn't wearing any underwear.

"Were you waiting for me?" He asked. His lips pressed higher up my leg, dangerously close to my core.

"No," I said. It wasn't a lie. I just forgot to bring underwear up here and had way too much shame to go back for them after storming upstairs.

233

He squeezed my thigh and I gasped. "You should dress like this more often."

I bit my lip. I wanted to yell, tell him to screw off. I was still mad and he didn't have the right to tell me how to dress like *anything*, but he ran his tongue up the center of me and I was pulled under his spell again.

"Is this helping you? Get to sleep?"

My dull laugh was swallowed by a moan. He circled my clit with his mouth.

"Fuck," I breathed.

He nipped at me, smiling when I jumped. "Dirty little mouth," he mumbled.

I gripped the sheets as his tongue slid inside me. "Not dirtier than yours right now."

His low chuckle scattered across my skin, threatening to break me. He took to his task like it was the most important thing in the world, licking me up and down and rubbing my clit. I moaned so loud I was afraid Rory would hear us.

Shit— Rory. I forgot he was even—

Darragh growled and shoved two fingers deep inside me. My back arched against the sheets, black spotting the edges of my vision. A wave of heat built up inside me, threatening to take over. His mouth tugged gently on my clit while his fingers pumped in and out of me. I took a deep breath, falling into the feeling and completely shattered.

I sucked in heavy breaths and melted into the mattress. Darragh licked me up and down one more time for good measure, pressed a kiss to my hip bone and then collapsed beside me.

Little arcs of pleasure raced up and down my skin, still reeling from the orgasm. In the few times Darragh and I had . . . gotten together, it was the first he actually had time to finish the job. And . . . well . . . I understood what he meant now when he said sex could be a perk for both of us.

Because if his fingers felt like that, his tongue, then what did his—

"You should drink some more water."

I couldn't help it. I burst out laughing. "Really? That's all you have to say?"

He shot me a boyish grin. It was so unlike him, I could only stare. "Excuse me for trying to take care of you." He traced little circles on my arm, sending goosebumps across my flesh.

I swallowed. "I'll get up in a second."

"I got it," he murmured, rolling out of bed before I could protest. Even though I just finished, my mouth watered as I watched him walk, still completely bare, to the bathroom.

He came back with a glass of tap water and rolled back into bed beside me. I was definitely in no state for anything more than what he'd just given me, but lust clouded all rational thoughts and apparently wasn't stopping.

I eyed his thick erection resting across his thigh. "Do you want me to . . . help you out, too?"

He followed my line of sight and tensed. Something dark and primitive took over his expression, and for a moment I thought he'd agree. He shook his head, like he was trying to knock the very thought from his mind. "When you're feeling better, you can make it up to me in all kinds of ways."

It boggled me how that sentence sounded like both a threat and a tempting promise.

I shook my own head, taking one from Darragh's book and trying to knock out any thoughts of exactly how I would make it up to him. We never even established that this is what we were doing now— messing around, but the best things went unspoken, I guess.

Dangerous. This was so dangerous.

We both lay in silence, still unclothed, staring anywhere but one another. I wondered if it would always be like this, so hot and cold. It was like one second we were normal and the next we didn't even know what to do with one another.

I ached to end the tension, so I broke the silence with the first thing that came to my mind, "We should have a codeword."

He snorted. "What?"

"You know, like, a codeword. Like something to say if one of us is surrounded by hostiles, or something."

He leaned on his side. "Hostiles? Am I James Bond now?"

I rolled my eyes. "All I'm saying is, I didn't know who Rory was and I almost shot you."

He shrugged. "It was kind of hot."

I gave a hard flick to his shoulder. He laughed, and again, I was so taken aback I could only watch. Laughing, smiling . . . it was different, but very, very nice on him.

"I'm serious," I said, fighting a smile while he continued to grin. "What if one of us is taken hostage or something? We need a code word."

"I don't think we need a code word, love."

"Test me any further and I'll make it Farrah Fawcett."

He groaned, falling back onto the bed. I couldn't stop the string of giggles that fell out of me.

"One," he declared, ticking off his pointer finger, "That's a terrible code word. How in the bloody hell are you supposed to work that into a normal conversation? Two, I'm gonna fecking kill Rory for telling you that."

I pressed the covers to my mouth to stifle my laughter. "C'mon . . . it wasn't that bad."

He cast me a look that had me breaking into fits of laughter all over again.

"Fine," he huffed. I laughed harder. "Our code word should be . . . 'I'm doing just fine.'"

I pulled the covers back off my face. "I'm doing just fine? Won't one of us, like, accidentally say that all the time?"

"Nope," he said, closing his eyes with a smug grin. "Whenever someone asks you how you're doing, you always say, 'Great, thank you.' Every single time. So, if you say 'I'm doing just fine,' I'd know."

I laughed. "Great, now I'm going to overthink it anytime someone asks me, probably say it on accident out of nervousness and you'll send the calvary in."

He snorted, "You'll be fine. You're too smart for that."

I hated that the compliment sent a feeling of warmth through me.

"You ready to go to sleep now?"

I nodded, yawning. "Yeah. Definitely."

Everything else . . . Andrea, Rory, illnesses, we'd deal with it tomorrow. Tonight, I just wanted to sleep.

It didn't occur to me until Darragh shuffled closer, pressing his chest to my back and wrapping an arm around my waist, this was the first time in our marriage we'd gone to bed together.

30

PINA

The next few days ticked by slower than sap. My burst of energy the night Rory arrived faded by the next day, leaving me hacking my lungs up and lying around most of the time. The second day was more of the same, but by the third, I felt like I gained most of my strength back. Darragh was busy with . . . whatever it was he did, leaving me and Rory alone at the safe house for most of the day after I started feeling better.

He didn't say when he planned on leaving, but I didn't really mind. The strange red-head had grown on me a lot the past few days. The longer we spent together, the more apparent it became he was Darragh's brother. Despite the happy and carefree demeanor, a shadow of darkness hung around him, rearing its head each time I asked something I wasn't supposed to and he steered the conversation in another direction. He was smart, beating me in cards so often we had to start playing two out of three to even give me a fighting chance. He even began to look a bit more like his brother, the same sharp jawline, nose and wide eyes becoming familiar, even though all the colors were wrong.

Besides, with Rory staying here, I was spending each night with Darragh. It never progressed more than him going down on me and falling asleep together, but I had no complaints about the

238

routine. Actually, I kind of enjoyed it. We never discussed what would happen when Rory went home, but the only two options would seem I went back to sleeping in the guest room or swallowed my pride and stayed upstairs.

I wasn't usually one to go for the latter, but I really did like sleeping upstairs.

Rory had just kicked my ass in our ninth game of rummy while I stared at the clock, wondering what time Darragh would be home. The casino was hitting peak season again, taking him away from home for what seemed like the entire day. It was weird to think part of his job entailed doing normal things, like running a business. You know, instead of murdering people.

Rory followed my eyes to the clock. "He should be back soon."

I tensed. "I wasn't thinking that."

He hit me with a smirk that screamed, *yeah, sure you weren't.*

I rolled my eyes. "Alright, tell me the secret. How do I kick your ass in this game?"

"No secret, just pure skill," he sang, laying out cards. "It also helps I'm not incredibly distracted waiting for my hot, Irish husband to get home."

I nearly choked on my water. "One, not how I think. Two, he's your brother."

"I was impersonating you, and I'm pretty sure it was accurate." He grinned. "Now, allow me to kick your ass for a tenth time, *per favore, signora.*"

I sighed, picking up my cards. "Don't roll the 'R' so much."

He looked positively delighted. "But I'm getting better, right?"

I plastered on a painful grin, nodding my head. It was enough to satisfy Rory's ego. Halfway through the game, I was already terribly losing. I threw down the cards in a huff, declaring, "That's it, we're drinking."

He winked. "Be careful, lass. Whiskey gives me power."

"Yeah, I believe it," I grumbled, searching for Darragh's not-so-secret stash. He made me promise not to let Rory drink him out, but I'd given up at this point.

I slammed the bottle on the counter along with two shot glasses. "Let's play a game, for every win you get, you take a shot."

Rory burst out laughing. "I already told ya, getting me drunk won't give you any advantages."

I shrugged. "It's worth a shot. Literally."

"Ha. Clever." He poured the little glasses and slid mine over to me. He held his in the air. "To my new sister-in-law, thank god she can drink."

I grinned. *"Salute."*

Two shots later and Darragh still wasn't home. The longer the minute hand ticked, the more my anxiety rose. He told me this was for normal business, but it wouldn't have been the first time Darragh lied. I wouldn't have put it past him to tell me one thing and completely do another.

We were supposed to go to Chicago a few days ago, but I hadn't heard anything about that. It was something we were going to do together. My first real hit. I wasn't itching to kill anyone or anything, but I'd be upset if he lied and handled that part of business without me.

Maybe Rory knew something.

I drummed my fingers on the counter. "Did Darragh tell you about our plans for Chicago?"

His utterly blank stare told me he knew something he wasn't revealing. My stomach dropped at the prospect I was actually right. Darragh had shut me out of something we were supposed to be partners on.

He tilted his head. "Minor details."

"What details?"

"I knew he didn't go when he was supposed to. That's about it."

240

I froze. What did he mean, *supposed to go?* As far as I knew, he'd just never heard back from the senator. He even told me that the other night when I brought it up.

"How do you know?"

He shrugged, casting his eyes at the counter. God, he made a terrible Made Man.

"Rory—"

"You ask him," he said. He poured himself another shot. "It's not my business, literally or figuratively. I overheard a bit of a phone call while you were sick, but that's it. I honestly don't know what he was thinking, so he should explain."

I didn't know what he was thinking either. And on top of that, he'd lied to me. Just another fucking half-truth to add to the growing list. I leaned back in my seat, crossing my arms.

"I don't think he meant to—"

"It doesn't matter," I said. My knee bobbed up and down. "It's business as usual, even if he lied."

Rory frowned, mirroring my position and leaning back in his own seat. "Whatever he said to you, I know my brother. He lies to others to protect the family, but he lies to himself to protect his own. Either way, he'd never want to hurt you."

I laughed bitterly, going for shot number four. "Then maybe you don't know him that well. You do realize we're not really married, right?"

His eyebrow shot up. "Whatcha mean?"

"It's a marriage of convenience," I explained. "We're more business partners than anything, nothing more."

He smirked. "Has Darragh told you that?"

"He doesn't have to. It's what we agreed on from the beginning." I shrugged. "We don't actually care about one another."

Rory shook his head, grinning to himself. "You are both complete fucking idiots, you know that?"

Before I had time to delve deeper on that, the front door flew open. Darragh came in, covered in a fine dusting of snow. He ripped his scarf and hat off and plopped down in the last remaining

241

bar stool. He glanced between us, a look of mock hurt crossing his face. "You started drinking without me?"

Rory laughed. "Blame your wife. She's a sore loser."

I tried to smile. I did. But once again, it felt like Darragh was so close, warm instead of cold, and suddenly he slipped through my grasp again.

———————

Rory left the next morning, promising to stop by again soon. Darragh was unusually quiet while the two men clapped each other on the back and Rory waved to us from his truck. We both stood in the doorway, watching the red-head peel off and disappear down the long driveway.

A long moment passed of complete silence. Darragh crossed his arms, leaning against the doorframe and puffing on a cigarette. For someone always so calm and collected, it was strange to think of how much must be going on in his head. How many secrets he harbored there. I wanted nothing more than to pull them out one-by-one, but I didn't think Darragh would ever allow that.

"We should train today. We lost a lot of time," he finally said.

I nodded wordlessly, heading back inside to pull on my warm winter clothes and collect my gear, the sniper rifle plus a pistol I was going to make Darragh show me how to use. A moment later, Darragh's cigarette hissed into the snow and the front door shut behind him.

The trek into the woods was also silent. The softly falling snow cushioned all sound except for the train blowing in the distance, puffing smoke into the sky as it threaded through the mountains. It almost seemed like a lifetime ago I hit Darragh with a frying pan and ran for the tracks. A lifetime where we'd come to some sort of understanding with one another. Where I learned to shoot a gun and planned to take Lucien Rocci down. It was hard to put my finger on exactly what happened, but now we felt like we were in some sort of in between. Not married, but married. Not friends, but close enough. Not enemies, but something far more dangerous.

"Why didn't you go to Chicago?" I asked.

He grunted, pushing a skinny branch to the side. "I told you, plans changed."

"That's a lie." I didn't accuse him, I told him. We both knew it was the truth.

"Pina—"

"Where did the bloodstain in your room come from?"

He sighed, turning on his heel. His crystal blue eyes shimmered in the dull, winter morning light. "Why all these questions?"

"What happened in Ireland?" I pressed on. "How come you never talk about your mother? Why is that after everything that's happened, you still don't seem to trust me?"

His face twisted into something I couldn't quite read. He stood before me, hands limp at his sides. Now would be the time to come clean. Tell me about what happened when I was sick, explain the truth about Chicago, all of it. But he stood in silence, his eyes seeing through me into some memory or thought he didn't care to share. He could be my business partner. He could be my fake husband. He could lie in bed with me each night, arms around my waist and mouth between my legs, but he couldn't just tell me the goddamn truth.

He shook his head. "Not now, Pina."

My hands balled into fists at my side.

We stared at one another.

A thought crossed my mind, an insane one. Just as insane as Darragh was making me. Because I didn't understand how through everything, he could still want to hide things. I didn't understand how he could say he trusted me, but not follow through on his word. But most of all, I didn't understand how even with this, I still wanted him to take me to bed tonight. Maybe even every night.

I grabbed the pistol at my hip and pointed it at him. His eyebrow went up.

"You trust me?" I asked.

He eyed the weapon, hands still in his pockets. His expression was bored, but that never fooled me. Always scheming, always calculating.

"I trust you."

"With a gun," I added. "Because you trained me to use it. Right?"

A withered expression came over him. "Pina, what—"

"But you don't trust me with anything else. Only what you can control around you. I thought maybe you were different from other men, maybe you really valued me for more than what you thought I could give you, but that's not true is it?" The words came out of me in an endless stream, one I couldn't just dam up and tuck away like Darragh always could. All my fears laid out on the table: that he didn't really think I was smart or strong or whatever other catchy words he liked to use. That I was back to square one, being nothing but the blushing, doting bride that served some sort of purpose to him. It was never the life I wanted. It was the life I fucking escaped by coming here, and now I was right back in it again.

I shot a bullet off into the snow.

He jumped, a scowl taking over his face. "Stop fucking around and we'll talk."

I nodded, smiling. "Okay, so now we'll talk. After I point a gun at you." I fired off another round into the trees to make my point. "What is this, Darragh? What the fuck do you want from me at this point if you can't even tell me what's going on? Forget your past, hide that if you want. What the hell happened with Chicago?"

He took a deep breath, nostrils flaring. Those calm blue eyes screamed murder now.

"I backed out."

244

"Why?"

He didn't say anything. I shot at a close-by branch, just missing his head.

He stepped forward for the gun, but I slipped away. Just like he taught me to.

"The blood belonged to a doctor I brought here to treat you. He recognized you, so I killed him."

Icy dread threaded through my veins. Not only had I unintentionally caused someone's death, but the way he said it was just how I imagined him from the start: cold, lifeless, empty.

"Just like that?" I murmured.

"I didn't want to tell you because I knew how you would feel." He shoved his hands in his pocket, the cool mask pulling over his face again.

"And Chicago?" I asked, my words coming out in a hushed stutter.

He shrugged. "I had shit to do."

I sucked in a deep breath. "You'll never tell me anything, will you?"

Silence stretched between us, a canyon that every bit of progress we've made these past two months completely swallowed. We were back at the beginning. Or more realistically, we never left it.

"Why did you even save me?" I whispered.

Again, that empty stare.

Nothing.

I absolutely fucking hated him.

I cocked the gun and pointed it right at his chest. "Why should I even trust you anymore?"

Fear, real fear, crossed his face. It was the first time I'd ever seen it. Maybe he was human, after all.

"Give me one good reason," I hissed.

Darragh turned to the side, refusing to look at me. "I called off Chicago because I didn't want to leave you. I thought you were going to die, and it was fecking terrifying, so I stayed."

My hand shook on the handle of the gun. It was a good answer. The perfect kind of sweet lie you told someone to make them spare your life. But if it was the truth, then why not just fucking say it?

I shook my head. "Why the secret then?"

His gaze turned back to me, the exact same look he gave the other night in the kitchen with Rory. That strange moment of vulnerability.

He closed his eyes. "I don't know."

Part of me believed him, but that other part, the more sensible one, knew deep down what he really was. That he could lie without a thought, manipulate, become a monster. It was the only way Made Men survived. And now that I pulled the gun and opened Pandora's Box, there was a chance only one of us would survive this moment. If I was wrong, he'd kill me once and for all. Because that's what men did in our world. They used, they destroyed and then they threw us away. Lucien Rocci did it, my father did it, even Andrea did it. My best friend was dead, and maybe soon, I'd be too, and the world will keep spinning and the men will keep killing and nothing would ever fucking change.

A hot tear slipped down my face. "There's something wrong with you. With all of you."

He nodded, agreeing. "Yeah, you're right about that, love."

"What am I doing here?" I asked again. I wasn't sure if the question was for him or for myself.

Darragh stared at me. Not through me, not past me, not around me. At me. Anger, violence, passion and everything in between laced through his voice. "Did my brother tell you about Ireland?"

I slowly shook my head.

His mouth pressed into a thin line. "Put the gun down. I'll tell you everything."

Too good. Too good to be true. I didn't waver a single inch.

He sighed and leaned against a tree. His hand reached for his pocket and I tensed, but all he did was pull out his pack of cigarettes and a matchbook.

Puffy smoke curled into the air as he lit the match between his lips. "I'm the youngest of four, you know that."

I nodded.

"My Ma was . . . a lot like you, actually." He frowned. "She didn't do well in this world, worse with Sean. She grew up in the IRA but never had a thing for violence. She was sold off to Sean to give the IRA some foothold in the states. And she suffered, a lot. She had three children she watched get molded and tortured by Sean. Then, she got pregnant with her fourth, and she made a choice."

"To leave your father?" I asked. I hadn't expected him to delve into his family history, had no clue where the hell this was going.

"To run away," he said. He took a long drag of his cigarette. "She didn't want another one of us to be hurt by him. So, she ran back home, hid with IRA people she could trust, and mostly just tried to disappear."

His hand shook around the cigarette. "When I was born, she told me she had no clue who my Da was. I never knew I had older brothers. She taught me how to use a gun, how to defend myself and hide, but mostly, it was a normal childhood. Until I turned ten."

"And Sean found you," I breathed. The gun in my hand lowered, just an inch.

He nodded. "Sean's men found us. Pat, actually, the passport lad. My Da didn't even believe I was his until he sent a photo back and he could see I was a spitting image of him. At that point, he only cared about getting back his runaway wife. But my Ma, she couldn't do it. She couldn't go back to him, back to the children she left behind to die under Sean's reign. So, the night before we were supposed to leave, she laid down next to me in bed, kissed me and wished me luck, and cut her own wrists."

His face scrunched, like he was a scared and helpless little boy again. He took a large breath and pulled a drag of his cigarette, lips shaking around the paper. "Rory never knew her. By the time we were found, my oldest brothers were both dead. Not even from the mob, just wrong place, wrong time. Killed by a drunk driver. So, I was the only one who knew what it was like to be loved. To have some kind of normalcy. And maybe that's why I fit in so much better than Rory ever did, because nothing killed me more than having it all stripped away."

He turned to me. "So, twenty years go by and my Da orders me to kill you. He wants to stop the Italian alliance and you're the key. So, I packed my shit and laid on a roof for half the day, waiting to put a shot in your head. But instead, I found you shivering and cold, wrists slashed and ready to die. Another woman. Another place. Another time, but the same exact shit. Lucien Rocci would have destroyed you, so you took another path instead, and it took me right back to that night when I was a kid. I should have left you die. It wouldn't be on my conscious if you did the job for me, but I've seen this all before and it killed me once, so I couldn't do it again."

Sticky tears dripped down my face. My hands shook with violence, but I kept the gun high. Darragh stood up, dousing his cigarette in the snow and walked towards me. I took a step back and he paused, resuming our little dance a moment later. I knew what he said was the truth, but it unraveled every part of him I thought I understood. Darragh never felt nothing, and somehow that scared me most.

"Pina," he said softly. "You of all people understand what it's like in this world. I was weak with you and I tried my best to make up for that mistake. I couldn't bring myself to kill you, so I brought you into the fold instead. I tried to right a wrong."

"And that's why I'm here?" I asked. He stepped closer, but I didn't slip further away this time.

"No," he said, voice unsure but eyes staring straight at me. "I think that was just the start."

248

I lowered the gun. He took it from my hands and disarmed it, tossing it into the snow. My breath came out in heavy clouds, blurring his face with each heavy contraction of my lungs. He was so close the warmth rolled off him. I was scared. The most scared I'd ever been in my life. We'd crossed enough lines already, but this was something entirely new. The most dangerous hurdle of all. If we kept going, then there would be no stopping the free-fall that came after it.

That was a lie. There was no stopping anything now at all. "What was the rest?"

A small smile crossed his face, almost sad. "I think you're here just because I want you to be." He smirked at the gun in the snow. "Craziness and all."

I shook my head. "I'm not the crazy one."

His eyebrow arched up. "How about we both qualify?"

That, I could agree on. Not because of the guns, the violence, the hit. Not because I married a killer and learned to become one myself. For one, and one reason only.

I stood up straight, leaning in. Before I had a chance to stop myself from falling over the edge, of re-thinking everything, his hands curled into my hair and his lips crashed against mine.

Every time I kissed him before I was overcome with his taste: whiskey, oak, salt, sweat, blood, fear. But this time it was different. The entire world melted away, leaving nothing but the feeling of Darragh's skin on mine. No snow, no thoughts, no cold, just his hands laced in my hair and warm mouth caressing mine. His touch slipped lower, cascading over my back and gripping my ass. Thick, calloused hands— the hands of a killer, a Made Man, my husband— gripped under my thighs and yanked me higher. I wrapped my legs around his waist and dug my own fingers into thick, black hair. It wasn't enough. I needed to be closer.

Like the mind reader he was, he sunk down, crashing into the soft snow at our feet. I came down on top of him, consuming him with my touch and hungry for more, more, more. His hands fumbled with the zipper of my jacket while I reached for his. He ripped the winter coat off my arms and yanked the thin fabric of my shirt high over my head.

A moment later, his own clothes were stripped, too. I ran my hands up and down his chest, savoring the warmth and the silky touch. He threw his jacket to the ground and flipped me over, laying me on top of it.

The kissing slowed. He didn't devour me anymore. He worshipped. His lips fluttered against my neck, tracing down to my chest. He took one hard nipple in his mouth and ran circles with his tongue. I groaned, digging my hands into his hair and trying to pull him back to me, but he took his time. His mouth moved to my other breast and showed it the same love. Then he dipped lower and lower until his mouth hovered at the hem of my jeans. In one movement he unbuttoned them and pulled them down my legs.

He pressed a soft kiss to the inside of my thigh, so unlike his next words. "You have one moment to decide. After this, there's no going back."

I swallowed, meeting his dark gaze between my thighs. Lust clouded his features, thick with want and the promise of danger.

I tensed as his finger ran down the center of me, drawing wetness like moth to a flame. "Decide what?"

His jaw set in barely controlled restraint. "Decide if I keep going."

I breathed heavy, need fogging all my thoughts. "What happens if you do?"

"I won't stop," he murmured. Two fingers pressed against my pussy and pushed apart the folds. He leaned down, lightly stroking my clit with his tongue. "This won't be like the other nights. I won't eat you out and stop. If you let me do this, you're not coming from my mouth. I'm going to fuck you. Then, I'm going to take you home and fuck you again. And again. And again."

A shuddered breath escaped me. I didn't know what to say. I didn't know how to form words. The need was so bad it was tearing me apart, cell by cell. I knew what I wanted, and I think Darragh did too. He tested his tongue at my entrance, before bringing his mouth back to my clit, sucking on the little bundle of nerves tenderly.

I gripped his hair in my hand and pulled him up to look at me. "Then don't stop," I snarled.

A hint of a dangerous smile tugged at his lips. He gripped my thighs and devoured me with his mouth. My hands curled into icy, cold snow as he stroked my clit, releasing one hand to shove two fingers deep inside me. I rolled beneath his touch, needing to feel more. I didn't want his fingers inside me anymore. I wanted him. I wanted his cock deep inside me and filling me up, stretching me as far as I could go.

Even then, my orgasm built low in my stomach. I breathed harder, ready to release when Darragh stopped.

He reached up and grabbed my face. "No," he murmured, stiller than death.

I nodded. Even without his touch, the orgasm threatened to tumble over. I whimpered as he gripped my face harder, pulling me close to whisper in my ear, "Don't even think about coming yet. I'll be buried deep inside you when you break."

He released me and pulled at his jeans, letting his thick erection spring free. My mouth watered at the sight.

He laid down on top of me, brushing hair sticky with sweat and snow from my face and kissed me gently. I moaned against his lips, loving the soft feel of him but still craving more. It was just like his training. This was designed to torture me.

He cupped my cheek in his palm and pressed his forehead to mine. "The night you were sick, I wanted you to promise me something."

I swallowed, staring deep into his icy, blue eyes. They still scared me, but in a different way now. "I'll promise you anything."

He smiled and hooked my leg around his hip. I gasped as the length of him prodded at my entrance, slipping in just a little.

"I have to amend it a bit," he breathed. I whimpered as he pulled out, then nudged himself against me again.

"I wanted you to promise me you'll never scare me like that again. That you'll stay safe."

I smiled. It wasn't what I expected. So selfless. So worrisome. I felt like an idiot for everything that led up to this moment, for thinking I could come to any harm.

"I can do that," I whispered, pressing a light kiss to his cheek. He answered it with kissing up my throat. He pushed inside me a little more, drawing a low moan from me. He shuddered above me, almost losing control. His hand gripped tighter on my face as he brushed his lips over the shell of my ear, "And for the second part, promise me this is a real marriage, that you're really my wife. That you'll never leave, and I get to do this to you every day for the rest of my life."

My hands tightened on his back, digging into his skin. So little of him was inside me, and I wanted— needed— more. But his promise wasn't one to give just because I craved his body. It was so much more.

Thankfully, I already knew the answer for that too. "I promise."

He took his time. His lips brushed against mine as he entered me, slowly. I felt every inch as he pushed in, and god, there was a lot of them. His thighs hit mine and I gasped, getting used to the feeling. It was so much different than his hands. So much more *full.*

He kissed me softly. "Does it hurt?"

I bit my lip as he pulled away. "A little," I admitted. "But don't stop."

He nodded, taking his sweet time again. He kissed everything, my lips, my hair, my cheeks as he slowly pulled out and rocked back in. The pain began to subside, numbing with each little movement and being replaced by something else. I moaned as he pulled out and buried himself back in, faster this time. My breathe came out in short gasps as the pace got quicker and more frenzied. He ran his hand down my thigh wrapped over his back and gripped my ass in hand, rocking me back and forth on his cock.

"Fuck," I groaned, digging my nails into his skin. Arcs of pleasure raced low in my belly, the orgasm building once more. He moaned above me, losing his focus and breaking the rhythm. I gripped him harder, breathing, "No— god, please don't stop."

He growled in response, fucking me harder. He pulled all the way out, leaving me empty and bare before shoving himself back in, all the way to the hilt. I screamed, but he swallowed it with a kiss. He took my mouth, sliding his tongue over mine. He reached down, rubbing my clit with his thumb while he fucked me again and again and again.

"I want you to come for me now," he murmured. He pressed his fingers against my clit and slammed deep inside me. I shook beneath him, unsure what to grab or hold or what to do. Fire raced across my skin as that pressure built up, ready to burst.

"Come on me, love," he growled. He took my lower lip between his teeth and tugged gently. "I want to feel you break on me."

I couldn't stop it anymore. My back arched against the snow as little tremors took over my body. Darragh breathed harder above me, pumping faster. I clenched around him, crying out as my orgasm took over and shockwaves coursed through me.

Darragh moaned deep and gripped me tighter, his own orgasm meeting mine. He trembled above me, breathing in heaving gasps as he finished, still buried deep inside me.

He collapsed against me, his chest moving in tandem with mine. He pressed soft kisses to my neck and hairline, warm breath cascading over my skin.

I stared up at the sky and laughed. "Oh, so that's what all the fuss is about."

He grinned beside me, turning my head to kiss my lips. "Don't worry, love. It only gets better."

31

DARRAGH

I made good on my promise to Pina the second we got home.

Her face flushed when she caught me watching her, already thinking of every dirty little thing I wanted to do before she even stepped in the door.

Despite the heat crawling up her neck, she didn't break eye contact as she slowly peeled off her soaking, cold layers of clothing. I'd make it up to her later. Now. I could barely breathe, let alone think as she stood in nothing but a black bra and thin, lacy underwear. I wanted to rip them off. With my teeth.

She reached behind to unclasp her bra when I strode forward, locking her wrists behind her back and tilting her chin up to look at me.

"Take that off here and we're not making it to the bed."

Her honey eyes darkened, a pout jutting out her lower lip. I closed my eyes, trying to contain myself as she shuddered against me. Never mind, we weren't making it upstairs no matter what.

I cupped her round, little arse and pulled her up, wrapping her legs around me. She gasped and clung to my shoulders, laughing softly as I sat her on the kitchen counter. The counter where we played cards, ate breakfast, where I taught her to read the books. I suddenly had a whole fresh set of ideas on exactly what I'd like to use it for.

She stopped laughing when she saw the look on my face, her own turning serious. Hooded eyes stared back at me as I ran my hands down the length of her thighs, wishing I could bottle up the feel of her satin skin under my fingertips. Hands that have killed far too many to count, hands that didn't deserve to touch a woman like Pina.

Her breath caught as I reached up and gripped the back of her neck. I stood over her, eyes focused on those cherry red lips and already thinking of everywhere I'd put them.

I ran my hand down the side of her face. "Tell me what you want, love."

I knew what she wanted, but I wanted to hear her say it. See those dirty little words form on the lips I couldn't stop thinking about. She glanced to the side, a little shy and a little unsure. It only made my cock swell harder in my pants.

"What you did in the woods," she finally said.

I smirked, leaning forward and hooking one golden leg around my waist. She gasped as my erection pushed against the thin lace of her panties. "Not good enough," I breathed into her hair.

She rocked against me, pressing her pussy against the bulge in my pants. I groaned into her hair and gripped her tighter. It took everything I had not to rip those lace panties off, but patience always got the best rewards.

I tilted her chin to look at me and ran a finger over underwear. They were already soaked through for me. Good girl.

"Tell me, love."

She whimpered and the sound nearly broke me. That must have made her realize the power she had over me, because her expression suddenly turned defiant. She shrugged, giving me a little smirk as she swung her legs off the counter and sashayed into the living room.

I reached for her, but she slipped out of my way. "Where the feck do you think you're going?"

255

She shrugged again, tossing a look over her shoulder before she settled on the couch. My cock throbbed watching her lean against the arm rest and spread her legs, knees up and feet planted on the cushions. She popped one golden finger in her mouth and sucked gently, closing her eyes like it was the best taste in the world.

I hovered closer, standing on the other end of the sofa while she licked up and down, then took her whole finger in her mouth and moved her lips down. Slowly. I'd never been more jealous of a finger in my life.

"I wanted you to do this," she breathed. She pulled one perfect breast out of her bra and palmed it, rubbing slow circles around and caressing her nipple.

I sucked in a furious breath, torn between ripping her off the couch and taking her on the floor or letting this go on. She released her tit and slid her hand down her stomach, stopping at a certain lacy, black hemline.

She pulled the fabric to the side, baring herself to me. Her tight, pink pussy gleamed back at me, slick with wetness. I'd slip right in. She ran her finger up her center, shuddering beneath the light touch.

I stepped closer. "And then what do you want me to do?"

A devilish grin broke out on her face. She didn't break eye contact as she slipped a finger inside herself with a low gasp. She'll be screaming when it's me doing that to her.

"I can handle it," she teased, shoving another finger deep inside herself. Then another. She came up to her knees and braced her free hand on the back of the couch. Then she started rocking, slowly, back and forth on her fingers. My mouth watered and my brain scattered, watching her fuck her own hand.

Her moans matched the roll of her hips. She watched me with an almost pained look, trying to get her fingers in deeper, faster, but we both knew it couldn't fill her up like I would. I smirked and fell onto the couch beside her. Her little display was entertaining. Let's see how long she could keep it up.

"You like that, love?" I gripped her face and forced her to look at me while she fucked herself. She nodded, gasping as I wrenched her closer.

"But you want something else, don't you?" She didn't respond, only staring at me with resistance in her eyes. She moaned loudly, trying to prove her point. Suddenly, I was much happier with her little game. If she wanted to try and play me, she had a lesson to learn.

"You know," I murmured, "Good girls get rewarded more than bad ones." I flicked her nipple, eliciting a little moan.

I ran my thumb over her lips. "Do you want to be a good girl for me?"

Sher shook her head, eyes turning to slits. She pulled her fingers out of her pussy and into her mouth, moaning deeply. Red spotted my vision as I honed in on nothing but the image of her tongue lapping up the taste I wanted so badly.

She grinned around the finger in her mouth. "Want a taste?"

Yes. No. More than fecking anything. But I wouldn't let Pina win at this little power game we had going. "I'll just watch you."

Her gaze turned near murderous. She shrugged, laying down on the couch and placing one leg over the back of it and the other across my lap.

"Fine." She ran two fingers over her center, pushing the folds apart and showing me exactly what I was missing. She slipped inside herself again, rocking on her fingers.

If hell existed, this was mine. I ran a shaky hand over her thigh, watching her thrust in and out of the tight, little space that was supposed to be mine. I was done playing games now.

"Get on your knees," I growled.

Her mouth formed an *O*. I stood up and lifted her off the couch with me, dropping her to the floor. She got on her knees like the good girl she was, but still wore that bratty little grin. It'd be hard to maintain it with my cock in her mouth.

I unbuckled my pants and slid them to the floor. Her gaze turned dark as I stroked up and down my shaft, right in front of her face. She gripped the back of my thighs, pulling herself up, but she was so tiny she just reached. I ran the tip of my dick over her lips.

"Suck it," I instructed her. For a moment, I thought she'd still try to resist, but one look at my face had her following orders again. She gripped my base tentatively and wrapped her little lips around the tip. She seemed unsure. I pushed my cock into her mouth another inch and fisted her hair.

"Take it in your mouth, love."

She pushed deeper, as deep as she could go before gliding her lips back to the tip. A little string of saliva hung off the tip, connected to her mouth. She took me again, circling around me with her tongue just like I did with her clit.

I moaned as the hand gripping me started sliding up and down. "That's a good girl, Pina."

I let her suck me off a few more minutes. She let out a surprised gasp when I pulled her up and threw her over my shoulder and walked down the hall. I knew exactly how we were going to finish this.

She giggled against my back. "Where are we going?"

I smacked her arse hard enough to leave a handprint. She yelped. "Just trust me, love."

I carried her upstairs to my bedroom— our bedroom now, because there was no fecking way she was ever sleeping in the guest room again— and threw her on the bed. She laughed as her back hit the sheets and raised her arms above her head. I flipped her onto her stomach and pulled her hips up to meet mine.

I grabbed her hair, pulling her face up enough to see our reflection in the mirror spanning the top of my dresser. I gave her arse another little smack just for teasing me earlier and nudged her legs wide open with my knees.

She swallowed. "What are you doing?"

"Actions have consequences, love." I let go of her hair, running both my hands down the smooth skin of her back. She

258

buried her face in the sheets, breathing hard. She wasn't getting off that easy.

"You tease me, I tease you." I pulled on her caramel hair again. "Don't look away from the mirror, Pina."

Her breaths got heavier. In the mirror, her eyes roamed over our bodies: her, chest to the bed and arse in the air, and me, gripping her hips like a fecking lifeline behind her.

I traced a little circle on her back with my thumb, prodding at her opening with my erection. "You're gonna watch. I want you to see every dirty thing I'm about to do to you."

I pushed inside her, grinning at her sharp gasp. She did what she was told and watched in the mirror.

I ran my hands down her back, rocking in and out. She whimpered around me, moving her hips to try and make me go faster but I was taking my sweet time. I wanted her to need it. And I wouldn't give her what she needed until she was screaming my name.

She let out a little frustrated huff as I stopped moving altogether, taking the opportunity to cup her arse in my hands and admire just how damn lucky I got in my choice of wife.

"Darragh," she murmured, rolling her hips. My vision darkened at the corners. "Please."

"What was that?" I pulled her up to her knees, pressing her back to my chest with my cock still buried deep inside her. She met my eyes in the mirror, giving me a pleading look.

"Please," she whispered again.

I kissed up the column of her throat. "Please, what?"

She swallowed, body tensing as I pushed deeper into her. "Please fuck me."

I grinned, wrapping her hair in my fist. "You think you deserve that, love? After your little show downstairs?"

She turned her head so she was staring at me. The look in her eyes was almost enough to make me crumble right there. "Darragh, fuck me. Now."

I was weak. Way too weak. I pushed her down and flipped her onto her back. As much as I loved the mirror, I wanted the real thing. I wanted to see exactly what her face looked like when she broke around me.

I shoved deep inside her and she moaned. I wasn't playing with her anymore, thrusting hard, pouring every bit of frustration and want that built up over the past few months into each stroke. She writhed beneath me, reaching for my face and pulling me down to meet her lips.

The taste of her, that did it.

My cock throbbed and pulsed as she finished around me. I pulled out when it was my turn. We hadn't been using condoms and as far as I knew, Pina wasn't on any pills. We'd have to fix that soon, because this was going to become a multiple time a day occurrence.

I rolled off her and reached for my underwear. She frowned watching me. "Where are you off to in such a hurry?"

I nodded toward the door. "Going to grab your things."

A perfect, latte-colored eyebrow arched up. "Why?"

I laid across her on the bed, kissing her forehead. "Because there's no goddamn way you're sleeping down there ever again."

32

———

PINA

December passed by in a blur of tangled sheets, gun practice, sweat-soaked nights and early mornings. Darragh was right, we had little time to make up for the training I missed, so we worked hard. But each morning before we left he took me in our bed, and each night when we got home we couldn't get the other undressed fast enough. Between meals, showers and forming plans, we talked about Ireland, my time in the compound, our families, and everything in between. If Darragh was a closed book before, now he was an open page, spilling words into every nook and cranny of our life. On Christmas, he bought me a camera, something state-of-the-art after I complained the walls looked too bare. Within days, they were filled up with pictures of the woods around the house, Darragh cooking breakfast, me lying in his bed, and a few terrible photographs of us together.

As the days came closer to New Year's, the plans poured in: we would travel back to the city on the 30th and meet with Sean as well as any other crew working the hit. Sean was informed a trusted accomplice would be helping on the operation, AKA, yours truly. The hit would take place at a neutral location, a party at a hotel outside of both mob's territory where Lucien Rocci was throwing a New Year's party. Darragh and I were to be posted on the roof of a bank across the street after attending the party, which would be our alibi if any police decided to look a little too closely.

As we packed our bags the morning of the 30th, Darragh filled me in on the other details of the hit— Sean.

I threw my suitcase into the trunk with a huff, watching the car fill up with my hands on my hips. "The plan was I'd take out Sean."

"Plans change, love." He threw our gun cases in the back and kissed me on the cheek. He did that a lot lately. Like even a few minutes without touching was unbearable.

I frowned. "We had a plan. I got one shot at Rocci and handled the rest."

He sighed, heading back towards the house to get the rest of our equipment. Sean had everything we needed, but Darragh insisted we bring our own. I wasn't sure if it was out of mistrust, or if he was just attached to his own guns.

"The layout Sean provided changes things. The best way to pull this off is for you to take out Lucien while I operate from another area and go after Sean. He won't be expecting anything if I'm supposed to be on the roof across the street with you."

I followed close behind, working double time to keep up with his long legs. "What if I miss my one shot?"

He turned around in the doorway. "You won't. And if you do, take another. You've been training for this. Lucien's on you."

Lucien's on you. I fumbled the words over in my head on the car ride down. For months, years, it was a dream of mine, finally getting my revenge and bringing justice for Paulina. So, I wasn't sure why felt so nervous. I'd trained everyday with the rifle. I got good. Even Darragh had to admit I was one of the better shots he'd seen. I could do this. I wanted this. But it didn't stop the anxiety brewing out of control in my chest.

Surely, a large part of that had to do with the first part of the mission— meeting my father-in-law.

I tried not to react when Darragh said our accommodations for the night would be the O'Callaghan Hotel. As far as I knew, any Delarosa's who went inside the place didn't live to tell the tale. Nobody but Darragh and Rory knew who I really was, but that didn't ease my fears. Not while Sean O'Callaghan was still alive.

Darragh and I had been walking a fine and dangerous line. The reality of it didn't hit while we were tucked safely away in the mountains, but now, as we coasted through the crowded Manhattan streets, it hit like a brick wall.

The O'Callaghan Hotel was massive, luxurious and looming. The golden light of the hotel's sign covered the sidewalk, illuminating every feature of those who dared to step inside. People in all manners of dress covered the sidewalk, gazing up at the monstrosity or happily stepping inside towards the grand, spanning lobby. Darragh and I sat in the car, watching little snowflakes flutter down from the street.

"Your name?" He asked me for the hundredth time.

"Annie McCormick," I breathed. The weight of what we were about to do squeezed all the air from my lungs.

"Where are you from, Annie?" He fumbled with a pistol beside me, screwing on a silencer and tucking it into the waistband of his dress pants.

"Boston. My parents are from the Northern Coast of Ireland. I did a few years of college in Dublin before getting recruited by the IRA and getting involved in gun-running."

He pulled on a thick pair of leather gloves. "And how'd we meet?"

"The Lombardo hit in '87. I sold them their guns, you recruited me instead of killing me."

"Good. And the final touch." Darragh held out a pair of silky, red gloves. They perfectly matched the sleek, maroon gown I currently wore, entirely ridiculous for the weather. The left glove had been outfitted with a special accommodation, a soft, round block in the pinky finger so my missing one wouldn't be apparent. I had several pairs of dressing gloves and thick, winter ones just like them.

I slipped on the gloves and adjusted the collar of my massive fur coat. The diamonds dripping from my neck— all real— along with the weight of my curly updo seemed to drag me down. *I can do this.* I repeated the words as Darragh opened the passenger side and offered me his hand. His own black suit was sharp and fitting. The wedding band on his left hand flashed in the streetlights as he pulled me from the car. *In two days, we'll be safe.*

Darragh waved his hand at a boy smoking a cigarette on the sidewalk. His brown eyes went wide, the cigarette dropping from his lips to the snow as he scrambled across the street to our car. Once we entered the lobby, it was easy to tell who was a guest and who was undercover, providing security for the mob. In a blink, about thirty sharply dressed men stiffened and pretended to look anywhere but us.

The bellhop nearly pissed himself as we approached the elevator and Darragh gruffly said, "The penthouse." He cast his eyes to the ground when I tried to look at him, staring directly ahead and shaking instead.

I crossed my arms when the elevator doors shut in front of us. "Are they afraid of you or me?"

He smirked, pulling out a cigarette and lighting it. "Both."

I frowned. "I thought no one knew who I was."

He shrugged, waving the little matchstick in his hand to a puff of smoke. "I may have made some threats about looking at my wife at the casino."

I raised an eyebrow. "I thought those guys were all your men? Why would anyone down here know about that?"

"Word gets around, love. And it doesn't matter if they're loyal to me or Sean, it's still one mob." He took a long drag of his cigarette. "We're assuming Sean knows you exist and has done thorough research, so be careful with your lines."

A throbbing pain suddenly erupted in my head. It wasn't until a few days ago I learned my alias— Annie McCormick— was, in fact, a living breathing person. Emphasis on *was*. Any information on her life up until she was killed in a shootout a few years ago was to be known, studied and perfected. Even though Sean knew Annie was an associate— he had to in order to clear both Darragh and I with FBI . . . which took damn long enough if you asked me, we still weren't sure if he knew the two of us were married. Darragh wanted to be sure I knew my lines in case Sean decided to do his own research on Annie to make sure she's— I'm— real now that I was officially *family*.

I drummed my gloved fingers on the elevator's railing, trying not to panic.

The elevator chimed and we both straightened. The door slid open and Darragh held his arm out for me to take. I draped myself across his elbow, counting my breaths, praying Darragh didn't get his inherent ability to read minds from his father. Three men with guns stood at the entrance of the elevator, nodding at

Darragh as we walked past. The short, golden hallway soon emptied out into a massive room complete with a skylight and floor-to-ceiling windows. Furniture carved from mahogany with gold and red cushions stood over an enormous Persian rug. Paintings I'm pretty sure belonged to the Louvre covered the walls and a spanning, crystal bar took up the back part of the room. The Irish loved to say the Italians were the flashy, gaudy ones, but I wasn't so sure. It was clear why everyone referred to Sean as the Kingpin—he clearly lived like one.

Four men were barely visible through the thick haze of cigar smoke. They sat on the lavish couches, an array of files, guns and whiskey glasses scattering the elegant coffee table between them. One I recognized immediately, mostly from the bright, red hair. Rory glanced up and waved happily at me, a cigar bobbing between his teeth.

The other three men were lost on me. Two were younger, tall and thin with raven black hair like Darragh's. The last was who I could only assume was Sean.

I wasn't sure what I expected when I saw him. Claws, horns, a nasty facial scar at the least? The O'Callaghan name was a curse in my childhood home. Darragh and Sean's, blasphemy to even think of. But even when my family spoke of Darragh, there was an element of respect among the fear and anger. When they spoke of Sean, they spoke of pure evil. A conniving *bastardo* who killed seemingly for sport. A dirty manipulator who made the devil seem like a good friend. They clinked their glasses to the death of Darragh O'Callaghan. They spoke in hushed whispers of who would exorcise the demon inhabiting Sean.

Yet, there were no horns, tails or claws to speak of. In fact, had I seen Sean on the street, I may have thought of him as a very normal, middle-aged man. Darragh looked a lot like him, though much more handsome than his father. The face was nearly the same, but for a nose that'd been broken too many times and skin bearing the brunt of the lifestyle he chose. A thick crop of gray and white hair covered his head over steel-blue eyes, chipped harder than ice.

He offered me a humorless grin and stood, holding out his hand. The smile looked all wrong on him, like he wasn't human, just merely pretending to be.

"I assume this is my lovely new daughter-in-law my son decided to hide from me."

Oh, you have no idea. I held out a gloved hand, allowing him to kiss the top. I resisted the urge to shiver as his lips came away and his soulless eyes met mine. "It's a pleasure. I've heard much of you and your family."

Sean smirked. "So proper. Your education in Dublin was well worth the cost."

My smile faltered before I could collect myself. We expected this, but it was still jarring. Sean had done his homework.

Darragh glanced between us with a bored expression. "Annie, this is my Da, Sean. Da, I'm assuming you already know who Annie is."

"I keep tabs on my children," was his only response. He drifted away from me like he was already bored, heading for the bar. I eyed him uneasily, wondering if he could sense all our plans and lies just by being near.

"Annie, you've already met my brother, Rory. And this is Finn and James. They work for us."

They work for us. If Sean found the wording strange, he didn't react. The old man came back to the group with a fresh cigar and a glass of whiskey in hand. I could use all the above right about now.

"So, Annie," Sean started. He clipped his cigar and popped it in his mouth. A snap of his fingers had a boy on the other side of the room running over with a chair. "Sit, sit," he insisted as the scraggly young boy, no older than fourteen, helped me into the chair.

"I have a few questions for my new daughter. To begin, how exactly did you meet my son?"

I launched into the made-up tale of how I was involved in the hit Darragh did last year. The lies came easy, easier than I expected. When Sean asked more questions, I was prepared to answer them. I even asked if he'd heard of my parents back in Northern Ireland. *I think there village was fairly close to you.*

Darragh gave me a small nod of approval from the window, where he looked out at the darkening sky solemnly. He twirled the glass of whiskey in his hand, pretending to be occupied with anything but this conversation.

Sean leaned back on the couch, his own glass in hand. I lost count of how many pours he gave himself after five or six, but it didn't seem to impair him much. Even with his relaxed stance I could see the muscles tensing under his jacket, ready to pounce at any moment.

"I hear you'll be aiding us on our . . . project."

I nodded. "Darragh thinks my expertise could be of use."

"Darragh thinks a lot of things." He winked. Darragh tensed by the window but said nothing.

I masked my frown with a cold smile. "As I'm sure you do, too."

He shrugged, releasing a dark chuckle. "That may be true. I certainly think . . . many things."

Darragh turned from the window, his face matching the confusion on mine. Sean only stared affectionately at his glass of whiskey, like it harbored all the secrets in the world. There were no other comments on whatever strange and cryptic line he just delivered.

"Rory, why don't you give your new sister a tour? I have some things to discuss with Darragh."

Rory plastered a pained grin on his face. "Sure thing, Da." I searched Darragh's face for any hints, signs, *anything*, but he was cold as stone.

I took Rory's arm and he guided me to the elevator. Just as we were about to step on, Darragh called out, "They were warned about what would happen if they look at my wife wrong."

I didn't know if it was a statement or a question. Rory gave him a mock salute. "I shall dig their graves myself."

I felt like I could breathe again the second the elevator doors closed.

I slumped down to a heap of red silk and diamonds. Rory gripped my shoulder, giving it a hard squeeze. "You did good, little Italian."

"What the fuck was *that?*" I huffed. Sure, Sean was strange, but things got *weird* at the end there.

Rory shrugged. "He's fucking nuts, who knows?"

I bit back a laugh, burying my face in my hands. "I can't believe we're doing this."

"Darragh has a plan. He always does. Just focus on the hit."

Darragh had a plan. A plan that even Rory didn't know the depths of. In truth, I probably didn't either. As insane as it made me, I trusted my husband though. If he said to get on a roof alone and shoot Lucien Rocci while he killed his father form another location . . . well, I'd do it.

I stood up as we reached the bottom floor and entered the bustling lobby. I worried I'd be overdressed for the Irish crowd, but if anything, my silk dress and fur coat looked drab next to some of these women.

We weaved our way through the crowd of glittering jewels, top hats and foreign textiles. I wasn't sure where we were going, but Rory was on a warpath. My legs barely kept up with his as he dragged me down a far corridor to an exit in the back.

We found ourselves in a snow-coated alley, teaming with garbage and ice. Smoke from the kitchen wafted out an open window, letting the sounds of clanging pots and pans and frantic waiters fill the night.

"Couldn't talk in there," Rory said, lighting a cigarette. He shot me a careless grin. "How've ya been?"

I frowned. "Good?" I gestured around at the alley. "Why are we outside?"

"Like I said, couldn't talk in there." He offered me his arm again. "Let's walk."

I glanced uneasily at the building. Darragh made it very clear I couldn't leave. We were deep in O'Callaghan territory, but on the slim chance I was recognized—

"We're not going far. C'mon, this is important."

I gave him a reluctant sigh and took my brother-in-law's arm. If this was something about Sean, I'd better listen.

We emerged on a crowded street, thick with holiday decorations, tourists, taxis, businessmen huffing heat into their palms and everything in between. It was so overwhelming in its chaos it was almost serene. The lights of Times Square flickered from three blocks away as we headed south. Stores pouring their goods onto the sidewalk glowed in the snowy night as steam rolled up through the subway grates and vendors yelled about fifty cent hot dogs. The skyscrapers crowded around us, so massive it looked like they could topple over onto our heads. From here, we could even see the massive World Trade Center on the south of the island. The city grew up, out and was stuffed with every imaginable thing. For someone who spent their whole life here, it was strange how little I'd experienced it.

I tossed a glance over my shoulder at 41st street, like I could see down the hundred blocks or so and recognize my old life. The multi-million dollar house planted squarely in the upper west side that was my prison for twenty-two years.

I was too mesmerized to realize Rory was guiding me towards a nondescript cafe that you'd miss if you blinked. The name of it was Chinese in glowing, red lights. The little room we stepped into was warm, small and occupied by no one but three older men playing a game in the back corner.

Rory ordered us tea and sat down at a little table, facing the door. His eyes darted back and forth with every person passing the foggy window.

"All the rooms are bugged," he said.

I crossed my arms. "I know." Darragh warned me most of the rooms in the hotel had wires, even ours. Only the top people in the mob knew, though some had to suspect. There was a reason any politicians, celebrities or high-profile businessmen suddenly found themselves being blackmailed after a stay at the O'Callaghan.

Rory smiled, thanking our waitress in another language as she settled a steaming pot of tea on the table. "Drink," he said.

I shook my head. "I'm—"

"Look normal, please."

It was probably the most serious thing he'd ever said to me. I sighed, pouring myself a cup. I held the little ceramic cup in my hand, grateful for the steam on my freezing face.

"I did you a favor, but no one can know. Not even Darragh. I broke a lot of rules here, so don't throw me under the fucking bus, capeesh?"

I nodded. "Sure."

He glanced around and leaned forward. "Last week, our boys cornered a few members of the Delarosa's. Caught them trying to raid one of our gun stocks in the harbor. Your brother was one of them."

My heart dropped to my stomach. "Which brother?"

He grimaced. "Andrea."

My vision darkened. Andrea. Was he—

"He's okay," Rory rushed. "The boys brought him back. Sean wanted to kill him but I convinced him keeping him locked up for info was the better move. They're hiding him on 51st street."

I gripped my teacup so hard it was a wonder it didn't shatter. "Is he okay?"

Rory shrugged apologetically. "A bit beat up, but he'll live. Sean's not concerned with moving him until after the hit is dealt with. Darragh doesn't know he's down there and he doesn't need to know, he'll beat my ass for making it seem like I have any Delarosa sympathies with Sean." Rory leaned back. "That's the best I can do, though. I'm assuming whatever plan Darragh has for making sure Sean doesn't kill you can extend to your brother as well."

I nodded, trying to steady my breathing. Right, everything would be fine. When Sean was dead Darragh would be in charge and he'd let Andrea go. If anything, this might be a good thing. It'll only strengthen Darragh's act of good faith and plan for an alliance.

Rory gripped my shaking wrist. "You alright?"

"Yeah, fine." I waved him off. No, I was not fucking okay. This wasn't supposed to happen. And what the hell was Andrea thinking, raiding an Irish warehouse? He was smarter than that, goddammit.

"We should get back," Rory said.

"I want to see him."

Rory stared at me like I was speaking in tongues.

I gripped his wrist. "Please, just let me see him. Tonight, after everyone's gone to sleep."

"It's not so simple—"

"He's my brother." I took a deep breath. "You'd ask the same if it was Darragh."

Rory sighed, hanging his head in defeat. "I'll see what I can do, but no promises. And no word about this to Darragh, okay? If, and this is a huge *if,* I can get you down to see him, expect it to be around three or four. Don't go to sleep."

I nodded. "Thank you."

"You owe me, sis."

I shook my head, pulling my coat on. "Who doesn't owe an O'Callaghan?"

33

PINA

Rory gave me a tour of the hotel, got us a few drinks and took me to my room. Several more hours passed before Darragh finally emerged, jaw set and eyes narrowed.

I jumped in the bathroom mirror as he appeared silently behind me, gripping my waist and burying his face in the crook of my neck. I scanned his white dress shirt for blood, but of that, he was clear.

"That bad, huh?" I whispered.

"We'll talk later," he breathed. He reached for the lacy hem of my nightgown, pulling it up my thighs. I shivered as his hands ran over my stomach and came up to cup my breasts.

"Not now?" I asked. I glanced pointedly in the mirror towards the bedroom, asking but not asking. I wasn't sure if this behavior was because the room was bugged to hell or Darragh really, really missed me. If it was the first and not the latter, I didn't exactly love the idea of any Made Men listening in on whatever Darragh had in mind.

He sighed and dropped my nightgown, shutting the bathroom door. He peeled off his expensive clothes and kicked them across the floor while he started up the shower. My mouth watered at the sight, but I reminded myself that his literal father could hear everything we were doing. Not my cup of tea, thank you.

He pulled the nightgown over my head and growled in approval. I swallowed as his thick erection bobbed between us.

"Shower. Now," he ordered, smacking my ass. All reason fled my brain.

The second I stepped in the shower Darragh had me pinned against the wall. His mouth brushed against the column of my neck as steam roiled around us.

"They can hear us," I whispered.

"Let them," he growled. His hands tightened on my waist and he hoisted me up, pressing my back into the tiles and wrapping my legs around his waist.

"That's what I'm counting on, actually." He shoved two fingers deep inside me. "Scream for me, love."

I had countless reservations about this plan, but I didn't need to fake the loud moan that echoed through the shower. Darragh pumped his fingers in and out, hard and fast. I tried to bite back the moans but my body wasn't having it. I rolled on top of him, needing to feel him fill me up deeper.

He wrenched his hand away and shoved his cock in. I screamed his name, panting heavily as he bounced me up and down against the wall.

His lips came back to my throat, caressing the shell of my ear. "Keep going, love." He shoved himself deep and I nearly broke. "He's made a bit of a mess of things in my absence. We'll have a lot of cleaning up to do after tomorrow night. The blood feuds have gotten worse."

I gripped onto his shoulders, half gasping and half whispering, "Sean?"

He grabbed my chin and forced me to look at him. "I don't want another man's name on your lips when I'm fucking you."

I nodded, gasping for air when he reached down to rub my clit and continued his thrusts. "Darragh— fuck."

He ran his tongue up the side of my throat. "We'll talk more when we have the chance."

I nodded again, panting. We could wait two days for the coast to be clear. Besides, I didn't think I had it in me to continue this conversation with Darragh moving me like this.

After the shower he took me to the bed. I didn't know how Darragh had this much freaking stamina but it never seemed to be enough, not that I was complaining. He pulled me tight against him, nuzzling his face into my hair and whispering something in Gaelic I couldn't even begin to decipher. A few moments later, he was asleep.

The next two hours were endless. I kept glancing at the door, wondering if Rory would show or not. When the bedside clock read 3:12, a note slipped under the door.

I carefully peeled Darragh off me and pulled on some clothes. When I softly opened the door and slipped to the other side, Rory was waiting, a finger pressed to his lips.

———————

Even at this hour, the hotel bar still crawled with patrons while a live band blasted music into the lobby. The streets were packed with people and cars. It really was the city that never sleeps.

Rory instructed me to pull the hood of my parka low over my face and walk with him. We looked like nothing more than a drunk pair of friends bracing the cold and stumbling home, but my heart hammered in my chest each time we passed a man in a suit.

"You'll only have a few minutes," he murmured, each word puffing clouds of condensation into the air. The wind picked up, burning every inch of skin not covered in thick clothing.

"That's all I need," I whispered. The rest of the walk was silent as we travelled up Broadway, passing block after block until Rory finally turned onto 51st.

The building we came to a halt in front of had seen better days. Construction signs and broken sidewalk littered the front, clearly stating the building was about to be condemned and no trespassers were allowed. I stared at the shattered glass of what used to be a front door, wondering just how long my brother had been forced to stay here.

Rory grabbed my shoulders, turning my attention back to him. For the second time this night, he looked completely serious and so unlike himself.

"We have things to discuss," he said.

I glanced around. No one was here, but that meant very little in the world of deceit. "We can discuss whatever you want after New Year's."

Rory gripped me fiercely, eyes turning wide and a little crazy. "This can't wait. I think my Da plans to take out Darragh."

I nodded. "Darragh already knows that."

"Soon," he whispered. He glanced around nervously before turning back to me. "After the hit on Rocci. I think he's going to use him for that and then be done with him."

I bit my lip. "We already figured that too. We have a plan—"

"What plan?"

I sighed. A plan Rory was supposed to know nothing about, just in case he had reservations about his father's murder. "I can't tell you right now. Just trust me, we're handling it."

Rory stepped back, a pained expression barely masked on his face. "You're turning out to be just like him."

"Is that such a bad thing?" I hissed. I didn't have time for this. Neither did he. I wanted to see Andrea, and after that, it was rushing back to the hotel before anyone realized we were gone.

"You're going to get yourself killed." He breathed deep through his nose, calming the rage filling his eyes. "Did Darragh ever tell you how our older brothers were killed?"

I sighed, glancing at the door. "We don't have time—"

"We do. Tell me."

I didn't like this serious Rory. The scared one. Any semblance of his happy-go-lucky attitude died as he stared at me.

"A car accident. Wrong place, wrong time."

"It wasn't an accident," Rory snapped. The air around us suddenly got colder. "Darragh has no clue, but I was there. Sean takes out anyone who threatens him, and he does it well enough

275

that no one knows he's the one who screwed everyone to hell." He took a deep breath. "He's trying to convince Darragh he's unhinged. That he hasn't been able to handle the business. It's all a part of the game and you've just started learning how to play. I can't get anywhere near Darragh without someone noticing so I'm trusting you to watch his ass."

The reality of it hit like a punch to the gut. I'd placed so much faith in Darragh I forgot how powerful the other players were. The players who taught him everything he knows.

"Why have you never told him?" I asked.

He shook his head. "Darragh's been through enough. He lost our Ma and I lost our brothers. They're our own burdens to bear."

Maybe, Rory wasn't as happy-go-lucky as I originally thought.

I shook my head. "I'll do what I can, but we're running out of time."

He nodded in agreement and pulled me toward the door.

The lobby of what looked to be an old office building was scattered with construction debris and broken glass. A few empty beer bottles and discarded cigarette butts littered the floor, covered with dust. Rory led me to a stairwell in the back and we climbed three stories. In the upstairs hall, the darkness was suffocating as we wound our way through broken desks and chairs, the only light coming from the bright, winter moon pouring through the windows.

We reached a room on the other side of the floor. It was so dark I didn't notice the two men with guns keeping watch until they were directly on top of us.

Cold metal pressed to my forehead.

"Stop, it's me," Rory said. He pulled down his hood so the guards could see.

"No one's allowed in here. Sean's orders."

"Yeah, well I'm still your fucking boss." He shoved the barrel pointed at my head to the side. "She's a doctor, let her in."

"Sean said—"

"Sean said to keep him alive long enough for questioning. Or do you want me to tell him you two are the assholes that beat the Delarosa to death."

My pulse fluttered in my neck. Rory said he was okay. A little beaten up, but okay. I waited for the guards to deny it, say that Andrea was fine and didn't even need a doctor, but they didn't. Instead, they stepped to the side, letting me pass.

"Go downstairs and watch the front. I'll keep an eye on her."

I barely heard their retreating footsteps as I laid a hand on the cold, wooden door to the office they were guarding. It was freezing cold in here. Dirty. How long had Andrea been kept like this?

Ten minutes, Rory mouthed. He pulled a revolver from his waistband and stood next to the door.

It opened with a gentle push, the lock long gone. There was nothing inside the room but more broken glass and debris. The broken window filtered moonlight into a small patch of dirty carpet. In that little strip of light, my brother slept in handcuffs, curled up on his side.

He was ten months older than me, but now he looked like a small child. The right side of his face had been bloodied beyond recognition, the left unseen where his skin dug into the dirty carpet. He shook in the cold air, pale skin on full display despite the fact it had to be below freezing in here. They didn't even give him a shirt. His bruised and bloodied chest heaved small, painful breaths.

I blinked back heavy tears. Sean would pay. He would pay fucking dearly for this.

I knelt beside him and laid a hand on his arm. His eyes opened in a flash, the light brown color we shared now drained and lifeless. He stared at me like he couldn't figure out if I was real or just another part of this nightmare.

"I was hoping they'd send you," he whispered.

I took a shaky breath, rubbing warmth into his arm. He felt colder than ice. "Who?"

"Death," he said. "Though I doubt I'm going where you are."

"Oh, Andrea." I couldn't stop the tears from brimming over. "You're not dead. Neither am I."

His dull eyes stared at me again, searching my face. "They sent your finger. Hair."

I pulled off one thick glove, showing him my missing finger. "I had no choice."

He sat up, staring at my hand. The cuffs at his hands and feet clinked. "You're not dead?"

I shook my head, biting my lip. I was afraid if I tried to speak, the tears would come and never stop.

"You're not dead," he repeated, tears filling his own eyes. He reminded me so much of Rory. Much too good for our world. If I thought he looked like a child before, it was even worse as tears streamed down his cheeks and he leaned forward, resting his cheek on my shoulder and sobbing into my coat.

"No," I bit out. I peeled off my coat and wrapped it around him. It was way too small and he was cuffed, but it was something. I wrapped my arms around his back, wondering how I could forget what it felt like to hug my brother. My shadow. The person I'd been inseparable from since the day I was born. My mother once told me Andrea would cry all night if I wasn't in the room with him. They put our cribs two feet apart. We were blood and so much more.

"You're getting out of here soon. I promise," I whispered, stroking his back. He shivered beneath my arms, shaking his head.

"How?"

"I don't have a ton of time to explain." I glanced at the open door. Rory could hear everything, so I had to be careful what I said.

"Are they holding you too?" I turned back to Andrea, the concern in his face nearly shattering me to bits.

278

"No," I whispered. "I have a deal worked out. It'll all make sense soon, I promise."

"A deal?" He glanced around like whoever I spoke of was about to appear from the walls. "A deal with who?"

"The Irish."

"You made a deal with the *Irish*—"

"One of them," I rushed. "I made a deal with one of them and soon it will all be worked out."

"Who?" He seethed. He peered through the doorway, right where Rory's shadow stained the ground. "Pina, what the hell did you do?"

"I'm trying to keep our *famiglia* safe," I said. "The blood feud has gone on too long. The Irish, Lucien, they'll kill us all. After tomorrow night we won't have to worry about that anymore."

He tensed. "How?"

I took a deep breath. "A marriage. We'll have an alliance with the Irish and Lucien will be dead."

"You—*what*—" His jaw set so hard the sound of his teeth cracking filled the room. His dull, brown eyes suddenly burned with fury. "Who the fuck are you marrying, Pina?"

Now would probably not be the best time to mention Darragh's name. Every night sitting in my room, ear pressed to the wall while the men discussed the Irish *Demone* came flooding back with a vengeance.

"You have to trust me."

"What happened?" The fury died and his face broke all over again. "What happened to you, Pina? We all thought you were dead. I thought they tortured you—"

"Nobody tortured me," I breathed. I wrapped my brother in my arms. "I'm safe, see? Better than ever."

"How can you be better? What did they do, force you, blackmail you?"

"None of that," I sighed. I didn't know how much time had passed, but I had to be close to running out of it. Rory's shadow danced nervously against the floor.

"After the engagement to Rocci I tried to kill myself. One of them found me, saved me and offered me a way out. I've been staying with him. He's been training me. I can protect myself now." I pulled up my shirt, showing the gun in the waistband of my pants. "I'm going to kill Lucien Rocci myself. We got married in secret, and when Lucien is dead we'll come clean and make sure the O'Callaghan's and the Delarosa's stick to the code. Nobody else gets hurt."

Andrea stared at the gun in disgust. "What did they do to you?"

"He saved me," I gritted. "Lucien would have killed me, we all know that. I'm fine where I am now. Happy, even. This is better for everyone, I promise you."

"Better? For who?" An ugly laugh escaped his lips, making me cringe. "We've been fighting ever since the day you left for your *better* life. The streets have run red, Pina, fucking red with Delarosa blood. We thought you were murdered. We were trying to avenge you."

"I never asked for any of you to avenge me," I snapped. The tone in my brother's voice was scary, hysterical. I'd never heard him like this before. Especially not with me. "Nobody avenged Paulina. In fact, father decided to marry me off to her murderer."

"The maid? That's what this is all about?"

I sucked in a sharp, angry breath. "*The maid* was Paulina. My best friend and a good friend to you, too. You of all people should have some respect for that."

"She wasn't blood," he growled. "You are. You're the Delarosa Daughter. We honor *you*. And all you've done is honor the fucking Irish and a nineteen-year-old maid."

My hands shook violently. I let them drop from Andrea's shoulders. We were running out of time. We could hash this all out when he was safe and Lucien and Sean were dead.

"I can't do this right now, Andrea." Rory's shadow flickered closer on the floor. The silhouette of his gun waved in the doorway. Time was up. "The alliance is happening. I'm married.

Lucien will be a threat no longer. Just hold on for another day and we'll be safe. Father, Mother and Alessandro included."

Andrea laughed. It was honestly the ugliest sound I'd ever heard. He howled, gripping the carpet threads in his hand as blood gushed from a wound on his chest.

I scowled. "What?"

"They're dead."

I must have heard that incorrectly. "What?"

"They're dead," he gritted out. He faced me again, nothing but anger and hatred in his gaze. "Not father, but he's dying. It started after mother. After your *husband* sent your finger back, she took one too many pills. We found her on the bathroom floor."

Blood roared in my ears. "And Alessandro?"

"They killed him and captured me." He coughed as hysterical laughter overtook him again, splattering blood onto the carpet. "Father doesn't have long, Pina. I'm the last one left."

I didn't have time to process it. Any of it. My whole family was dead. Father, Alessandro . . . we never got along, but they were family. And mother was a victim just as much as me. A woman born to the wrong bloodline.

I blinked back tears. There was no time to dwell on it. I had a hit to focus on, we had to go back to the hotel, and I had to protect Andrea.

"You're not the last one. I'm here. We're here. Everything is going to be okay."

"Fuck you, Giuseppina."

I reeled back, the sharp sting of his words burning more than a backhand to the face ever could.

"Andrea—"

"Our family is dead because of you. All because you couldn't suck it up and do as you were told. We've all lived and died by honoring this family. You've done nothing but destroy us."

Heat crawled up my neck. I flexed my fingers, red dotting my vision. "You decided you weren't my family the day you sent me off to die."

"At least you would have died with a shred of fucking honor. At least your family would still be alive."

He was hurting. He was sick and cold and everything was fucked, but we'd fix it later. We had to.

I stood up. "I'll be back soon. Just wait a little longer."

I'd just reached the door when his voice called out behind me, "Don't bother."

I whipped around, fingering the edge of my sleeve. "Don't bother what?"

"There'll be no alliance, Pina. The Delarosa's are dead."

I blinked, fighting back the tears burning behind my eyes. "There's still the two of us."

He shook his head. "You're dead to me, too."

The tears fell now, unstoppable and hot and heavy. Rory grabbed my arm on the other side of the door and led me down the hall. I could barely see through the darkness and sobs, so even though there was no doubt Rory heard everything, I was still grateful he was here. We passed the guards at the bottom silently while Rory waved them back inside. I wanted to tell them to keep Andrea more comfortable— doctor's orders— but I couldn't will the sounds out of my throat.

"He'll be okay. You just need to focus on tomorrow. The rest we'll deal with afterwards."

I nodded my head, holding onto those words even as they slipped through my fingers. Because even as I clung to the hope I hadn't made the biggest mistake of my life, I knew those words of comfort were just as dead as the rest of my family.

34

DARRAGH

The room was dark and quiet. Too quiet. I knew the sound of Pina's breathing better than my own, and the soft sounds that followed her into sleep were noticeably absent. The space next to me on the bed, cold.

I sat up, eyes adjusting to the darkness immediately as I ran for the bathroom. She wasn't there, and she wasn't in our room.

I swallowed as panic began to take over. There were only so many places she could go in the hotel. Maybe she just woke up and needed air or something to drink. But intuition had kept me alive this long, and my gut was saying something was definitely fecking wrong.

I pulled on my pants and threw a shirt on, not bothering to button it up. I slung my pistol holder over my back and stormed into the hall. There was nothing but bright, synthetic lights in either direction. I stormed to the end of the hall, where a nodding out Kieran stood to attention, gun slung loosely across his chest.

"Have you seen Annie?"

He shook his head. "I just got here an hour ago, but she didn't come this way."

Shit. This was the only exit off this floor, and if Kieran hadn't seen her . . .

I stumbled down to the hotel lobby. At this hour, everyone was either too drunk or too tired to care what I looked like. The clock above the desk read 4:38 AM. Pina had been missing since at least 3:30 in the morning.

I scoured the hotel bar, the restaurant, ballroom, even the damn alleyway, but she was nowhere to be seen. I couldn't stop the panic now, the rage filling my head. Like a complete fecking idiot, I'd taken her to a hotel full of people who wanted her dead. Somehow, without me even noticing, she was gone.

If something happened to her—

Before I could even think of what I was doing, I found myself in the elevator, pressing in the keys to take me to the top floor. If Pina was gone, there could be only one explanation. That explanation was about to have the barrel of my gun shoved down his throat, consequences be fecking damned.

Sean was passed out on his couch, an empty glass of whiskey and a snuffed cigar in his outstretched hand. The guards at the top of the elevator didn't stop me, only giving one another a side eye as I told each of them to get out. The hall cleared and I stormed down, eyes set on the person I hated most.

Sean's eyes snapped open before I even reached him. He wasn't quick enough, reaching for his gun as I grabbed his shirt and yanked him nose to nose. *"Where is she?"*

I couldn't tell if it was sleep, drunkenness or confusion written all over his face. His hand hovered at his waistband, fingers twitching. His expression cleared and he raised an eyebrow. "Who?"

"Annie."

My heated breath was the only thing that passed between us. No one else was here, Pina included, but that didn't mean anything. He could have brought her anywhere. There was no way to know if he found out the truth or this was just another way to toy with me, but either way, she was gone and there was only one person in this building with the balls to cross me.

The corner of his lips curled into a half-smile. "Haven't seen her."

"I'm not fecking around," I huffed. I yanked him closer, the smell of his whiskey breath turning up my nose. "Where the feck is she?"

His eyes narrowed into slits. This was no longer entertaining to him. I didn't care. If he did something to her, I'd kill him right fecking now.

"Darragh."

Sean and I both snapped to the hall. Rory stood with hands out like I was a wild animal. "Darragh, what are you doing?"

"Where is she?" I grit out.

He gave me a pained smile. "She couldn't sleep. I took her down to the bar for a few drinks. She's back at your room now."

My fingers uncurled one at a time from Sean's shirt. The old man fell back to the couch with a huff, a full-blown shit-eating grin on his face. "Maybe you should worry less about me, and a little more about what your brother is doing with your wife, boy."

The temptation to pistol whip him was at an all-time high. I may have done it, too, if Rory didn't step forward and say, "Don't put any weird ideas in his head, Da. Annie is a sister to me, Darragh knows that."

He took another tentative step down the hall. "She's a bit drunk, you might want to check on her."

I gave Sean one more murderous look and stepped away from the couch. He had nothing to do with it, but Rory was a fecking liar if I'd ever seen one. He rightfully earned the new place of enemy number one in my head, but I was more concerned with what Pina was doing. I pushed past him as he went to Sean and stormed down the hall.

I hit the button for the elevator with all the pent-up rage I had. The chiming bell of the doors opening almost covered the soft sound of my Da calling my name.

I took a deep breath, not turning around. "What?"

A beat of silence passed. "You ever pull some shit like that again, I'll shove my pistol down your throat. You understand, boy?"

I nodded to nothing but the open elevator. "Understood."

285

Outside our room, I leaned my forehead against the cool wooden door. I wasn't sure who I was angrier with, Rory, Pina or myself. My reaction had jumped the gun, and I'd given two vital things away. One, I actually cared for Pina. With that knowledge, Sean would no doubt try to use it against me. Two, I was hiding something. Sean had no reason to suspect anything was off. Now he did.

I punched one hard fist into the door and grunted. Such a fecking idiot. He probably knew the whole time Pina was off with Rory and I walked right into it.

The sound of soft sobs dropped the second I pushed through the door. It was dark, but Pina's silhouette sat up in bed, gripping the comforter harder than I punched the door.

I battled back and forth on what to do next. I was angry. She left, it was dangerous, and I specifically told her not to. On the other hand, she was crying when I walked in, and now that I stood in the doorway, she was eerily silent.

I gripped onto the edge of the door and waited for her to say something. She always spoke first, which I hadn't realized until now made my life a lot easier. It was always good to know what you were walking into.

She didn't speak now. I shut the door softly behind me. Before I could flip the light on, her voice came out, soft, slow and terrifying, "Did you know?"

I leaned against the door. "Know . . . ?"

"About my family."

My eyebrows scrunched together. Did she think I was someone else? Yeah, I knew all about her family. Lorenzo Delarosa, Alessandro, Andrea, the whole fecking brood.

"Did. You. Know?" Her voice went down an octave, taking on an icy chill.

I walked toward the bed, moving to sit beside her but she stood up and pushed me away. My back hit the wall, not expecting her tiny hands to shove me as hard as they did.

I gripped her wrists and pulled them away. "Know what? I don't know what the hell you're talking about."

"Don't lie to me." Something shattered against the ground, but it was too dark to see what it was. "You know everything about the business, everything that's going on, so don't tell me for a goddamn second you didn't know."

I gripped her and pulled her close. She thrashed in my arms, so I clenched her tight to my chest. She screamed, and it was only then I remembered the damn wire in the room.

"I don't know what you're talking about but let's figure it out somewhere else."

She snorted, still trying to wrench free. "I found the bug ten minutes ago. It's gone."

I sucked in a deep breath, trying not to let my anger show when clearly we already had enough of that in the room. "Pina, that's going to look very fecking suspicious."

"So let it!" She threw her body to the side, breaking my grip.

I tried to reach for her again, but she fell to the bed in a heap of sobs.

"They're all dead," she whimpered.

I sat beside her, not attempting to touch her this time. "Who?"

She pulled her hands away from her face and hissed, "My family."

Ice shot through my veins. What did she mean, *her family*? Her whole family, one person? If the O'Callaghan's had something to do with it, I'd know.

I gripped her hand in mine, squeezing softly. "Is it Andrea? Did something happen?"

She laughed, the sound only broken by the occasional sob. "Andrea is being held on 51st street by your father. But Alessandro, my mother? Both dead, and apparently my father has very little time left."

She turned to me, glittery tears glinting in the dark. "If you knew, Darragh, if you had any part in this— I'll kill you myself."

I shook my head, hand slipping from hers. "That's not possible."

"It is," she snapped. "Rory knew. He took me to see Andrea tonight. He told me himself."

A low growl emanated in the back of my throat. "Rory took you *where?*"

"You're not my fucking keeper," she snapped. She stood up, pacing back and forth in front of me. "Andrea was at one of your gun warehouses and Rory convinced Sean to let him live. Alessandro is dead and my mother died days after you sent—" She stopped talking, stopped pacing. She stared at the wall, lost in the image of something I couldn't see.

"Pina." I stood slowly, wrapping my hands around her forearms. The gaze she gave me was empty and that was the scariest thing of all.

"I didn't know," I whispered. The wire may have been gone, but who knew who was listening through the walls. "I swear on my fecking mother's soul I didn't know. I don't know how Sean managed to keep this from me, and the fact that he did means we're in a lot more fecking trouble than I thought."

She bit her lip, eyes darting back and forth. My eyes adjusted now, taking in the way her hair captured the little bit of moonlight coming through the window, the streaky red of her cheeks, the small bleeding wound on her lip where she kept biting it.

I gripped her tighter, forcing her to look at me. "I didn't know."

She shook her head, more tears coming to the surface. "You know every—"

"I didn't know." I took a deep breath. "But Sean knows something that I don't."

Her eyes widened, real fear in them now. "Do you think he knows who I am?"

288

I shook my head. There was always the possibility, but I had my doubts. He would have killed us both the second we walked through the door. "No, I highly doubt that."

"Then what?"

I had the sudden urge to bite my own lips. I never got nervous, not since I was kid, but this new development sent me on edge. We were in danger. *Pina* was in danger, and I had no bloody clue where to begin sorting out this mess. Sean was playing me, and I'd been too goddamn distracted these past few months to even notice.

"You don't know," she whispered. It wasn't a question.

"We'll figure it out." I pulled her against me, resting my cheek on her hair. The scent of her was like medicine, instantly calming.

"This isn't going to end well."

"It'll end fine."

"No, Darragh." Hot, tears fell onto my chest. "Andrea . . . Andrea he—" She sucked in a shaky breath. "Fuck."

I smoothed her hair out along her back. "What?"

"There won't be any alliance," she whispered. "My brother hates me. The rest of my family is dead. He told me himself this would only end in blood. Even if we pull this off tomorrow, we'll have no allies, no friends. We made a mistake, Darragh. We really fucked up."

I wanted to tell her she was wrong, we didn't screw up, everything would be fine. And that may have been the truth if I didn't slip. I was never distracted like this. Never preoccupied. The entire time I'd been with Pina, Sean had been working hard right under my nose. The truth was, we didn't feck it up. I did.

"I have a plan," I lied. Her breath caught, like she was about to say something, but she didn't. She knew it was bullshit, but she wouldn't say. She'd put her trust in me one more time.

I didn't deserve her.

I brought her into the shower to wash off the tears and cold and blood I could only assume was her brother's. I had slow, quiet sex with her, laid in her bed, and pulled the curtains tight as the sun started rising on the horizon.

She slept deeply, like the weight of everything dragged her under and wouldn't let go. I couldn't say the same for myself as I stared at the ceiling, arm slung over my head.

I couldn't protect her. I'd just proven that, and not even with Sean hiding all this shit from me, but the way I reacted when she went missing, the fact I didn't even fecking realize she went missing. She was a distraction, a weakness, and it didn't matter how much I wanted to keep her around me. I couldn't.

Tomorrow, she would kill Lucien Rocci. I'd kill Sean O'Callaghan. After that, I was getting her on the next plane out of here with a new name, a new passport and a new life. I'd drug her and throw her on the damn thing myself if I had to. She'll hate me forever. She'd given me enough of her goddamn speeches about independence and being equals, but she'd never forgive me if I killed Andrea, and the second I released him he'd be gunning for her. Anyone else who realized the weakness she was to me would be too.

I was going to lose her. The only woman I've ever wanted to be with. The only woman I've ever cared about. Pina wasn't bad. She didn't deserve this. She deserved life, and I'd rather she hated my guts and lived to talk about it than watch her drown in the blood of my own mistakes.

I turned on my side, wrapping my arm around her and burying my face in her hair. She was beautiful, strong, passionate, and I lied that day in my kitchen, because she made the best goddamn wife in the world.

I regretted the day I saved her in that alley. I regretted taking her home. I should have known better. I shouldn't have let myself fall in love.

35

PINA

Today was the day.

The day I waited for the past three years.

The day I killed Lucien Rocci.

I pulled on my blood red, satin gloves and stared in the mirror. It was the same dress from the other night, the red one, but somehow I looked different. The diamond choker glinted at my neck, my hair pulled into an elaborate updo of curls with little diamond pins stuck throughout. Darragh said they looked beautiful. I picked them because they were another weapon to use.

Darragh came up behind me and wrapped his arms around my waist. He held one gloved hand in his palm, the left one with the fake pinky finger stuffed inside. He pulled my engagement ring and my wedding band from his pocket and slipped them one-at-a-time over the silky fabric.

His black tuxedo fit in all the right places, his normal five o'clock shadow neatly shaved. His black hair was gelled back and his blue eyes held the icy glint that once terrified me. I'd seen him with guns, I'd seen him kill, but it was in this moment he finally looked like a true Made Man to me.

He kissed the side of my neck. "*Bòidheach.*"

I smiled. "What does that mean?"

"Beautiful," he whispered, pressing a long, grazing kiss to my jawline. "If we had time, I'd teach you a few dirtier ones, too."

I smirked. "Save it for tomorrow. We'll have all the time in the world then."

He turned his face away, burying his lips into my diamond studded hair. "I'll hold you to it."

Down in the lobby, Rory waited for us in his own tux. He wouldn't be joining us tonight, but he was on back-up just in case. He gestured for us to follow him out to the street. A black Ferrari idled on the sidewalk.

Rory leaned down and kissed my cheek. "The trunk is loaded with all your shit. Be careful and don't fuck this up. And watch my little brother, he's an idiot."

I smiled and leaned back, offering him a little wink.

Darragh and Rory only nodded at each other.

I ran a silk glove over the dashboard. "I didn't think your family would drive Italian cars."

"We drive fast cars," he said. He tapped his fingers on the steering wheel. I must have been rubbing off on him. "And tonight, we're trying to blend in."

"But he knows we'll be there."

"He knows Sean will be there and a few others, but not me." He took a deep breath, gripping the steering wheel tighter. "I don't know if whatever Sean has planned is supposed to happen after tonight, but either way I don't want to take any chances. I spent all morning figuring out placements and here's what we're going to do."

I frowned. "Won't it look even more suspicious if we don't follow Sean's plan?"

"I don't care about suspicion, I care about getting this done as fast and efficiently as possible."

I side-eyed my husband. He gripped the steering wheel with ferocity, white knuckles tense against the leather. He was . . . nervous. He never got nervous. His own tense mood should have affected mine, but I couldn't let that get in the way now. We had a hit to complete.

I took a deep breath. "Okay, so what's the plan."

He careened around a taxi. A horn blared and lights flashed above us. "Originally, we were supposed to attend the party for an hour and a half, then excuse ourselves at 11:30 and get ready on the bank opposite *The Ritz*. From there, you were going to shoot Rocci and I was going to go back inside to find Sean at midnight."

I nodded. "Yes, okay. And now we're not doing that?"

He took a hard left, slamming on his horn as a group of tourists tried to walk in front of him. "I'm setting you up above the ballroom. I'll be on the floor with Sean when you target Lucien. I'll tell him the first location was discovered and use the chaos from your shot as cover."

My mouth went dry. "I have about three problems with your new and improved plan."

His eyebrow went up.

"One," I said, lifting up my pointer finger, "it's fast, sure, but efficient, no. Two, there's supposed to be somebody on the bank roof who radios Sean. He'll report if we're not there. Three, I'm not killing anyone from inside the hotel we have to clear. There'll be cops all over the place within minutes."

"Rory's working on that now."

I whirled on him. "Rory's in on this?"

"He knows what he needs to." He took a deep breath as we rolled to a stop in front of the hotel. A stiff valet with a thick mustache approached the window, but Darragh waved him past.

He turned to me. "Don't worry about Sean's men on the bank. I'll handle it. I know this isn't ideal and it's going to be a logistical nightmare getting out, but we've prepared for this and I'll do whatever I can. Sean can't know we're onto him. If he suspects we'll do anything tonight, he'll use this opportunity to bring us down. If I'm directly within Sean's sight, it'll be the only way to convince him we're still on his side."

I tapped my fingers on the door handle, trying to think of what to say. "Can you really kill your father, Darragh?"

His eyes narrowed to slits. "I've been waiting for this for a long time."

Our heavy breaths filled the empty space between us.

"There'll be witnesses," I said, "if you're standing right next to him."

He nodded. "Enough chaos on the ballroom floor and no one will notice at all. Get creative with it. I trust you."

I trust you. Three little words with infinite meaning.

I blinked. "We're not using the guns Sean supplied, right?"

The corner of his lips turned up. "Such a smart girl."

I swallowed. "So, the supplies?"

"Kieran's on it." He opened his door, letting an icy breeze blast inside. A moment later, my door opened and he stuck out his hand. "Are you ready, Mrs. O'Callaghan?"

I placed my hand in his. "Let's fucking do this."

We slid our venetian masks over our faces as we approached the hotel entrance. Darragh had chosen gold and white for me, a bejeweled and feathered monstrosity with actual diamonds hanging off little chains from the bottom edge. For himself, a black mask with gold embroidery that swooped up and covered half his forehead. I once called him the Angel of Death. Now we looked like both sides of that moniker.

The attendant at the door smiled. "Are you here for the masquerade?"

Darragh gave me a side-glance and I resisted the urge to laugh. He stayed silent and handed the attendant our invitations, each paper card engraved with what I could only assume was real gold. Lucien Rocci had so much money, he could literally dispose of it.

The attendant waved us through, not bothering to check if we were really James and Kaitlyn Ferguson. It would have been an easy catch, too, since the happy couple who would unfortunately be held up at a police stop all night were well over the age of fifty.

"You look good for your age," Darragh teased, looping his arm through mine. I made an over-exaggerated laugh as a group walked by and placed my hand on his bicep.

"Botox, bourbon and *Buns & Thighs.*"

He snorted. "I'll be sure to let our middle-aged friends know."

The decadent hallway we walked down boasted thick red carpets and gold emblazoned wallpaper, covered floor to ceiling in paintings. Partygoers drifted up and down, dripping in diamonds, emeralds, rubies and anything else that screamed money. I recognized a few faces that had taken off their masks, people who worked for Lucien. It was no surprise so many of his people would be here tonight, but it still made me extremely uncomfortable.

The hallway eventually led into a massive ballroom, fit for kings and queens of the past. But the only royalty here tonight were the kings of New York City, Lucien Rocci and Sean O'Callaghan. Soon, the man beside me would wear the crown.

I spared a glance upwards. The high-domed ceiling was mostly covered in a massive painting that looked like it belonged to the Renaissance, dotted with enormous crystal chandeliers. Balconies high up on the wall were filled with drunken onlookers, little flutes of champagne held in slender, gloved hands. The only breaks in the ceiling were where the dome met the vertical wall, little windows where speakers and cameras jutted out of. It was safe to say I'd be there tonight.

"Relax," Darragh said, rubbing my arms. "In another hour, this will all be done."

I looked to a huge clock in the center of the room with alarm. It resembled the one in Grand Central, presumably put in the center of the room for tonight's event only. It was already 11:00 PM. Everything was happening so quickly.

I stole a few deep breaths and looked up into Darragh's eyes. He was on high alert, barely paying me attention as he scanned the room. A bit hypocritical after telling me to calm down, if you asked me.

"Come on, let's dance in the meantime."

I raised an eyebrow behind my thick wooden mask. "To observe the room better or to pass the time?"

He smirked. "Both."

Darragh was a terrible dancer, which wasn't all that shocking, but it was nice to be better at something for a change. I led us around the room, observing the way Darragh subtly glanced around with each spin and turn, watching but not watching as more people filtered into the ballroom.

I leaned my head on his chest as a slower song came on. "Where's Rocci?" I whispered. Even through a mask I would recognize him. He was yet to appear.

"He'll be here closer to midnight," he said, pushing me away and twirling me around. He pulled me back to his chest, completely out of time with the music. "Just wait."

It was so much like Lucien I wanted to laugh. To pretentious to even attend his own party.

Twenty minutes later, Sean O'Callaghan, wearing a terrifying demon mask, entered the ballroom. Darragh leaned down, whispering. "I'm heading to the bank now. Be upstairs by 11:40 and go to sound room 4B. If anyone asks what you're doing, get creative. Meet me outside the service elevator as soon as it's done. I'll be back soon"

I nodded, my mouth drying out. "Okay."

"Deep breaths," he whispered, tucking something into my hand before pulling away. "I'll see you soon. "

He was swallowed by the crowd within seconds, leaving me alone on the dance floor. I looked down to see a little revolver in my hand, one I had used several times in the house upstate. It was small, quiet, and efficient, but only held one round.

It didn't matter, I told myself, slipping it into a lace garter at my ankle and letting the fabric of my dress fall back over it. Kieran would have the production room stocked with the weapons I needed. I'd shoot Lucien Rocci through the window. Darragh would kill Sean. This would all be done and over with. I just had too fucking breathe.

God, why was I so nervous?

Darragh would probably kill me if he saw, but I couldn't think of anything better with the way my nerves were acting. I rushed over to the bar at the far end of the room, asking a masked waiter in a tux to pour me one of the heady glasses of champagne. Several women next to me gave me sidelong glances as I downed the entire thing in one swallow.

"If I knew you were such a fan of champagne, I'd have had some for you at the hotel."

I nearly spit out the last of the drink. My eyes drifted up, meeting the cold-hard gaze of a man in a demon mask. The eyes of Sean O'Callaghan.

I covered my surprise with an embarrassed smile. "Just a bit nervous," I said. It wasn't a lie.

He nodded empathetically, though none of it reached his eyes. "It's a big event."

I nodded, wondering what could be said without raising suspicion in the curious onlookers around us.

"James left about ten minutes ago. He was feeling a bit ill," I said, using Darragh's cover name.

Sean nodded. "I heard. Will you be leaving soon too?" AKA, *I got the radio signal from the bank and when are you going to meet him?*

"In a moment." According to Sean, I would meet Darragh on the opposite roof by 11:40. Only my husband and Kieran knew I'd actually be upstairs, and Darragh, down here.

"While I have you, I'd love to share a dance. I've hardly gotten to spend any time at all with my new daughter."

I glanced at the clock in the center of the room. 11:25. I'd only have a few minutes before I had to leave. It'd take me at least ten to find where I needed to be.

But I didn't want to raise any suspicion in Sean. I held out my hand, setting my glass on the crystal bar top. "Of course."

He led me to the middle of the throng, close to the clock. He placed his hands on my waist lightly and kept a healthy distance. Respectable. But even with the minimal contact, I wanted to shudder.

He took my left hand in his and began the waltz around the room.

"You're a better dancer than your son," I said to break the tension. He stared at me in a way that made my skin crawl. Like he could see beneath the fancy clothes and right through my lying teeth.

"It was something I picked up on my own, later in life. When you deal with these types, you need to learn their ways."

I plastered on a fake smile. "These types?"

He leaned in, a vicious smirk on his face. "Italians. They absolutely love showing off."

"Oh," I murmured, covering it with a nervous giggle. "I've noticed that, too."

"Hm." He schooled his face back into neutrality, watching me like a hawk once again. I turned my head to the side, pretending to take in the extravagant display of masked dancers.

"Have you met Mr. Rocci before?"

My attention snapped back to Sean. "No, I haven't. Have you?"

"A few times," he said. His hands tightened on my waist. "He approached me for the first time in October, actually. Right after his bride went missing."

I swallowed, feigning confusion. "His bride?"

"Yes, the daughter of another businessman in our area. I believe you were familiar with her. She went missing shortly after your trip to Vegas."

298

Right. I was Annie McCormick, gunrunner and associate who helped in Giuseppina Delarosa's death.

I nodded. "I have a vague memory. I didn't know she had ties with Mr. Rocci."

"Many ties. Ties made in honor and blood." My foot nearly slipped as Sean veered us to the left, taking us in a dizzying turn around the clock. "Poor Lucien didn't believe his bride to be dead, though. He's approached me several times, asking me to help look for her. It's a shame, seeing such a great man be so taken by grief."

I pressed my lips together, trying to look somber, trying to cover up the pounding of my heart. Where was he going with all this? Lucien would be dead within half an hour. The massive, black minute hand of the clock ticked to 11:34. I had to leave.

"I hope Mr. Rocci finds peace." *In hell.* "But James is waiting. I think I should be heading out."

Sean gripped me tighter, keeping me from escape. "Just one more minute."

I glanced around the room. The crowd was getting thicker the closer we got to midnight. Nothing but unfamiliar, masks faces swam around me, taunting. I was alone. Darragh should be back any minute now, informing his father the spot was compromised and the hit was off. And I needed to get the hell out of here.

"I don't think Lucien will ever stop looking," Sean said.

I met his cold, dead eyes. There was nothing, absolutely nothing, behind them. "That's very unfortunate."

Sean leaned forward again. "You see, men who have power don't like when things are taken away from them. It shows weakness. And there can be no weakness in powerful men."

The heat of his breath made my head swim. 11:35. I needed to leave, now. I needed to find Darragh. Something was wrong. Sean's words, the room, this entire hit.

"It was lovely dancing with you," he said, pulling away. He clasped my hand in his. A look of surprise flashed over his face as he brought my left hand in front of his face. "He gave you his mother's ring."

I gave him a tight smile. "I'll take good care of it."

His thumb ran over the diamond. "I'm sure you would have, Giuseppina." He slipped it off my finger and disappeared into the crowd.

I stood in the middle of the dance floor, breaking the ebb and flow. A woman hissed at me as her and her dance partner bumped into my side, but I didn't move. I didn't breathe.

He didn't say that.

He couldn't know.

Blood pounded in my ears as I ran for the ballroom exit. People gave me strange looks, but I hardly saw their narrowed eyes and pursed lips. Darragh was in danger. We were both in danger.

I moved on autopilot, taking the service stairs three at a time before reaching the sixth floor, where the production room would be. Darragh would know by now our position was compromised. He'd know to meet me there.

The hallways meant for employees only was clogged with workers. The crowd thickened ahead, so dense with black and white uniforms I couldn't see past. Shouts of alarm went around as someone yelled to call the police. The pounding in my head got heavier.

A sweaty-faced waiter grabbed my arm. "I'm sorry, miss, but you can't be here."

I rocked onto my tiptoes, trying to see over the crowd. "What's going on?"

"We have a medical emergency, miss. You really shouldn't be in this wing."

"I'm meeting someone," I hissed, wrenching my arm away. I pushed through the workers, who were all too distracted to notice my presence. Some were crying, some held hands to their open mouths. One young boy retched loudly into a corner.

I broke through the wall of tuxedos and aprons, sucking in a breath of open air. It was short-lived.

Kieran . . . or what was left of him, slumped against the wall in a pool of blood. It covered his face and neck so thickly it took a moment to recognize him. His lips moved in a quiet murmur, eyes closed while several workers around him pressed dark clothes saturated with blood against his wrists. My eyes drifted to the other side of the hall, where two hacked up hands were thrown against the wall.

Bile rose in my throat. His hands . . . they—

There was so much blood.

Too much blood.

If they did this to Kieran—

I shoved someone to the side and collapsed to my knees in front of him. Hot blood soaked through the thin fabric of my dress, drenching my knees in it.

He turned his head to the side, eyes opening into nothing more than slits. His nostrils flared.

"Sean," he mumbled, voice thick with rasp and pain.

"Sean," I repeated, stuttering around the word. "Where's Dar—"

"Sean," he repeated. Blood dripped out of his mouth, streaming out the corner of his lips. Most of his teeth were gone too. "Took him."

"Where?"

He blinked, slow and empty, then his eyes rolled into the back of his head. Tremors overtook him, shaking his limbs violently as he thrashed on the floor.

"Go!" A worker screamed at me, trying to hold him down. I stood on shaky knees, violent breaths threatening to explode my lungs. Kieran took a final gasp and slumped against the wall.

I backed up, shaking my head. The workers moved out of my way, their cries and shouts of horror raising in a deafening crescendo. He had Darragh. Sean had Darragh. Sean was going to kill Darragh.

I broke into a run back down the hall. My bloody dress smacked against my shins, smattering blood all over my legs. I had nowhere to go, nowhere to hide, and I had no clue where Darragh was. Maybe Sean didn't have him at all. Darragh was smart, a fighter—

I wheezed in a breath as I smacked into a tall, lanky man in a mask resembling the sun.

I was about to scream before I took in the red hair, the hunched build. Rory's green eyes widened in alarm.

"Rory—" I panted. "What—"

"What's happening?" He looked over my head, but there was no way he could see past all the people.

I grabbed his arms and snapped him back to me. "Where's Darragh?"

"I came to ask you." He glanced around, like his brother would materialize from thin air. "I never heard from him, so I came."

"Your dad has him. Kieran is dead and Sean took him—"

"Why would Sean take him?"

I stared at him trying to find the words to explain how badly we fucked up. That Sean knew everything. Thankfully, I didn't have to.

"I'll find him," he breathed. He clenched my arm. "Wait for me outside, we have to get the fuck out of here."

Before I could protest, he was running down the hall.

Wait outside. Wait fucking outside. When Darragh— my husband— was . . . was possibly already dead.

I shook my head. No, I couldn't even go there. Not now. I had to help find him.

The blood blended in with the color of my dress enough I didn't stand out. I practically fell down the stairs, getting strange glances from bellhops, waiters and management, but none of them stopped me. I ripped the mask off my face and discarded it on the stairwell.

The service door led me back into the main lobby of the hotel. Down the hall would be the ballroom, but Darragh wouldn't be there. Someone shouted behind me the countdown would begin soon and a swarm of people gushed toward the dance floor at my

302

back. I pushed through the crowd, yelling at people to get out of my way as I ran for the elevators on the other side of the vast lobby.

If Sean was hiding him, he'd likely be in one of the hotel rooms. I'd have to swipe a master key off of someone to check each one and with the amount of rooms in this place, it could take hours to search. I wracked my brain for any indication of where I should start, where Sean would be keeping him. The penthouse, maybe. Made Men always had to have the best.

The elevator door opened, still twenty feet away. People grumbled and moaned around me as I tried to shove them out of the way, the surge of the crowd resisting each step I took. Two men stepped onto the elevator, only the black backs of their jackets and grey hair visible. But when they turned around, two faces stared into the open space, smiling as they spoke with one another and shook hands. The two faces of my nightmares. The faces that took everything from me. Sean O'Callaghan and Lucien Rocci. And they were shaking fucking hands.

A loud cheer echoed behind me as the countdown began. All at once, the crowd screamed at the top of their lungs, *TEN*.

A woman in a gold dress screamed as I knocked her to the side, spilling champagne all over her dress. The cry of, *You'll pay to have this cleaned!* was overshadowed by the crowd screaming, *NINE*.

EIGHT.

SEVEN.

I don't think Lucien will ever stop looking. Sean's words echoed in my mind. He knew this entire time. So did Lucien. This entire thing was a set-up. The alliance with my family between the Rocci's probably never existed. Sean knew right from the start who I was, what Darragh had done, and he cut a deal with the enemy to hand me back. What was he getting in return, money, weapons, territory? The chance to kill his own son?

SIX. Ten feet away. The doors of the elevator trembled, preparing to close. Neither men had noticed me, still laughing and conversing like old friends. Like they weren't murderers. Demons.

Sean would kill his own son for discovering him. For showing mercy. For . . . falling for someone.

FIVE.

The elevator doors began to slide shut, the thick golden emblems on the metal appearing from the walls. If Sean lived, he would kill Darragh. It would be the first thing he did, and if Rory didn't find him in time—

FOUR.

Only a few feet away. I reached for my ankle, pulling the little gun from its holster. One bullet. One shot. I waited for this day for three years. This moment sang me to sleep each night I sobbed into my pillow, picturing Paulina's terrified face as Lucien took her. As he ripped off her dress and forced himself on her body. As he slammed her head into that goddamn dresser and took her short, beautiful life. My best friend. The only reason I survived as long as I did. The only reason life didn't crush me all those years being locked away inside the Delarosa home. She died for *me* and I swore to avenge her.

THREE.

Paulina, Andrea . . . they were all I had. Lucien Rocci took them away. He killed my friend and double-crossed my brother. He tore my family apart. His blood was on their hands as much as it was on mine. But Paulina and Andrea, they were gone. Dead to me, either through true death or through calling it so. But I still had one person left. The Angel of Death. The cursed O'Callaghan. The youngest son. The man with the blue eyes and black hair, the man who held me in my sleep, the man who put a gun in my hands and told me he believed in me. My husband, my partner, my equal and my friend. The man I didn't even realize, that after all these months, I was deeply and madly in love with. And I never even got to tell him

TWO.

Three feet away. The men looked up as I broke through the crowd. It was now or never. I had to make a choice. *There can be*

304

no weakness in powerful men. I was Darragh's weakness. I led us here. But as much as I was his, he was irrevocably mine.

I shoved my way into the elevator.

The doors closed behind me.

Neither man said a word as I stood before them. The petite brunette. The daughter. No one.

They still wore there mocking smiles when I raised my gun and put a bullet between Sean O'Callaghan's eyes.

ONE.

HAPPY NEW YEARS!

1989

EPILOGUE

TWO WEEKS LATER

DARRAGH

The 60-inch screen of the TV was the only light in the penthouse. With the migraine I'd had for the past two weeks, I ordered all the men to keep them off. I stared at the screen as I hit the rewind button, the recording of the news special I took playing again so I could read through each word, observe each little movement, and play the scene over and over again in my mind.

It aired three days ago, right after Lucien Rocci announced his official engagement to none other than Giuseppina Delarosa. The tabloids had been going nuts with it, posting the smiling couple's faces over every goddamn magazine cover in the city. *New York's richest bachelor is taken!* and *Daughter of Lorenzo Delarosa finally shows us her face!*

I rubbed my temple while the recording rewinded, the blue light covering the TV screen making me want to put my fecking head through a wall.

Quiet murmuring echoed behind me and there was a hand on my shoulder. I'd told my boys— previously Sean's— to not let the little fecker in about a thousand times. I didn't know if it was New Year's or the fact that our Da was dead that made Rory suddenly grow a pair of balls. He went from the fun-loving idiot to

317

the terror of the O'Callaghan's overnight. Even the boys he used to drink and laugh with now feared him, especially after he cut someone's face last week for breathing wrong.

Even with his newfound anger, he still handed me the crown.

The first thing I did was empty Sean's penthouse of all his shit. I wanted it gone. It was replaced with newer furniture the same day, straight from the store. I didn't want anything with my Da's scent still clinging to it, anything that still held memory.

It only took a few days to get everyone in line. After Rory found me in the hotel, I killed every one of the feckers that had me tied up. That was all it took to scare the rest into realizing who their boss was now. That, and my brother/ right-hand man threatening all their lives daily.

By the time I emerged from that hotel room covered in blood, Pina was already gone.

"You won't see anything new," Rory mumbled.

"Piss off."

"We have things to do." Rory fell into the seat beside me, signaling without looking for the guards I had posted around the room to leave. Their quiet shuffles sounded like thunder against my head.

"I talked with Finn tonight. Lucien is gearing up. There's war coming."

War. That was an elegant name for the impending misery. This wasn't war. I would know. This was revenge, this was spite, and this was going to end with me bathing in Lucien Rocci's fecking blood.

Rory sighed, deeply. "Look, I know you don't want to hear this—"

"Don't."

"Someone has to say it," he snapped. He leaned forward, resting his elbows on his knees. I wouldn't meet his eyes.

"There's a possibility she's not in danger. She may have been in on this the entire time."

318

"She killed Da," I mumbled, hitting the pause button. The scene that played in my head every waking moment flared to life on the TV. A pretty, blonde morning host sitting in an armchair, and beside her, Pina O'Callaghan. My wife.

I hit play.

"That may have been part of it," he said, eyes glancing between me and the TV. "Maybe she did it for intel, or to get Lucien close to Da or you, who knows."

"She wouldn't betray her family."

"She hated them."

The host smiled as a round of applause thundered through the penthouse. She waited a few moments for the silence to die down, cheeks straining with the effort of looking delighted. Beside her, Pina wore her own smile, strained and cracked at the corners. She crossed her legs.

"I just want you to consider—"

"Pina didn't betray me." I whirled on my brother, who had the brains to shift as far from me as he could. "She didn't do this willingly. She's my wife. Mine. And I'm fecking getting her back. If I have to torture every goddamn son of a bitch in this city, I'll do it. Consider *that.*"

Rory frowned. His eyes cast to the ground and he shook his head. "I hope you're right." Without another word, he shuffled out of the room.

I knew I was right. All my doubts erased when this special played. When I sat on this couch and listened to my wife speak. When she said the words I was looking for.

The host grinned and gestured to the crowd. "Good morning!" The audience echoed it back. "Today we have a very special guest. The luckiest bride in the city and the woman you're all dying to mee. I'd like to introduce the future Mrs. Giuseppina Rocci!"

The audience clapped and cheered.

I leaned forward.

The host turned to Pina, folding her hands in her lap. "Good morning, Ms. Delarosa. How are you doing today?"

Here it was.

The moment I'd been waiting for.

My wife looked at the camera.

She smiled.

"Good morning, Cindy. I'm doing just fine."

AUTHOR'S NOTE

Writing a book is never an easy endeavor and a lot of the time, it can be a very lonely one. Thankfully, I had a few people on this journey who made putting out *Hit* one of the best experiences of my writing career.

First of all, a huge thank you to my husband, B, for not only explaining everything on weapons and sniper training but being my biggest support through writing and just about everything else. I love you and thank you for tolerating my insanity and bringing me coffee on all my late writing nights. Also, you're sexy as hell (and about my dedication to Tommy Shelby in the beginning . . . I totally think you're better).

A huge shoutout to my writing buddy and great friend, Kate King, for always being supportive and being an endless fountain of writing knowledge. Without you, I'd be pretty lost in the sauce on just about everything.

Also, thank you to Jaime at Rock Star Book Tours for getting the word out about *Hit* and doing a killer job promoting this book I worked so hard on.

But most of all, thank you to all the readers who took the time to read this book and became invested in Darragh and Pina's journey. Without you, this novel would be nothing more than a draft sitting in a word doc, never seeing the light of day. It's the readers who truly bring a story to life, and I can't thank the people who fell in love with this story enough for it.

With that said, I have one more favor to ask of the readers who really enjoyed this story and want to see more of Darragh and Pina in the future. Reviews are the best way for a book to get noticed and allow writers to continue doing what they do: write! Whether you have something good or bad to say, reviews help me figure out what the story needs or show others that they can enjoy this book as much as you. It would mean the world to me to take a few moments to write a review on Amazon or Goodreads, or even just post a picture of the book on social media and write about what you think. Seriously, it would be pretty fucking cool. *Wink, wink.*

If you read all this, thanks for listening to my rambling internal monologue. You're a real one. Once again, thank you, thank you, thank you for taking the time to read *Hit* and I hope to see you soon for the conclusion of Darragh and Pina's tale in *Marked.*

XOXO,

Mallory Hart

MARKED

The heart-pounding conclusion to the Mafia Born Duet is available for pre-order now.

Want a sneak peek of it? Join the newsletter at malloryhartromance.com for an advanced read of the prologue! Also coming up in the newsletter: *Hit*'s playlist, behind-the-scenes info and more.

Printed in Great Britain
by Amazon